GW00949841

HOUGHTON MIFFLIN HARC~~OURT CHILDREN'S BOOK GROUP~~
BOSTON :: NEW YORK

ADVANCE READING COPY

IMPRINT:	HMH Children's Paperback
TITLE:	Swoon at Your Own Risk
AUTHOR:	Sydney Salter
ILLUSTRATOR:	
ISBN:	978-0-15-206649-9
PUBLICATION DATE:	April 2010
PRICE:	$8.99 / Higher in Canada
TRIM:	5 x 7
PAGE COUNT:	368
AGES:	12 and Up
GRADES:	7 and Up

*These are uncorrected galleys. Please check all quotations and attributions
against the bound copy of the book. We urge this for the sake of
editorial accuracy as well as for your legal protection and ours.*

Reviewers may reprint cover illustrations to accompany reviews with the following credit:
Courtesy of Houghton Mifflin Harcourt Publishing Company

To obtain an electronic image of the cover of this book,
please visit www.hmhbooks.com.

Please send two copies of your review to:
Caroline Litwack | Publicity Department
Houghton Mifflin Harcourt Children's Book Group
222 Berkeley Street | Boston, Massachusetts 02116

Swoon

at your own risk

Other books by Sydney Salter

Jungle Crossing
My Big Nose and Other Natural Disasters

Swoon
at your own risk

BY SYDNEY SALTER

Houghton Mifflin Harcourt

Boston   New York   2010

www.hmhbooks.com

Text set in TK
Library of Congress Cataloging-in-Publication Data TK

Manufactured in the United States of America
TK 10 9 8 7 6 5 4 3 2 1

*F*or the one who always
makes me swoon—Mike

the way) my dad with Mr. *River Runs Through It*? I barely like *thinking* about my dad. I'm definitely not going to talk about him.

Sawyer pushed himself out of the beanbag. "Why won't you open up with me? You're hard like a golf ball." He made a ball shape with his hand, again squeezing his fist tight. "But I know you've got, like, layers."

"Maybe I'm like a tennis ball." I jumped up, faking a grin. "No layers but I bounce real good." I flung my arms around his neck.

Sawyer shook me off. "I don't know, Polly. You seem like a smart enough girl, but I don't think you're deep enough for me." He grabbed his car keys off his dresser. "Maybe I better take you home."

I laughed. "Just watch me go deep when we work at Wild Waves this summer. I'm all over that deep end." I made a swimming motion with my arms. "Fun in the sun, right?"

But Sawyer hadn't laughed. He drove me home, walked me to the door, and said that maybe we'd be better off as friends. He needed someone who valued intellectualing and found inspiration in the wilderness, et cetera, et cetera. So I joined the Nature Club, ended up hiking during spring break, and had a fling of sorts with Gareth Miller. But I don't want to think about that now.

Not while I'm pardnering up with my good old buddy Sawyer in the Lazy River. I squint into the sunshine, shouting at kids to stay on their inner tubes. None of them listen to me. I'm not good at sounding mean. I shuffle my feet against the rough concrete bottom. My water-logged toes look as wrinkled as that thousands-of-years-old ice man they found in the Alps, making my pink nail polish look so wrong.

A group of girls from my mom's just-graduated fifth-grade class float past me. "Hey, Mrs. Martin's daughter!"

I wave. "Hi, guys!"

I feel good for a minute, but then the little divas start a water fight with a group of boys. I scream and blow my whistle, but they listen to me about as well as they listened to my mom in the classroom. A hugely pregnant woman holding a toddler on her lap floats into the fray. The little hellions don't notice her. Water swishes back and forth, sloshing up the sides like a physics lab experiment. The pregnant woman is stuck in her tube. A wave of water smacks the toddler in the face and he starts crying. Then the mom's tube tips to the side like a boat listing in a storm of bratty fifth-graders. The kids laugh, oblivious. Sawyer blows his whistle. But they don't care. Little monsters! Kids spill out of their tubes, crashing into the water, squealing. I run toward the fray, but it's like one of those slow-motion dreams. This is why I should be standing *outside* the pool!

"Stop it!" My voice grows hoarse.

Boys dunk girls. Girls dunk boys. Water rolls back and forth. And the toddler goes overboard.

"My baby!" the mom shrieks. "He can't swim!" She struggles to get out of the tube. Not a pretty sight. Her butt is so stuck. I dive under and swim, getting there in time to pluck the kid out of the water. Gagging, the kid grips on to me, climbing me like a ladder. Legs clutching my torso. Arms grabbing my neck.

Sawyer stands on the side of the pool screaming instructions. "Get him out of the water fight!" He blows his whistle.

The kids splash some more. I trudge through the mess. The kid bawls, sputtering a nasty mixture of snot and regurgitated pool water onto my shoulder. His hand claws at my hair, pulling painfully. I can barely see with the kid climbing all over me, so I don't notice that I'm heading toward the drop-off below the Coyote Cliff jumping ledge.

Holding the sobbing kid, I plunge ten feet deep. Next thing I know, Sawyer leaps into the water, yanking me upward, practically bisecting me with my own swimsuit. We break the surface, and Sawyer tries to take the kid. But he won't let go. So

Sawyer pushes me—both of his hands on my butt—over the side. I sit on the hot pavement, gasping for breath. The kid has swallowed so much water, he vomits all over me. It's warm. Apparently he ate scrambled eggs for breakfast.

Sawyer pats the kid on the back, cooing, "You okay, little buddy?"

The mom waddles over, hugs the kid so tight he quits crying, but now *she's* sobbing. A small crowd gathers around us.

Sonnet Silverman saunters over. "Damn. I need a waterproof video camera. Words aren't going to be enough to describe this. Polly Martin wearing her swimsuit thong-style while her ex's hands—"

"Please don't make *me* hurl." I brush a gooey glob off my arm, grimacing at the sour stench.

Sonnet giggles. "I already love working with you."

```
Dear Miss Swoon:
Help! I dated a coworker. Then we broke
up. Should I look for another job? I'm
not sure I can maintain a professional
relationship with this person. But the
job market is tight.
—Working With X
```

Dear Working:

No need to hit the highway. Take the high road and move on. Next time yield when it comes to dating in the workplace.

—Miss Swoon

Not Shakespeare's Sonnet!

Blond count: a depressing 0

EX-change of Information:

Polly Martin (see <u>Polly-Wants-A-Beer</u> here) dove into the deep end at Wild Waves, leaving *her* deep end exposed, if ya know what I mean. Sadly, no image available—use the old imagination, folks. Polly's curvy, but she stays in shape. Anyway, our Miss Martin managed to snag the attention of a certain jocky blond from her past (see <u>Random Locker Room Fantasies</u> here). Let's just say the guy had his hands *all over* her deep end. I sense a rematch, Polly! Next time ditch the Eau de Spew in favor of a more sporty citrus scent.

Chapter Two

A sound like a zipper opening the pavement on our street wakes me. I blink into the sunlight brightening my room, angry with myself for not sleeping in while I have the chance. Part of me almost jumps out of bed to look out the window but I don't. I'm sure it's just some neighbor's newfangled hybrid, and I'm so over anything remotely automotive since breaking up with Kurt. I haven't even changed the oil in my car since our breakup. It's a matter of principle. Besides, I like how that little red check-engine light reminds me—like a stoplight—to avoid the male half of the species.

Thanks to the Lazy River incident, I have the day off. My boss wanted to fire me for not "maintaining proper control," but Sawyer talked him out of it. He even used his sweet-talking ways to remind the angry pregnant woman that I'd actually *saved* her kid's life. That and three years' worth of season passes convinced her not to call a lawyer.

I would have rather been fired, even though I totally need the money for little things like, um, college tuition. Now I'm going to owe Sawyer a big debt of gratitude. I never should have dated a coworker. Grandma is always telling people that in her columns; it's so basic. But back when snow fell practically every day and I wanted to spend every single second with Sawyer and I knew we'd be together forever—yeah, whatever—applying for the same summer job sounded amazing.

I plop my pillow on top of my face. Oh God. Now he's calling me Pollywog, a name that conjures up the image of a metamorphosizing amphibian that eventually sprouts warts and puffs out its throat when it talks. Disgusting!

I'm inventing terrible nicknames for him—Chain Sawyer Massacre, Saw-Yer-Coming so I left—when my ten-year-old sister, Grace, bursts into the room, flapping the newspaper's Style section in my face.

"They left Grandma out of the paper!" She plops her little prepubertal butt on my bed. "I searched every single section. No Miss Swoon! We've got to call the paper and make them fix it."

"Why aren't you bugging Mom with this?" I make a big

deal of rolling over, crushing my pillow over my head. "Leave me alone."

Grace tugs on my shoulder. "Mom left for her job interview."

I bolt up. "Job interview? I thought she was joking."

Grace shakes her head, looking solemn. "Nope, she even wore her silky parent-teacher conference shirt. It's the real deal."

Last night Mom had said something about applying to be a server at Hamburger Heaven, but I thought she'd just been saying it to torture me. Like I hadn't had a bad enough day anyway. But Mom likes to joke people out of a bad mood. It's the hazard of teaching ten-year-olds. (Let's just say she uses the word *Uranus* much too often). *Everyone* in town eats at Hamburger Heaven. Sure I'd seen more unopened bills lying around, but Mom isn't exactly—what do you call it? Organized. I assumed she'd spend her summer vacation taking teacher classes at the university, volunteering at the library, maybe tutoring a bit, and acting like, you know, a grownup. Kids from *school* get jobs at Hamburger Heaven.

Grace flaps the paper at me again. "What about Grandma? We have to call."

I grab the newspaper out of Grace's hand. Sure enough, in the place right above the horoscopes (which are completely unscientific and give people false illusions about finding love), there's an advice column. Not Miss Swoon but the Sassy Sage. I quickly scan the first letter about a desperate woman trying to attract a coworker. The Sassy Sage tells her to start wearing shorter skirts to work. This *is* an outrage. No one should date a coworker; you break up (because no relationship lasts) and they end up shoving your butt out of the pool, watching kids vomit on you, and calling you embarrassing nicknames.

I jump out of bed, clutching the paper, and immediately search for the phone. I finally find it stuck between the sofa cushions covered with crumbs. I dial the Style editor. An angry diatribe runs through my head: how dare you allow an irresponsible fool to proffer advice to idiotic love-obsessed women, et cetera, et cetera. But when a person actually answers the phone, it goes more like this: "Um, what happened to Miss Swoon?" "Oh, okay. Thank you."

"Ugh!" I toss the phone down. "I can't believe I actually said thank you!"

Grace's eyes go wide. "What happened?"

"On Mondays, Wednesdays, Thursdays, and Fridays, Grandma will be replaced by a 'hip and edgy, younger syndicated columnist' due to 'decreased reader relatability.'"

"But Grandma is so good!"

"I know! What's the deal? People only need solid advice on the weekends and Tuesdays?"

I shred the rest of the paper into pieces fit for a hamster cage. At least that's what Grace says as she gathers them to save for her best friend, Amy. The pair of them are like Siamese twins with different addresses. But I've overheard them plotting to ask to be adopted by each other's families—that is if their fantasy of being shipwrecked on a tropical island where they become twin queens doesn't pan out. Thinking about their happy little friendship reminds me that I haven't called my supposedly best friend, Jane, since school got out. Not that she's called me, either. Not since I ignored her during my all-too recent and brief relationship with Hayden Steele (after I'd ditched her for that hiking adventure with Gareth). Things aren't too copacetic between Jane and me. But that can all change now that I'm standing on the side of the dating pool. Like Miss Swoon says, "Boyfriends come and go. Girlfriends are forever."

I dial Jane's cell but hang up when I realize that it's only eight o'clock in the morning and she's probably sleeping because her summer enrichment classes don't start until next week. I look around at the mess in the living room.

"How can Mom leave the house looking like this?" Crusty

dishes clutter the coffee table, along with stacks of school papers, newspapers, magazines, and, of course, bills. Grace's backpack has been in the middle of floor since the last day of school. "Oh God, my student council petition. Ugh!" I crumple the page of signatures.

"But I thought you were excited about planning dances and stuff." Grace twirls around the living room. "You said it would be so romantic."

"Only because I was tricked by my hormones."

Grace wrinkles her forehead. "But you said you were going to buy a purple dress."

I shrug. "Things change. Boys suck. And I will not be attending a prom during the Holocene Epoch."

"What?"

"It's a geology term."

"Well." She holds up a catalog for me to see. "I think you should get a blue dress."

I roll my eyes. "Oh, Grace."

"To match your eyes."

I dated Hayden during election season, unfortunately, and got talked—maybe kissed—into running for the student council. (I didn't exptect to win!) Now I'll be stuck spending every Friday lunch planning the prom. Hayden didn't think I was deep enough, either, except he called it "not committed to a cause." His cause includes banning books from schools due to "negative content." I was a little too fixated on his dark hair and the way he always used SAT words correctly (so unlike Saw-Me-In-Half).

"How am I going to figure out my life if I live in a junk heap of my past?" I grab the catalog and sweep it into the pile of discarded school papers. "Grace, we're cleaning the house."

She tilts her head skeptically but then, dragging her back-pack, runs off to organize her stuffed animals. I tune the radio to a country music station, since I've never dated anyone who indulged in that particular genre. I don't really like the twangy sound, but at least it doesn't bring up any bad memories. Besides, those gals are totally right about men done gone and leaving you high and dry and stuff. I'm singing along, making up my own words, and collecting stacks of recycling. I open the mail, putting the bills aside for Mom.

Way too many of them have ugly red past due notices stamped on them. Why can't she get her act together? How difficult is it to sort through a few envelopes, sit down with a calculator, and pay the bills like an adult? This is the woman who goes ballistic if the first letter of the alphabet shows up on my report card with a minus sign attached. Mom flunks Housekeeping 101, that's for sure!

I notice an envelope with Dad's handwriting. It's the only one that's already been opened. I peek inside hoping for a note, but it's empty. He used to hand deliver the child support checks when he came to drive me to my dance lessons. Now he mails them. No note. And he never drives Grace anywhere. Too busy, he says. He bought me a car at the start of junior year so I could "help out." It should've made me happy; everyone wants a car, right? Except it felt more like he was buying me off. He can ignore me guilt-free; we now have an e-mail relationship based on forwarded articles from *The New York Times*.

Cleaning feels good, as if vacuuming the floor has sucked all the negative thoughts out of my mind. By the time Mom walks through the door around lunchtime, our cozy little abode looks like we're expecting company. I'm lounging on the de-crumbed sofa reading my autographed copy of *Miss Swoon's Best Columns, Volume 3*. I giggle over her advice to "ditch the dogs," "abandon the bums," and "leave 'em on the front porch like a pair of worn-out loafers." I love how she tells Jilted Jill to "emphasize the positivity." Yeah, I should focus on *my* good qualities, not Sawyer Later Alligator's various possibly appealing traits. Green eyes = so what?

Mom comes in with Hamburger Heaven To Go bags. "Good news!" She sets the bags on the counter, and I smell cheese fries.

"Meet your new lunch shift Angel." Mom's smile can't hide the strain at the edge of her mouth.

"That's such a demeaning label, Mom." I hold up my *Swoon* book. "Grandma says titles are how we talk about each other; 'angel' might even be worse than using 'girl' in the workplace." I'm not sure where "deputy" fits into the mix, but it can't be good.

Mom frowns. "It's just a silly title. And two dollars above minimum wage plus tips." She already looks tired. "Besides, it makes me feel young and gorgeous." She fluffs her hair. "I always wanted to be an angel—like on *Charlie's Angels.*"

Grace bursts out of her room. "Yay! And yum! Do you get to bring home treats every day?" She hugs Mom then immediately goes rooting through the bags. "Can Amy come over to help celebrate?"

Mom nods. "Sure."

Grace runs for the phone, and Mom looks around the room. "So, aliens from the Planet De-Clutter invaded while I was gone?"

I fake a smile. "Yeah, first I couldn't find the phone, then I lost Grace, so I figured . . ."

"Looks great." Mom flips through a stack of bills. "Except for these. This decorating trend is quite passé."

"Just open them on the day they come. That's easy enough, right?"

"You betcha. I just saved these because I was thinking about wallpapering the bathroom in Old American Phone Bill." Mom slides the Styrofoam container of fries over to me. "You enjoying your day off?"

I shrug. "Cleaning beats standing in a pool of pee and squealing kids."

"But you were so excited about working at Wild Waves."

"Yeah, well." I munch a soggy, slightly cold french fry. "You're not going to have to wear wings and one of those halos, are you, at your age?"

Mom rolls her eyes. "Standard uniform."

"Wait, Mom. What about Grace? With my work schedule and yours she's going to be home alone." Unless I quit my job and stay home, learning about the evils of love by watching soap operas and talk show repeats all summer. "I could always, you know, take one for the team and stay home with her."

"Oh!" Mom clapped her hands. "I completely forgot. Good news. You get to keep your summer job in the sun, and I can hustle my hiney at Hamburger Heaven because"—Mom makes a drumroll sound on the counter—"our very own favorite advice columnist is coming to stay with us for . . . awhile."

Grace drops the phone and jumps around the room. "Grandma's coming! Grandma's coming! Omigosh. What kinds of presents will she bring this time? I hope she brings me the new . . ." Grace lists must-have critters from her Internet-based stuffed animal obsession.

I watch Mom's face. "Grandma?"

"She called about needing a place to plop while her condo is renovated. And she's working on a new book. So I offered her your room and—"

"Not my room!" How can I find the positivity in that? With all the stuffed animals invading Grace's bunk bed, I might end up sleeping on the couch. Well, I did just vacuum the sofa cushions.

"Your room's bigger, so she can use it as an office of sorts, to write her column and work on her book."

Grace bounces across the sofa cushions. In her shoes. But I'm *not* going to think about the billions of bacteria clinging to her feet. "Yay! Grandma!"

"I guess it will be good."

"Good? It's going to be grrrrreat!" Mom lifts her fist in the air like that cartoon tiger in the cereal commercial. She really does spend too much time with ten-year-olds. Maybe having Grandma around espousing her sensible advice will help Mom get back on track. Me, too.

And soon we're all jumping around the living room imitating that obnoxious tiger.

Dear Miss Swoon:
We finally got the kids out of the house,
but now my mother-in-law wants to move
in. She has the means to purchase a home
of her own, but she says she's afraid of
living alone at her age. How do I convince my wife that we need a little
empty nest time of our own?
—Too Many Birds In The Nest

Dear Nest:
Don't push Grandma out of the nest! Life
flies by. When Grandma's gone, you will
have your love-nest back. And you might
just miss the old bird!
—Miss Swoon

Chapter Three

We're spread out across the O.K. Corral practicing lifeguard techniques. An hour before work. An *unpaid* hour before work. But I'm emphasizing the positivity: my little incident is helping the entire staff, because now we're all required to take extra training. It might save lives. I'm *not* hearing the snide comments about drowning Pollywogs. I'm also going to forget Sonnet Silverman's blog post about Sawyer putting his hands all over my butt—she completely left out the near-drowning aspect of the situation. Six people e-mailed me last night to congratulate me on "getting back together." I only knew one of them.

The EMT instructor yawns, looking as thrilled to be here as everyone else. "Okay, partner up."

Several guys make a move toward Sonnet because that curvy little gossip rarely worries about pulling up her swimsuit.

"Looking forward to a little mouth-to-mouth action?" Sonnet asks me. "Maybe reignite your lost love?"

"Yeah, because resuscitation is so romantic."

Sonnet waggles her eyebrows. "It's all about who you're with, right?"

I giggle at the look on her face when she finds herself paired with a completely unblog-worthy sophomore. "Exactly."

She flips me off.

The other girls, including dance team diva Kipper Carlyle, head over to Aaron, the older lifeguard. Yeah, he might look exactly like an underwear model *if* you were the kind of person who noticed that kind of thing. That leaves me standing next to Sawyer.

Sonnet says, "So, mouth-to-mouth can lead to making out, right?" Her partner blushes the color of a Wild Waves bandana. "I'm just asking, because Polly and—"

"Ahem." The EMT clears his throat and points to Sawyer and me. "We'll use you two as an example." I lie on the grass, pretending to have nearly drowned. Sawyer leans over me, shaking my shoulders with big warm hands. But so what? I have hands. Everyone has hands. Except that guy in that horror movie . . . I'm envisioning the movie's bloodiest scene, *not* the way Sawyer's looking at me like he still cares, his green eyes wide and concerned. So what? I have eyes. Everyone has eyes. Except for those blind cave fish. Sawyer leans toward me, lips slightly parted. Lips = making out. *No!* I sit up, completely revived. "Thank you for saving me. That was great." I ignore *those* kinds of feelings now pulsing through my body.

"Uh-uh," the instructor says, frowning. "You've got to start chest compressions and mouth-to-mouth."

Sawyer stares at me, mouth gaping—unattractively, I might add. I pull my knees to my chest. "No need. Look." I take a few deep breaths. "Breathing just fine." I jump to my feet. "Next victim."

One of the girls who missed out on Aaron runs over. "I'll do it."

"He's all yours. I mean, it's all yours." I slink to the back of the group, partnering with a kid who's always quoting *Star Wars* and could be an acne cream model. No temptation there.

I spend the rest of the training session mentally focusing on the positivity about saving lives, learning new skills, and, you know, giving my partner the opportunity to touch a girl who isn't a relative. When Sawyer gives us the daily assignments, I get garbage duty.

"We're going to keep you out of the water for another day." Sawyer talks to his clipboard, and that's fine with me. Really.

Let's keep this ex-ex-ex relationship strictly professional. And keep his green eyes and full lips out of it, too.

"Great!" I say with forced enthusiasm. "I'll get those litterbugs."

By my afternoon break I've touched more used drinking straws than the health department should allow. But at least the babies crawling around on the grass won't choke on them now. Still, I'm fantasizing about dipping my whole body in a vat of liquid hand-sanitizer. Not a bad fantasy, really. It's totally clean. (Get it?)

I keep my eyes on the ground, weaving between beach-towel encampments and clusters of women sitting in foldup chairs bragging about their kids between shouting reprimands to those same amazingly talented little prodigies. And even though, after working here for three days, I've pretty much decided never to reproduce, I am glad that Wild Waves caters to the elementary school crowd. No one I know would come here unless forced to attend a family reunion or company picnic. I'm almost content in a finding-inner-peace sort of way, stabbing plastic sandwich bags, hamburger wrappers, paper napkins . . . I enjoy the crunchy sound the metal post makes as it slices through paper. Stab, stab, stab. *I'm cleaning up a gold mine o'litter, pardner.*

But then, just as I'm bending in a totally cleavage-exposing way to pick up a cluster of squashed grapes, I see Xander Cooper. Sitting on a beach towel. Biting his lip to trap the smile that completely shows in his eyes. Brown eyes that are several shades darker than his kinkyish, curlyish, sun-streaked hair.

What is *he* doing here? He flashes his eyebrows up at me before leaning—hair flopping over to cover his face but not his huge smile—to write something in a little black notebook.

Quickly I turn around and stab more and more litter, pretending the laughter I hear is coming from a bunch of scabby fourth-grade boys, not tall, lean, mocha-colored Xander Cooper. When did he start looking so—struggling for vocabulary here—hot? Why am I suddenly *feeling* so, um, hot? The guy lives up the street from me. I've known him since he routinely licked Kool-Aid powder off his desk in third grade, stuffed his chubby body into Spider-Man sweatpants, and hummed during silent reading time. He's such a geek—a hot (come on, brain!), sexy geek.

"Hey!" a lady yells as I pick up a few french fry cartons. "We weren't done with those! Do you know what those cost me?"

I ignore the angry lady, even though she's still ranting about concession prices. I turn back toward Xander Cooper. Did he see that? Hear that? He's occupied with blowing up a floaty. A little girl hops around jangling, as gobs of beaded braids brush her dark shoulders; a little boy stares at me through his swim goggles. I'm all confused. What's with the kids? But then I remember Xander has an older sister. He's an uncle.

"Deputy Polly?" The woman's voice sounds really—how do you say it?—sarcastic.

I finally look at her angry red face; her hair has dried funny, giving her an almost rabid demeanor. "Here," I say, pulling out of my pocket the five-dollar bill I'd gotten as change during lunch. "Buy more fries."

"It's the principle of the thing," she huffs, taking my money.

I decide to clean up the other side of the good old O.K. Corral, steering clear of Xander. Just real quick, I glance over at him. He's holding that little notebook again, but now he's watching a baby giggle as a woman blows soap bubbles. Oh, to be so easily charmed. I'm talking about the baby, *not* the guy and certainly not me.

I tug the front of my suit up, my shorts down. Maybe if I were a deeper thinker, I'd be able to come up with a simple biological explanation for why someone like Xander Cooper would send my body chemistry into such a frenzy. I did read somewhere that biracial faces are more symmetrical or something. As I look over at Sonnet patrolling the Lazy River, I see that I'm not the only one noticing his hotter than hot (please, brain cells) presence. She's most definitely not concerned about the state of her swimsuit. So what? He's just a human being. A regular person with flaws, even if they aren't visible to the, you know, human eye.

After my shift I walk over to the employee locker room. Someone's phone rings, playing an intensely grating tween pop song. It's mine. How many times have I told Grace not to mess with my phone? Ignoring the dirty looks I'm getting from fellow employees (what else is new?), I fumble with my locker combination and dig around for my phone. It's Jane.

"So, hey. I noticed you called me yesterday?" She sounds way more confused than a best friend should. "Is something wrong?"

"No, of course not." I grab my tote bag and exit the locker room without changing into regular clothes. Too many ears listening. Too much Sonnet Silverman hoping to score another blog entry. "What? Do I only call you when I'm having a crisis?" I laugh, *not* thinking about my teary post-Gareth, he-doesn't-think-I-appreciate-nature-enough phone call. Or my post-Hayden, so-what-if-I-don't-have-an opinion-on-school-vouchers phone call.

Jane's quiet for a few moments, as if she's also listening to my thoughts. "Um, well, lately? Yeah."

I feign a laugh as I cross the parking lot to my car. "Well, the new me is all about you! I was just calling to see what you were up to, because, you know, it's Friday. The first— well, I guess the second Friday of, you know, summer vacation. And—"

"You called on Thursday morning."

"Oh yeah. Well, I was still thinking—"

"Don't you work on Thursdays?"

I click my doors open. "Had the day off." I slide into my sauna of a car, thighs burning on the leather seats. "So, you know . . ."

Jane barrages me with questions. Did you get fired? No. Did you quit? I wish. Was there an incident? Sort of. Sawyer? Sort of. Are you over him? Yes. Is he over you? Big yes.

Jane sighs. "Well, what happened?"

As I drive home, I tell her the short version of the incident, the one that makes me look heroic and worthy of her friendship. "But I really did call because I wanted to hang out with you."

"You're not crushing on some debate team guy, are you?"

"No! Why do you always think it's about that?"

"Hayden."

"But that was, like, weeks ago."

"Three weeks ago."

"Well, in dog years that's practically eighth grade."

Jane laughs. "A group of us *is* getting together tonight."

"Oh, great. Debate team people?"

"Polly! You said—"

"Joking."

"Actually, yearbook staff."

I mentally go over the yearbook staff, visualizing the group photo. *Crazy, red-haired dude. Nope. Math class guy. Nope. Lurking photographer. Nope.* "Sounds great. And hey, Jane. Just for the record, I've sworn off guys. For good."

Jane guffaws—in an entirely unfeminine manner, I might add. I try to do all the traditional see-you-later, good-bye stuff, but she's laughing so hard she can't breathe. I tell myself she's watching something funny on TV. It's *not* about me.

```
Dear Miss Swoon:
Why are girls always attracted to the
jerks who don't treat them right?
—Not A Bad Boy

Dear Not:
Rebels = fun!
—Miss Swoon
```

Toothless grin, a chubby hand, reaches for the ethereal. The temporary. A soapy bubble bursts in her hand. A quick frown pops her smile. But with each new bubble the baby giggles again and again.

—XC

Chapter Four

Yes, I think as we sit in Rowdy Cox's basement with a bunch people from the yearbook staff. *This is why my friendship with Jane is so good for me.*

Several of us sit squished together on a plaid 1980s sectional that smells like it's stuffed with wet dog hair, watching the second installment of *The Lord of the Rings* trilogy. I'm completely bored, but I'm bonding with Jane; our flesh practically melds as I sit crushed between her and a dweeby freshman kid who keeps moving his leg away from mine like I've got cooties or something. Cooties = good. I've got to find my inner cootie catcher again, maybe return to a more third-grade view of romance. Boys = yucky. (Think Xander Cooper licking grape Kool-Aid powder off his desk.) We're all taking big handfuls of stale popcorn out of a bag the size of a five-year-old. And it's probably about that old. I hold a handful of stale kernels in my hand, not wanting to, you know, ingest them. A few of the guys take sips from *one* shared beer. There's no way I'm going to get myself into trouble here.

"Jane." I whisper since these guys take the movie quite seriously. "Where's the bathroom?"

"Upstairs near the kitchen."

The freshman looks palpably relieved when I extricate myself from the sofa.

"We're not scaring you off, are we?" Rowdy asks.

His friends laugh nervously.

"Nope. Just using the ladies' room. Don't want to miss it when that Egghorn guy comes back riding his stallion."

Blank looks.

Whatever.

In the kitchen I immediately find the trash under the sink, ditch the stale popcorn, and wipe my greasy hands. I spend a few minutes looking at the stuff pinned to the refrigerator. Rowdy has a sibling who loves to draw stick figures. I peer into the family photos, noticing how smiley his parents look. One big happy family at the beach. We don't have recent photos like that at my house. We haven't taken a vacation since my parents divorced, other than a few trips to visit Grandma. I do spend a couple of days each summer up at the cabin with Dad. Other than that he's real busy and I'm supposedly busy. I lean closer, examining their faces to see if these people are really all *that* happy. I hear the front door open and immediately grab a glass out of the dish rack as if I'd come upstairs to get a drink of water.

"Polly?" The voice sounds confused, and familiar.

I spin around. "Oh. Uh, hi, Hayden. Didn't realize you were part of the yearbook staff."

He furrows his eyebrows in a way that makes me want to study SAT words with him again. "I'm not." He sets a two-liter bottle of Coke on the counter, along with a bag of pretzels. "Rowdy invited me over for a *Lord of the Rings* party."

"Like, duh. I just thought everyone knew each other from yearbook or something. I'm here with *Jane*." I emphasize her name to make it clear that I'm *not* noticing his crisply ironed khaki shorts.

I turn around and fill my glass with water and drink it above the sink, even though it's warm. Not quite as warm as my cheeks. "Everyone's downstairs," I say. "Egghorn's about to save the day again."

"Aragorn."

"Hmm?" I fill my glass again because it's the only thing I can think of doing.

"Polly? What are you doing here? You hate fantasy films."

"No, I don't. Besides, I think it has enough battle scenes to be called a movie not a *film*."

Hayden's mouth curves into a slight smile. "You sound just like that critic on NPR. You're still listening to her, aren't you?" He looks far too pleased about influencing my media habits.

"Only because I haven't gotten around to changing my presets." I shrug. "Anyway, I'm here to spend time with Jane. Better get back to the *movie*." I turn and run downstairs, *not* thinking about how arguing with Hayden makes me want to do other things with him, or to him.

Jane's now sitting on the floor close to Rowdy—intentionally close. Maybe she just wants to avoid taking on the scent of the sofa. She would have told me if she'd started crushing on someone like Rowdy, right? That *so* isn't Jane. She's focused on the future: SAT prep, applying for scholarships, taking university classes to get her prerequisites out of the way, and things like that. Not doofus boys like Rowdy who join the yearbook staff to avoid taking more—how do you say it?—academic subjects.

I plop down on the sofa next to the freshman; he holds a cross-stitched pillow across his lap like a shield. I'm not going to even think about why. More blood and guts spill onscreen. Hayden steps down into the basement holding a bowl of pretzels, a stack of cups, and the bottle of Coke.

"Hey, hey, Hayden!" Rowdy shouts. "You almost missed it."

"Told you I had to volunteer, my man." Hayden glances around the room, sees me, looks at the group sitting on the floor, and joins me on the sofa. Freshman guy hugs his pillow tighter. I brace my foot on the floor to prevent myself from sliding up against Hayden, but the worn-out cushions don't cooperate.

I try to watch the movie, but watching Jane is far more interesting, although frankly more disturbing, than losing the battle for Middle Earth or whatever. I'm not worried about all those gobbledygook creatures, but I am worried about Jane's judgment. Rowdy makes a joke and Jane laughs, leaning her head against his shoulder.

Hayden whispers to me about the student council, as if that topic still interests me even remotely. I nod every time he pauses, only mildly impressed by his correct usage of two- and three-syllable words.

Soon Rowdy has his arm behind Jane's back, barely touching her, but I recognize the basic Hook Up at a Party 101 move.

"So, I thought I might start a student council listserv for the summer. Get the ideas flowing," Hayden says, sitting so close that I feel his breath on my neck. "What do you think?"

"Yeah, whatever. Sounds good." Hayden makes me uncomfortable, acting like we're still in some sort of relationship even though he made it clear that he has more "pressing priorities for the foreseeable future." When he rests his hand on my arm, I lean forward.

"Hey, Jane." I poke her in the back. "You wanna get going?"

Rowdy whips his arm back into his lap, and Jane looks as crestfallen as she did the time I accidentally sat on her graham cracker gingerbread house in fifth grade. "Not yet." She scoots a little closer to Rowdy. "Oh, I love this part," Jane says. Onscreen Frodo's friend goes for the Ring. Little traitor! Doesn't Jane see the irony here? I sink back into the couch, sighing deep.

Hayden leans back next to me, smelling squeaky clean. "I knew you hated this movie. I mean, film."

I fold my arms across my chest. "Shut up."

Hayden laughs to himself, popping a piece of peppermint gum into his mouth. It does *not* remind me of kissing him. He offers the pack to me. "Want one?"

"No, thanks." I'm not falling for all that minty fresh business again. No way.

I poke Jane.

"What?" Rowdy's got his arm around her again.

"Can we, um, talk for a second?"

One of the guys makes a crude remark, and Rowdy punches him in the arm, destroying Jane's cozy little snuggle-fest. She stands up to avoid being crushed by the impromptu wrestling match that's broken out on the floor. "Okay, fine."

"Hey, you scared of the Orcs?" Rowdy teases. "I'll protect you!" He reaches for Jane's arm, but the other guy tackles him again.

Jane glares at me. Doesn't she realize that I'm protecting her? Dating Rowdy would be like going out with an Orc, not to mention a complete social disaster worthy of its own trilogy. I push myself off the sofa, not saying anything to Hayden, and follow Jane out of the room. I can still feel the warmth of his leg on mine, *not* that I'm noticing; it's just that the air conditioning is turned up high and the basement is freezing. I rub my arms.

Jane stops halfway on the stairs. "Okay. Talk."

"Can we at least go upstairs?"

I glance back at Rowdy—now throwing handfuls of the greasy, stale popcorn at people.

"I don't want to leave yet." Jane's mouth is tight. "I'm having fun."

I nudge her in the ribs with my elbow. "Then why aren't you smiling?"

"If this is about Hayden, just deal with it."

"What? No. I don't even care about that. It's *so* over."

"Really." Jane huffs. "Then let's get back to the movie."

"It's just that I'm kind of tired: you know, long week at work soaking in urine, nearly drowning and all."

Jane peeks at her cell phone. "It's only eight thirty."

"Yeah, well." I bite my lip. I'm not going to admit that Hayden *is* freaking me out—what with smelling all bathed, brushed, and kissable. Why didn't I drive? Then Jane could have her ill-advised Orcish moment or whatever, and I could go home, hide under my covers—while I still have my own room—and detox from a week's worth of ex-boyfriend contamination. "I've got to clean out my room, what with my grandma coming and all."

Jane raises her eyebrows. "Maybe Hayden will give you a ride?"

"Jane, don't."

"Don't what? How many times have I been stuck, left, or ignored because of your—"

I put my hand up. "Don't. I get it."

"Do you? Because it doesn't seem like it. Seems like you're only thinking about Polly."

"That's not fair," I whisper. The back of my throat tingles. So do my eyes. I turn and watch Rowdy dog pile onto the sofa with the other guys, screaming about Orcs. What could she possibly see in the guy?

Jane turns her back to me, flipping her hair. "Maybe you can walk home like I did that night you left the basketball game with Sawyer." She walks down a couple of steps. "Too bad it isn't snowing."

I feel slapped. Did I do that? Yes, but—

Jane runs across the room and flops onto Rowdy's lap, giggling. I walk upstairs. Maybe I do deserve this. I *will* walk home. It's good exercise, right? Positivity. On the way home I can figure things out, Zen-style. I remember that fortune I saved from a cookie a few weeks ago that said something about enjoying the journey.

I grab my purse and stand in the foyer debating myself. Just walk home. That will show her. No one should be stuck in a dark basement with a fresh ex. Jane can't expect me to stay, right? I'm going to walk. I hope she feels totally guilty. I had hoped to have some girl talk time. Well, I'd listen to Jane talk, anyway. I like thinking about her sensible ideas. If I'd spent more time listening to Jane last year, I could have avoided a whole heap of ex-ex-ex-ex-ex trouble. But with the way she's now going after the great Orc clone, I'm not sure she'd have much to say tonight. I'll wait to talk to Grandma; she wrote an entire book, called *Swoon for Yourself*, about living single and happy, even though she, you know, ended up marrying her publicist.

As I walk down the front steps, I'm surprised that it's still light outside. I look around and gather my bearings, searching for my neighborhood in the valley below. Really it's not that far, especially if I walk along the highway for a bit and cut down Apricot Avenue. The air feels warm, and I relax a little, thinking that a long walk might do me a lot of good. Across the street, a couple saunters past walking a pair of fluffy golden retrievers. I decide to walk in the other direction.

At the bottom of the hill cars zoom past on the highway. Ignoring the air whooshing past, I step onto the sandy shoulder. My heart pounds slightly as a semi truck takes up too much room. I wish I could call Mom, but she's covering a co-worker's shift at Hamburger Heaven. Really the woman can't say no. She reminds me of Stretched Too Thin from Miss Swoon's Tuesday column. Mom's on practically every single committee at her school and then spends time tutoring kids on the weekends. Sure, I've got obligations like organizing the Nature Club trail cleanup, Hayden's book drive thing, and planning that pathetic prom, but it's not the same.

About a half hour later Hayden's car zips past me. Bumper stickers cover bumper stickers, making Hayden's car resemble that nasty plaid sectional, except the car is patriotic red, white, and blue. I've always wanted to ask if he joins political causes for the stickers the way Grace still orders Happy Meals for the toys.

Hayden's Ford Focus swings to the side of the road, kicking up dust. What now? Right after a rumbling cement truck passes, Hayden's door swings open, and he runs down the road toward me.

He gasps. "What are you doing out here?"

"Painting my nails." I roll my eyes.

"Jane said you left, but she didn't say you were walking. You live miles from here." Hayden jumps into a patch of weeds as a Corvette cruises past. "I'll give you a ride."

"No, thanks." I suck in my breath as a minivan swerves away from the shoulder, but I keep walking. Hayden follows behind me, stumbling in the thick weeds growing along the shoulder.

"Polly, this is crazy. You're going to get us killed."

I turn around. "I didn't ask *you* to be here." I reach Hayden's car; red paint gleams between the bumper stickers. I keep walking.

Hayden follows. "Please get in the car, Polly. Please."

I ignore him and keep walking, sticking a little closer to the shoulder when I realize that the sun is going down and I'm walking in the shadows. Hayden finally gives up and runs back to his car. As he speeds past me, I wave cheerfully.

The car pulls over, brake lights flashing red. Again, Hayden gets out, jogs toward me. "Just get in the car, Polly. Let me drive you home. As a friend, if that's what this is about."

"This isn't about anything. Can't a girl walk home in peace?" A passing sedan honks at me, a little too angry sounding.

"Be careful!" Hayden pulls me by the arm into the weedy section. I shake him off, but now we're both stumbling along in the dusky light. Really Hayden's precious City Council should get someone to mow this stuff down, maybe install some good lighting. Sidewalks.

Hayden makes a move to grab my arm when we reach his car again. But I run ahead of him, now jogging along the side of the road, feet slipping in the sand. I hear Hayden make an exasperated sound like he does when he's displeased with some politician's gaffe. Why does he care? He decided *not* to care about me three weeks ago when he told me we should "take a break during campaign season and see where we are in November." I apparently distracted him too much, taking away precious volunteer time. I think he freaked because he got a B plus on a civics exam. Making out ≠ studying.

Hayden's car roars ahead of me. His break lights flash, but he doesn't pull over. A pickup honks, nearly hitting him, before swerving into the other lane. Hayden speeds up. But then I see those break lights flash one more time. He pulls over to the side of the road. In the darkness I hear his car door slam. Traffic has thinned out a little, but it's pretty dark now.

"I hope you know that I can't even see you from here!" he shouts. "You're wearing rather dark clothing."

I look down at my jeans and purple T-shirt. So what if I can't, um, see my own legs? I hear Hayden's feet crunching along toward me at a slow jog. "Polly." He sounds breathless. "You will get into my car. And trust me, I'm not doing this because I—" He takes another deep breath. "It's just that I like to think of myself as a decent human being. I don't want your death on my conscience."

He's probably afraid it would end up in the newspapers, forever tainting his political legacy like that Kennedy guy who crashed with a girl on a bridge way back when.

Another driver beeps on the horn, swerving quickly into the other lane. "Polly? Please."

"Okay, fine. But no peppermint gum."

Next to me Hayden lets out a way too dramatic sigh of relief. "What was that about gum?"

"Nothing."

He walks to the passenger side of the car to open the door for me, but I brush him away. "I can open the door for myself, thank you."

Hayden's car smells new even though it's two years old. He turns on the engine, holds his hands in the correct ten and two o'clock positions, waiting for a break in traffic. I realize that I smell like dust and exhaust fumes. Maybe walking home was a stupid idea. Hayden signals, checks over his shoulder twice, and pulls on to the highway.

As we pull in to my driveway, Hayden reads his odometer. "Eight miles."

Sitting in the dark, I calculate that it might have taken me two hours to walk home.

Hayden pops several pieces of gum into his mouth at once and chews them: *chomp, chomp, chomp.* His hands go back to gripping the steering wheel.

"Um, so, yeah, eight miles. Guess I should say thanks. For

the ride. It's getting so late that if you hadn't come along a vampire might have gotten me or something."

He doesn't laugh.

"Polly, look. Having a fight with Jane doesn't justify harming yourself. Am I glad that I saw you on the road? Yes. Because I feel fairly certain I prevented you from coming to harm, with possibly fatal consequences. But I'm also tremendously disappointed. You're a smart young woman, Polly. But the lack of judgment you've displayed tonight, well . . ."

"Oh God, Hayden. Give me a break. It's not that dire."

"Let me finish."

"Fine."

"Well, it's just that I'm concerned that you lack the judgment required to serve responsibly on the student council."

"As in planning the senior prom?"

"Our budget is more than most couples spend on their weddings."

The front porch light blinks on, and I see Grace's face in the front window. Why isn't she at Amy's house? Mom can't keep leaving her alone—she's only ten years old!

I open the car door a crack, and the overhead lights blink on. As I open my mouth to mumble another apologetic thank-you, I notice the vein pulsing on Hayden's temple. "Hey, don't stress," I say. "Everything turned out fine."

Hayden turns away, shrugging. "That was completely reckless."

I reach out to touch his shoulder, but pull my hand back as he faces me again. He looks as pissed off as when his favorite city council candidate lost the primary.

"Don't worry. We'll still have the best prom ever."

"Yeah, okay. But that's not—"

Grace watches from behind the curtains. Poor kid. "Look, I've gotta go. Thanks again for the ride and everything."

As I step out of the car, Hayden grabs my hand. "Don't do that again . . ."

His expression is way more intense than it is even when he's taking an essay exam, studying chemistry formulas, or trying to convince me to agree with some obscure ballot measure.

"Yeah, okay." I rub the goose bumps on my arms. "So . . . Okay, bye!" I jump out and run toward my house, forgetting to close the car door.

Oh God. I'm a mess. Grandma will be here in just seventy-two hours. Let Operation Rescue Me from Myself begin.

```
Dear Miss Swoon:
My girlfriend and I agree on almost
everything. Mushrooms don't belong on
pizza. Squeeze the toothpaste from the
```

top. Vacations mean sunshine. But we
disagree about politics. Can an elephant
live with a donkey?

—Political Uproar

Dear Political:

I'm not sure I can deliver a speedy solution. You can't brush away these kinds
of problems. But they will rain on your
paradise. Looks like you need to talk
more, argue less.

—Miss Swoon

Not Shakespeare's Sonnet!

Blond Count: 0.5 (a fifth-grader felt me up)

HOOK-UPdates:

- Confirmation that Kipper Carlyle shared her
  lip-gloss with a certain football player at last
  Saturday night's bonfire.
- Precocious Lass *invented* the bikini incident
  (see Swimming With Skanks here). Watch out,
  honey; you're not in junior high anymore.
  You're playing with the big girls now.

• Polly Martin, you're not as dumb as you like people to think you are. Maybe you can give us lessons on how to get a hot guy to read your butt like Braille in order to score cushy, nongrope-fest work assignments?

Chapter Five

It's only six in the morning, on a Saturday, in the summer, but I'm thinking positive. Moving into Grace's room gives me the opportunity to purge unpleasant memories. I'm going to eliminate everything that reminds me of junior year: photos, newspaper clippings, school assignments, gifts from various ex-boyfriends, and a significant portion of my wardrobe. Why did I have to wear my blue hoodie around so many guys? I put it in the giveaway pile, along with a pair of PJs in which I'd had a *way* too vivid dream about Gareth.

I roll a Matchbox car back and forth across the carpet. Kurt stuck it in my locker with a ticket to a stock car race. And even though I hated all the roaring engines and the fumes in the air, I loved sitting in the stands listening to Kurt talk about different engine parts. Okay, so automotive technology completely bores me, but Kurt looked so cute and passionate. And he had complete knowledge of various kissing skills. If only he hadn't wanted our entire relationship to go from zero to sixty quite so soon, things might have worked out. I roll the car over to my trash can. *Clink.* I make an explosion sound deep in the back of my throat.

"And relationship number one crashes in an inferno— okay, wrong word." I crawl over and *thunk* the car into the trash can. "It crashes and dies when he calls me frigid for not wanting to go all the way after the Homecoming dance."

That and he didn't approve of the way I let my car go too long between oil changes. (Given my engine's age and my driving habits, every five thousand miles *is* entirely acceptable. Ask any expert.) But I'm done with automotive maintenance now, no matter what my check-engine light says. I pull several glossy copies of *Road & Track* magazine out from under my bed. I subscribed (which *did* benefit Grace's school) so I could whisper sweet automotive nothings to Kurt. Instead we argued about the new Audi's front/rear torque split.

Mom peeks into my room. "Nice to see you making so much progress," she says. "Maybe you'll inspire me to go through my room. Or my office or my classroom . . . or my brain!" She laughs. "You have no idea how hard it is to memorize the names and ingredients of twenty different hamburgers. And I thought my master's thesis was difficult!"

"Whatever, Mom. Maybe just make sure those bills are paid?"

"Oh, look who's grumpy." Mom walks into my room and sits down on my bed, messing up my neat piles of un-ex-contaminated T-shirts. "Grace says that Hayden drove you home last night? Does that—?"

"No."

"So, you haven't rekindled?"

"Absolutely not."

"Oh, I thought maybe that's what inspired you to get rid of Car's—I mean, Kurt's—"

I shoot her a *don't-even-go-there* look. Mom saw my six-week relationship with Kurt as an opportunity to polish up all her automotive jokes. The low point: knock, knock. Who's there? Cargo. Cargo who? Cargo beep beep. She said it every time he honked for me in the driveway.

"No. I'm getting rid of it all. But I'm going in order. And I only let Hayden give me a ride home because Jane was acting completely selfish and immature." I find the Homecoming dance photo in the pile, but just as I'm about to rip it up, Mom snatches it from my hands.

"You looked so pretty that night, in racecar red." Mom laughs. "Zoom, zoom."

"Yeah, well." She has *no* idea! It was more like stoplight red.

"Don't rip up the photos. You'll want these memories someday."

"Uh, no. I won't. Why would I want to relive the pain and agony?"

Mom looks at her hands. "It won't seem so painful in the future, honey."

"Oh. So, explain to me again why you bashed your golf clubs against the driveway until they bent like paper clips?"

"That's different. I only took up golf because of your father—seeing those clubs made my stomach turn every time I pulled my car in to the garage."

I wave a newspaper clipping in front of her face. "Well, this brings back bad memories for me." Sawyer took me to the state basketball championships, and our picture ended up on the front page of the newspaper, plus the reporter interviewed us—but only quoted *me* in the article. Maybe Sawyer shouldn't have used a hockey reference while talking about basketball! He totally overreacted.

"Hey, you sounded so intelligent in that article! And you look adorable." Mom grabs the clipping from my hand, reaching down to scoop the rest of the detritus into her arms. "Why don't you just let me keep these away from you?" She smiles. "I mean *for* you—for a few years?"

"How about a few centuries, millennia, eons . . ." I shake my head. "Mom, the last thing you need shoved in your closet is—"

"You leave my closet to me, okay?"

"You and the health department." Mom crams her closet with all kinds of papers and boxes of old crap—pretty much everything except clothes. She keeps those in the middle of her floor. She's been on a laundry-folding strike since the divorce seven years ago.

"Very funny. *Not!*" Mom cackles at her own stupid joke, but at least she leaves me alone.

I sift through my school papers and toss them into the trash. *Take that, Gareth! I'm not going to recycle.* I find a trail map from the spring break trip and crush it into a ball. I spent six months of baby-sitting money on all that outdoorsy clothing—and those pricey boots still gave me blisters. I pluck *The Guide to Western Wildflowers* off my shelf. Who cares about the difference between golden pea and lupine? All those weedy plants inflamed my allergies. I toss the book next to my blue hoodie. Let some other fool memorize wildflowers to impress a guy.

The only thing I keep is a piece of ripped-out notebook paper that has just a hand-drawn smiley sun above the word *you*. Sawyer passed it to me in class on a snowy day right after our first official date. It had made me feel he liked me for *me* and not just for liking the same stuff he did. (For the record, I didn't start watching ESPN with Sawyer; I used to watch it with my dad. Mom and Grace just don't remember.)

Two hours later a Tibetan monk could have moved into my room—if he had a thing for pink curtains, floral wallpaper, and rock posters. Ex-ex-ex-ex Jack listened to every single one of those bands, and since we spent a lot of time at the mall's music store, I ended up with quite a few mementos. I like Linkin Park. *Not!* (That's for you, Mom.)

I walk another armload of stuff into Grace's room; she doesn't have any space for more posters on her walls. I'll be living among puppies, kittens, and horsies, all espousing logic that sounds remarkably similar to the stuff Grandma writes in her columns. I'm all for it—how can I go wrong with the advice to *hang in there* scripted above an adorable kitten? I especially love the "Back Off If You Know What's Good for You" poster of a spiky little hedgehog. I look around Grace's floor; that might be the only stuffed animal species she *doesn't* have. My move to Grace's room is displacing an entire phylum of critters that used to live on the spare bed. I toss an armful of Webimals off my bed.

"But these meat eaters can't live with the plant eaters," Grace says, holding up a stuffed moose, a deer, and a skunk. "You're ruining my system!"

I shove a fluffy blond doggy the color of Sawyer's hair onto the floor. "Well, I'm not sleeping with that! I didn't before and I'm not going to now."

I still get twitchy when I think about how I attempted to push things forward with Sawyer in *that* way only to avoid talking about difficult subjects. Talking = bad. Making out = good. Besides, how could sharing my feelings with Sawyer make my mom less depressed? Or stop my dad from dating a series of interchangeable Bank Teller Barbies?

I glance at Grace's bunny poster: *Just Relax.* I take a deep breath, close my eyes. Good advice. Early morning sunlight streams through the window, warming my face. And then I hear that zipper sound.

Gliding down the street on his skateboard: Xander Cooper. His body leans into the curves, so graceful. He's not wearing a shirt, and I stand in the window gawking at his smooth dark skin. Muscles. I don't move a single one of my muscles. I don't care that he can probably see me if I can see him, but he doesn't look up. He takes wide turns across the steepest part of the hill, effortless. After he passes the window, T-shirt hanging from the back pocket of his pants, I close my eyes again, listening to the sound of his wheels unzipping the asphalt.

Grandma will be here in how many hours?

"Why is your face all red?" Grace looks up from redistributing her sea animals under her bed, which has now become the "ocean zone."

"What? It's not." I shove the handful of underwear I'm holding into my shirt drawer. I'll sort it out later: the skateboarder and the tees. Not that I'm a *tease*. Jack was so wrong about that. I hung out at the mall playing video games because I was interested in improving my hand-eye coordination, not just to see him. It's not like playing video games together is the same as actually dating, even if you do end up fooling around a bit. He really doesn't count; I was simply confused after breaking up with Kurt. Plus, I could walk to the mall from my house and avoid driving my car, which, you know, reminded me of Kurt. I only played for like three weeks—long enough to get the high score on Donkey Kong. And win a series of posts on Sonnet Silverman's blog: Polly Martin Scores Again (and Again) (and Again).

Suddenly I can't wait to get to work just so I can rush home again and have Grandma talk some sense into me. "Gracie, dear," I say, "I'll give you ten bucks if you finish moving stuff from my room to yours."

"I'll do it if you buy me a new Webimal. The manatee or the killer whale."

After taxes that's equivalent to three hours of monitoring screaming, wet kids. "Fine!"

"If Amy helps, will you get her one, too?"

"Yes, but now you have to organize my drawers."

Grace sticks out her hand. "Deal!"

On the way to work the little red check-engine light blinks on my dashboard. "You totally saw me staring at Xander Cooper, didn't you?"

I will beg to patrol the Buckaroo Pond, unofficially known as the Poop Pit. Just stick me with babies and toddlers; otherwise I can't be trusted.

I try to talk to Sawyer before he hands out the assignments, but he's acting like I hurt his manhood during lifeguard training by not wanting him to faux save me. He won't look at me. "No special requests. We all work all park features."

"Just this once, you know, a favor for a friend?"

"Friends? Right." He glances at me through his hair, "Only if you tell me why."

What is it with this guy and talking, and reasons, and having to know the stuff lodged deep in my psyche? It's none of his business. It's not like I can even put it into words.

"I'm having *issues*," I say. The word *issues* is nice and vague and covers many possibilities.

Sawyer looks at me, and this time I look down to avoid his big green, stare-into-your-soul eyes. "Are you saying you want to avoid deep water today?"

I have no idea what he's getting at, but we seem to be talking in some kind of code. "Yes, that's exactly what I'm saying."

"Fine. You can have the Buckaroo Pond for four days. Is that enough time?"

"Yes." Four days should be plenty of time for Grandma to help me devise a plan to avoid male temptation. Only moms and dads venture into the Poop Pit. "Thank you very much, Sawyer." And then since I'm feeling grateful, I add generously, "I'm sorry about yesterday. I was just feeling a little—" I don't know how to express it.

"Moody."

I wrinkle my nose. "Yeah, I guess."

"That's okay; it's all clear to me now. Go and get 'em, Pollywog."

"Sure thing, Saw—Sawyer." I'm not going to piss him off by trying out one of my new nicknames. Not today.

It's only after I've had to evacuate the pool due to a leaky swim diaper and I'm waiting for the chlorine treatment to kick in that I realize why Sawyer relented. He thinks I'm menstruating! I'm so humiliated that I want to die. I would never tell a guy *anything* about that kind of situation, even though it *is* a natural biological process. I blow my whistle to signal that it's safe for the infectious tots to return to the water.

Sonnet saunters past. "What're you doing to score all the cushy assignments, huh?"

I shrug.

"Do you think if I let Sawyer fondle my ass, I could get out of that stinking Lazy River? I'm sick of fifth-graders grabbing my boobs all day. So are you back together with Sawyer or what?"

"No. He thinks I'm"—I vaguely tilt my head back and forth—"having my, you know."

"You told Sawyer you were on the rag? Priceless, Polly. Priceless!" Sonnet chortles. "You don't get enough credit for your intelligence."

Oh God. What have I done now? I need to keep my mouth shut!

Dear Miss Swoon:

My boyfriend doesn't like my little dog. He's always teasing my pup, making fun of him, calling him a wimpy little rat and worse. I don't know what do to do? —Doggone It!

Dear Doggone:

Ditch the dog. The big one, not the small one! —Miss Swoon

Chapter Six

Grandma's shuttle arrives just as I'm trying, for the septil-lionth time, *not* to think about the way Xander Cooper said, "Hey, nice to see you again, neighbor," as I walked to my car after work. I managed to raise my hand slightly before collid-ing with a toddler, knocking the poor kid to the pavement, and getting chewed out by her mom. The ever-present Sawyer rushed over to intervene.

But that's not the embarrassing, must-churn-it-over-in-my-mind part. Xander must have *seen* me *seeing* him from my window. Wasn't I holding a bunch of my underwear? Oh, I don't even care. He simply uttered a greeting. He does live in my neighborhood. It's nice to have friendly neighbors. That's all that means. I'm not about to go lusting after the old dude who's always out mowing his lawn even though I always say hello to him, too. Besides, Xander's the one who used to tuck his sweatpants into his tube socks in fourth grade. And come to think of it, I recall an incident in which his Incredible Hulk boxers made an unfortunate appearance at recess.

I perseverate about Xander, even as I race out to the shuttle to greet Grandma. Grace beats me to her, leaping at Grandma, wrapping her arms around her neck. "You're here! You're here!"

"Mmm. Hmmm." Grandma nuzzles into Grace's hair, but then her bright blue eyes turn to me. "Polly, you gorgeous thing, you. Come here!"

I don't even care that we're having a weird group hug in the middle of our driveway. The shuttle driver grins at us as he lines up suitcase after suitcase. *Having Grandma here will fix everything*, I think even as she whispers, "I bet you have to beat the boys off with a stick, huh, gorgeous?"

"Um, about that." But I realize it's not the right time.

"Charlie, these are my beautiful granddaughters," Grandma tells the shuttle driver.

"They take after you." He winks at Grandma. "Let me carry your bags inside, Sharlene."

"You're too kind." Grandma smoothes a hand through her freshly reddened hair. "Ooh, look at those muscles. Popeye must be jealous."

I'm only a little freaked out by the fact that Grandma is on a first-name basis with the shuttle driver after a thirty-minute drive from the airport, but whatever. That's why she gets paid to give advice in hundreds of newspapers across the country. People love her.

"I can get them," I say, attempting to heft a bag, but Charlie takes it from me.

"It's my job, little lady." Then he turns to Grandma, "This must be the feisty one, right? Like her redheaded grandma?" More winking. Winking = creepy. I'm a brunette. Grandma was a brunette before "updating" after her last divorce.

"A gal's got to learn to stick up for herself without a big strong man around."

Exactly! I ignore Grandma's flirtatious shoulder shrug— maybe she just had an itch or something.

When the shuttle driver leaves—after a few too many minutes making small talk in our living room—Grace ransacks the bags, searching for the gifts Grandma always brings.

Grandma sits on the sofa, laughing. "Oh no. I think I forgot this time, Gracie Pie." Then she reaches behind her back and pulls out the manatee Webimal *and* the killer whale. Grace practically seizes. I might have to use my newly acquired life-saving skills at home, but then she recovers and races to phone Amy; really I'm going to have to discuss their co-dependent attachment with Grandma.

"I brought this for you." Grandma dangles a delicate gold

chain in front of me. A small pink heart swings at the end. It's all wrong! I detest superficial symbols. Plus, it looks almost exactly like the necklace Sawyer gave me for Valentine's Day. The one Mom snuck out of my giveaway pile. Grandma frowns. "You don't like it?"

"Oh no. It's completely pretty, it's just that—"

"Your boyfriend gave you one just like it?" Grandma nods. "I should've known."

"Yeah, sort of, but—" This is *not* going how I imagined.

"Why didn't you say so? We'll exchange it. Maybe for earrings to match."

"Um, Grandma?" I listen to Grace yapping about stuffed animals on the phone with Amy. "I kind of wanted to talk to you about guy stuff."

"Miss Swoon at your service! You juggling too many beaux?" Grandma smiles.

"No!"

"Trying to figure out how to let him down gently? You little heartbreaker."

Why isn't she listening to me? "Grandma, a guy just broke up with *me*."

"Oh, honey. Just get right back in the saddle. That's the only cure for a broken heart."

"I kind of tried that, um, unsuccessfully."

Grandma knits her eyebrows, finally listening.

"Five times unsuccessfully."

"Oh my." She's nodding. "Looks like you need a Miss Swoon relationship evaluation."

I exhale a long, cleansing breath. "Yes, exactly! That's what I need."

"These boys wanting too much hanky-panky?"

"No!" My face warms. "Not after the first two, anyway."

Grandma folds her arms, nodding. "Okay, then we'll move straight to Learning the Love Lessons. Find something you can learn from each relationship. That way you turn a negative into a positive. It's all about positivity, right?"

I smile. "Exactly. I've already started thinking about that—I've been reading your columns."

Grandma rolls her eyes. "Glad someone has."

"I've been trying to, you know, focus on the good things in my life."

"Make a list, dear. Things you learned about yourself from each relationship. There's magic in putting pen to paper." Grandma lifts herself off the sofa. "I'm going to freshen up. Unpack a little. What are we doing for dinner?"

"Mom wants us to go to Hamburger Heaven, since she has to work. Things have been a little, um, different around here this summer."

"It's a good thing I've come, then."

"You're telling me. Thanks so much for the advice, Grandma. I mean, Miss Swoon."

Grandma laughs, pulling a suitcase behind her. I head into Grace's room, but I can't think clearly with all those beady, stuffed animal eyes staring at me. I go into the kitchen, grab a notepad and pour a glass of iced tea.

The birds flitting from tree to tree make me feel upbeat and hopeful as I sit on my front porch steps. I start at the beginning with Kurt. Hmm. I'm not even going to think about the whole sex fiasco (he rented a hotel room without telling me). That was really more about him than me. I tap my pencil against the paper. What did I learn about myself? I write down:

```
1. Kurt. I'm surprisingly good at
   memorizing engine specifications.
2. Jack. I kick ass at level three
   in Donkey Kong.
3. Sawyer. I'd rather kiss than read
   or talk about fish.
4. Gareth. My feet blister easily.
5. Hayden. I'm popular enough to get
   elected to the student council.
   (Although maybe it was Sonnet's
```

I'm blushing, wondering why I did all that stuff—memorizing paragraphs from *Road & Track*, climbing mountains, begging people to sign my campaign petition—to make guys like me (and I'm stuck planning the prom!). I look up to see forever-shirtless Xander Cooper walking in front of my house carrying his skateboard. He glances sideways at me, through all that curly hair, and raises his eyebrows.

In a rush to hide the humiliating list I knock over my iced tea, breaking the glass, splashing tea all over my bare feet. I pick up shards of glass, glancing at Xander every few seconds. He strolls uphill, not looking back, but I notice that he's taken that little notebook out of his pocket. Holding his skateboard under his arm, he scribbles something. Maybe he's designing the ultimate superhero hideout like he used to in elementary school. If only he still wore his pants hiked up too high—and not so low slung on his slim hips.

I sweep the wet, broken glass onto my soggy list, go inside, and throw the whole thing into the trash. Lists are completely ineffective! I haven't learned anything about myself from my past relationships.

Dear Miss Swoon:

My boyfriend dumped me six months ago,
but I just can't recover. I keep thinking
I could have saved the relationship if
I'd only changed like he wanted me to.
—Too Late To Change

Dear Too Late:

It's never too late to change! Change
can be a good thing—but only if you're
doing it for yourself! Make a list of
the things you've learned about yourself
from this relationship. And put it to
good use in your next one. (There will be
a next one!)
—Miss Swoon

*Broken glass. Sharp shards. Little weapons to prick and make
you bleed. Symbols of past pain, broken relationships . . . Or is
it as simple as a nervous girl knocking over her beverage? And
a fragile object hitting hard cement steps?*
—X.C.

Chapter Seven

Sunday morning I get up even earlier than usual to meet Jane at the veterinary clinic where she volunteers to walk the animals on the weekends. I like it that Jane has maintained her love of everything animal; unlike me, who got hit with hormones and moved on to a love of everything Neanderthal. Jane walks a poodle recovering from hip surgery—with the neck collar, weird puffs of hair, and bandaged bald spot, it looks more alien than canine. I've got a pug that's more interested in sniffing my sneakers than doing his business. At least I think it's a he; some dog breeds always look like boys the way some skateboarders always look—

"Jane." I tug the pug toward Jane's poodle. "I need you talk some sense into me."

The pug growls at the poodle, so she stands a few feet away. "Who is it *now*?" Her voice sounds weary.

"No one." I'm *not* thinking about how I waited in bed listening for that skateboard, in a safe nonromantic, simply-interested-in-the-physics-of-sound-waves kind of way. "I told you I've sworn off guys."

Jane scoffs, "Yeah, right. So *that's* why you were all cozy with Hayden on the sofa the other night."

"It was the only place to sit. Besides, he sat next to *me*."

"You could have sat with me on the floor."

"Did you see that floor? It was disgusting. Who knows what those dorks do down there when there aren't regular humans around."

Jane's cheeks go pink. "That's not nice," she says quietly, letting the poodle wander back toward the kennel door.

"I just mean that I'm over Hayden—and he's way over me. He's the one who broke up with me, remember."

Jane opens the kennel door. "Oh, I remember. So does my GPA."

The pug still won't do his business. "Come on, you little beast." Yeah, so I begged Jane to come over and study for the AP Bio final, and, you know, listen to me rant about how men should be classified lower than single-celled bacteria. We did study! She resents the fact that I outscored her, despite being an emotional wreck and everything. I couldn't sleep, so I studied—I *asked* her to stay up with me.

A few minutes later Jane emerges with a pair of angry-looking rottweilers that match her mood. The pug immediately squats and goes. I look down at the nasty little pile. "Um, Jane?" I nod toward the stinky heap. "What now?"

She glowers at me like *I'm* the big pile of crap. "You pick it up. That's what the plastic bags are for."

"Oh." I practically gag on the stench and the texture of the stuff as I scoop it into the plastic bag. I hold it away from me as the pug makes a beeline for the kennel door.

"Bring out the Lab next. Be gentle. He was just neutered."

The pug jumps into his empty wire cage before I can get the leash off. Part of me feels like joining him. Dogs do have that sixth sense thing, right? Jane is not in best friend mode. She's looking to pick a fight. I should've stayed home, even if it meant succumbing to a lascivious Xander Cooper fantasy. The black Lab starts wagging his tail as if he's been waiting all day for me to arrive. I've always been a sucker for dark hair, I think, unlatching the cage—and light hair and medium light hair, and not-quite-so-dark hair. Maybe I'm just a sucker. I've got to make Jane understand.

The black Lab yanks me through the door. "Jane. Let's start over, okay?" The Lab pulls me across the lawn, breathing heavy with enthusiasm. "I'm not interested in Hayden anymore. And I'm trying to avoid all contact. That's why I left early."

Jane shakes her head. "Oh, so that explains why he gave you a ride home?"

"How—?" I wasn't about to get into that whole situation. Just stick to the facts. The bare minimum of facts. "He insisted."

"And you, with your expanded vocabulary, forgot the word *no*?"

"Expansive. I have an expansive vocabulary. Besides, I did say no. About three times. But he made me get into the car."

The rottweilers nip at each other's ears, and maybe they're playing, but it's not reassuring. "Made you?"

The friendly Lab flops on the ground, rolling over for a belly rub, and I oblige. "After I, you know, almost got hit by a truck."

"God, Polly! Can't you drop the drama queen act for one night?"

"I was just walking home. Like *you* told me to."

Jane doesn't look one little bit guilty. Her lips pull back into a snarl. "Oh, so you didn't even think for one moment that Hayden would shoot out of his seat as soon as he found out precious Polly would be walking home all alone?"

"No! I'd been walking for almost an hour before he offered me a ride. I figured he stayed until the end of the movie."

"No. He spent that hour driving around trying to find you. He practically put out an AMBER Alert." Jane yanks a rottweiler away from a dried piece of crap. "He kept calling Rowdy to see if I'd heard from you."

"Really?"

"Really. So, my evening was completely ruined."

"It's not like I planned for that to happen. I was leaving you alone like you asked." The Lab leans against me. "Besides, you've seen that movie so many times."

"It's not about the movie!" Jane sounds so exasperated that the rottweilers both look up at her. "I wanted to spend time hanging out with Rowdy, but instead I ended up involved in yet another big Polly drama."

"I'm sorry."

"I'm not sure that's enough anymore." Jane leads the dogs back into the kennel. A bunch of angry barking ensues. I focus on the black Lab. Not the bad feelings welling in my chest, threatening to pop out in a burst of embarrassing emotion. I pat the Lab on the head. "What's the secret to happiness, little buddy, huh? Maybe I need to get neutered like you."

Jane comes up behind me, almost smiling. "Believe me,

I've thought about it." She's carrying one of those froufrou dogs that seem incapable of self-ambulation. "Polly, the way you were acting, I figured you were still into Hayden."

"I'm not." I bite my lip so it won't tremble. "I'm really trying to focus on *not* having a boyfriend, because I totally suck at it."

Jane sets the tiny dog on the grass. "Can't argue with that."

I feel as jittery as that little froufrou dog shaking on its pencil-thin legs. "I want to be a better friend, too."

"Yeah, well. Maybe you could start with telling me stuff. I feel like I barely know you these days. One minute you're rushing off to stock car races, the next you're obsessed with video games—"

"You don't need to go on." The Lab lies on the grass with his head resting on my feet. I wonder if I can convince my mom to get us a dog. Dogs = love (the safe, unconditional kind).

"I don't even know where you're applying for college."

My stomach flutters like a thousand unopened credit card bills. "I'm probably just going to the U," I say. "Stick close to Grace and Mom and stuff."

Jane looks like I've just suggested we feed the frou-frou dog to the rottweilers. "But you've always talked about getting *away* from your mom and Grace."

I shrug. I haven't even told her about Mom's new job at Hamburger Heaven; it's just too humiliating. Jane's mom does volunteer work and stays home, making crafts and preparing delicious meals, because her dad owns a successful accounting firm.

"The U's really strong in science." I have no idea if what I'm saying is true. But we've dropped the college talk at home, and Dad avoids the subject like e-mail spam, so I've stopped thinking about it.

Jane rolls her eyes. "You know you have the grades to go anywhere. And Grace doesn't need you, she's got your mom and Amy, right?" Jane scoops up the little dog's microscopic doo-doo.

"Why didn't you let me walk that one?"

"Come on, Polly. I thought we were both going Ivy League? That's been the plan since, what, seventh grade?"

"Yeah, I guess, but . . ." I scratch the Lab's belly again. "Hey, where are *you* going to apply?"

Jane takes my lead like a retriever chasing a ball. I listen, nodding, making funny quips and serious comments in all the right places. That's what good friends do, right? Jane keeps up the college discussion until we've finished feeding and watering the dogs. Jane locks the clinic door and smiles. "So, now that I'm not completely pissed at you anymore . . ."

"What?" I'm hoping she'll suggest we go to her house to hang out and let her mom make us salads for lunch; all that's been served lately at my house are Hamburger Heaven reject orders.

"My night wasn't totally ruined."

I find my inner Labrador and fake enthusiasm. "Oh, really? Details, please."

"So, after Hayden called to say he found you and everything, Rowdy pulled me aside and said that maybe we should finish watching the movie together sometime. Just the two of us! Omigod, I almost died." Jane touches her hands to her cheeks. "But I totally channeled you—and acted all coy and said maybe I'd think about it. It worked! He looked about as hungry as those rotties!" Jane starts laughing. "He's already texted me three times this weekend. You totally know how to hook 'em." She giggles. "Maybe I can figure out how to actually keep them."

"That's a compliment, right?"

Jane shrugs. "If you think so."

Dear Miss Swoon:
I really hate my friend's boyfriend. I
don't see what she sees in him or why
she chooses to spend time with him when

she could be spending time with me. How
can I make her see that I need her too?
—My Friend Is Blind

Dear Blind:
Are you sure that you're seeing 20/20?
Jealousy could be clouding your vision.
Time to focus on *yourself*.
—Miss Swoon

Chapter Eight

My voice cracks as I scream at kids to stop: spitting, running, pushing, shoving, splashing—basically violating every single Wild Waves rule and inventing new ones like seeing how fast ice cream melts in pool water.

"Where do you think you're going?" I say to a kid about to take a corn dog on a ride through the Lazy River. "No food allowed in the pool."

The kid looks at me like I'm a big loser; he's even younger than Grace. His eyes fixate on my plastic sheriff's badge. "You're not a real sheriff. That's so fake."

"Well." I hate myself for feeling intimidated by this kid. "My authority is real."

The word *authority* means nothing to him. He takes one more bite of the corn dog, tosses it toward the nearest trash can, misses, and walks into the pool. My face turns the color of the ketchup now dripping from my hand as I pick up the disgusting, half-eaten, nitrate-filled food product. I'm seriously considering becoming a vegetarian—simply because Hamburger Heaven doesn't seem to have any vegetables on the menu and Mom might be forced to, you know, buy something at the grocery store. I half expect her to make us shampoo with Hamburger Heaven washroom soap.

I spot a kid about to snap a girl's swimsuit straps. "Hands to yourself!" The kid looks at me with wide-eyed innocence. "Yeah, well, I saw you!" Little perverts like him should be branded so girls like me won't try to date them in high school. I'm sure Kurt snapped swimsuits!

I tug my swimsuit up, shorts down. "Is there a single person here who isn't compelled to break the rules?" I say it too loud, and a couple of mom types glare at me like *How dare you talk about* my *snot-dripping cuties?*

"What rule am I breaking?"

I spin around at the sound of Xander Cooper's voice, *not* that I recognize it or anything, but he *has* been bringing his niece and nephew here all week and I've heard him talking to them. This is the first time he's talked to *me*. He smiles with one eyebrow raised in a question. I look into his eyes—

big brown eyes—because he's not wearing a shirt. His lips curve into a smirk, and I realize that my witty response is way overdue.

I tilt my head. "I think you know."

That makes him laugh. "Yeah, but do *you* know?"

I gawk at him. My mind goes blank. My eyes flash down at his chest. No, not there. I look up at his hair. Not there, either. I focus on his wrist. How can a wrist be sexy? Fingers. Smudged with black ink. He's been writing in that notebook on and off all morning, *not* that I'm watching, but it is my job to patrol, or whatever.

"Do you?" he asks, touching inky fingers to his kinky-curly hair.

Yeah, I *do* know. He's broken the rule of standing so close to me that I can smell his sunscreen and see the mole on his left wrist, the chapped spot on his bottom lip, the reddish streak in his hair, the way his skin is the color of tea with milk. Grandma drinks a lot of tea. Thinking about Grandma is much preferable to thinking about—Wait! He's the kid who once ate an old piece of chewed gum from under my desk. I take a deep breath and draw myself up a bit taller, in spite of the way it makes my swimsuit pull downward.

"Oh, I think I do know." I resist tugging at my suit, my

shorts. "But you should know that I like to follow the rules."
Rule number one: avoid guys!

I ignore a group of kids running past screaming, whacking each other with their towels, and clearly violating Wild Waves regulations one through three. Well, maybe they don't *all* have communicable diseases, but whatever.

Xander cuts his eyes toward them. "Clearly some rules are made to be broken."

Sawyer's whistle blows but who cares? I ignore the screaming, splashing sound echoing off the walls of the Lazy River. The whistle blows again. "Polly!" Sawyer screams. "Take action."

So I do. I look straight into Xander Cooper's eyes and say, "Don't mess with the deputy, Mr. Cooper." I head over to the melee in the pool, but over my shoulder I say, "Or I'll have to lock you up."

Now he's the one who's speechless.

I cannonball into the water—yeah, breaking the always-enter-via-the-stairway rule, but I'm an employee, right? And we have a situation. Plus, I need to cool my hot face, skin, hot all of me. I stay underwater for a few seconds, but Sawyer's still blowing that whistle, so I pop up, brush my hair back, and swim the few strokes toward the boys who've created an inner tube barricade under the Shot-Bucket Waterfall—about once a minute a gunshot pings, and the bucket dumps water into the Lazy River. These boys have got a younger kid trapped, and they've decided it's funny to steer his head under the streaming water. I recognize Corn Dog Boy.

"Hey, you!" I try to blow my whistle, but it's full of water. "Stop right now!"

The victim gets dunked by another bucket of water.

I reach over and yank one kid's tube out from under him. "I said stop!" But of course, that kid doesn't hear me because he's under water. So I knock another kid off his tube. If they're all concerned with staying afloat, they can't torture their victim, right? With my foot I give the victim's tube a good shove so he drifts away.

The other kids have turned on me. One says, "Hey! I'm telling my mom you pushed me into the water!"

"I'm going to tell her that you were engaging in unnecessary roughhousing."

The kid looks at me like I'm speaking a foreign language. "My mom is going to be so mad at you! I almost drownded."

"The word is *drowned*! You almost *drowned*. I mean, not really. Argh!"

Sawyer blows his whistle loud. Right next to me. Deafening.

"Out of the pool, boys."

"Okay," Corn Dog Boy says. "But did you see what *she* did?"

"You're still in the penalty box." Sawyer points to the pool stairs. "Back to the twenty-yard line."

Now I look at him like he's speaking a foreign language, but the kids seem to understand his well-churned sports metaphor. And he thinks he can become an ESPN commentator!

"You, too, Pollywog. We need to discuss procalls."

Protocol. The word is protocol.

Sawyer waves Sonnet over. "Here's the lowdown. I need you to man the Lazy River for a few minutes."

"Gosh, Sawyer. Can't you tell that I'm a girl?" She throws her shoulders back, exposing even more mammary tissue. "Isn't that kind of sexist? Shouldn't I 'woman' the Lazy River?"

"Yeah, sure." Sawyer runs his hand through his hair. "Just do it, okay?"

"'Do it.'" Sonnet snickers. "Who with?"

Sawyer puts his hand on my shoulder—what gives him the right?—and steers me toward the employee break room behind The General Store.

"You owe me one, Sawyer," Sonnet says. "There's a totally cute dad in the Splash Pasture."

I look back over my shoulder. "Um, gross."

"Don't judge, Pollywog. What about that single dad of *yours?*"

I shake Sawyer's hand off. "What?"

"That tall iced coffee of a man who doesn't seem to own a shirt?"

"Xander Cooper? He goes to our *school*. And those aren't his kids; they're his niece and nephew."

Sonnet's mouth gapes. "How come I've never noticed him before?"

I shrug. "He's more of an academic guy. And maybe he finally had his growth spurt?"

"Well, hell, sign me up for the physics club!" Sonnet chuckles. "Spurt? Good one, P.M."

"Sonnet, please?" Sawyer's all business. "I just need a few seconds alone with Polly."

Sonnet winks at me. "So, is *that* why you kids broke up?"

I roll my eyes. Sawyer ignores her—more likely he didn't get the joke.

"Look, Sawyer. Can't you yell at me here?"

"Is that what you think? I'm not going to yell; I just want to talk deep."

"Can't we just talk in the deep end?"

Sawyer knits his eyebrows. "No, we're going to the employee break room."

I sigh. "Never mind."

On the other side of the O.K. Corral I spot Xander Cooper sitting in the shade, writing in his notebook while watching a sparrow struggle to fly with a french fry in its beak. He snaps the notebook shut as we pass. But when I look back reflexively, he makes his fingers into a gun and shoots me then blows on his finger. What a doofus! So, what's wrong with my palpitating heart? He used to be so . . . so not hot. Xander tips an invisible cowboy hat to me. Freak.

I'm jittery as Sawyer motions for me to sit in a plastic chair. "You can get your towel first."

"I'm okay." I look at the Wanted poster hanging on the wall displaying the employee of the month: Acne Cream Guy. I want my brain to cooperate: stop sending all these chemical signals to my heart, stomach, quivering knees.

"You're shivering."

"Just because I'm nervous." I try to rub my goose pimples away. "Going over the big protocol and everything." How can Xander Cooper have this effect on me? I know way too much about his sordid elementary school habits.

"This is serious, Polly. You're having trouble controlling with control."

I look at him, confused. Does he know about Xander Cooper? Did he totally see me flirting? Was I blushing that much? Sure, I felt hot, but it's ninety-four degrees outside. I let my guard down a bit. "I know. But I'm working on it."

Sawyer's forehead squishes into a frown. "Kids just don't listen to you."

"Oh, the kids." I shift in my chair. "Well, yeah, those little brats don't listen to anyone. Have you seen the way they treat their mothers?"

"Wild Waves safety depends upon your ability to lead the team."

"Well, hey, I told you the deputy should be allowed to carry a gun. And a lasso."

"That wasn't funny this morning and it isn't funny now." Sawyer pulls a chair out, turns it backward, and sits down, draping his arms over the backrest. "Polly, if you want to keep this job, you've got to learn how to act like a coach, you know? Ruling with rules. And you can't dump kids in the water."

"Fine. I obviously suck at this job. So fire me." Yeah, I totally need the money, but who needs the temptation—I mean, aggravation? I'll never save enough money for college anyway.

Sawyer rests his warm hand on my clammy arm. "I know how much this job means to you. You were so excited about it back—"

"Before I got in over my head in the deep end?" I hate the way he acts like a concerned dad—not that I have much experience in that department, but whatever. He keeps looking at me with his big puppy-dog eyes, all interested in my well-being. What a poser.

He doesn't even smile. "I don't want our relationship, what used to be our relationship—a more involved, yet not quite that involved, involvement of sorts—to dampen your summer employment enjoyment."

"Employment enjoyment?" He sounds like a poorly written English essay, the kind he writes all the time. "Dampen?" I look down at my still-wet swimsuit. "We work at a water park, Sawyer."

"Stop trying to use humor to disabuse the situation."

I stand up. "I think you mean *defuse*. I use humor to *defuse* the situation—as in lessen the tension. Look, Sawyer. I have no problem working with you." I scoot my chair back under the table. "And I'll work on increasing my leadership, or whatever. Now, please let me get back to work before one of those brats kills someone."

Sawyer stands up. "But we're not finished, Pollywog. We have to go over an incident management plan."

"Write it down on a little piece of paper. And I'll take it home and memorize it, okay? But right now I'm freezing, and I want to get back to work. Outside. In the sunshine." I turn and wave. "Saw-yer later!"

I run—yes, breaking the rules—through the concession area, glancing briefly at Xander Cooper—shirt on—packing up his stuff. Normal guys don't take baby-sitting jobs. They mow lawns, sell fast food, videos, coffee.

When I get back to the Lazy River, Sonnet is forcing a kid to pick up a bunch of spilled ice cubes on the sidewalk. How does she manage to have so much authority? "So, how did that go? You were gone long enough!"

"He's my ex, okay? No need to post anything on your blog about it."

"Omigod! You read my blog?" Sonnet sounds way too excited, but then her face grows stern as she points to a melting ice cube. "You forgot one," she tells the kid before turning back to me. "Maybe you should tell Sawyer to read my blog. He's doesn't act like he knows he's your ex."

"He broke up with *me*. So, yeah, I think he knows."

Sonnet laughs. "Then why does he always assign himself to your station? I haven't worked with him once." She sticks her hand on her hip. "And I'm on a mission to hook up with blonds this summer."

"Probably because he thinks I'm incompetent." I glance at Sonnet's bulging bosom. "And you probably scare him."

That makes Sonnet laugh loud enough to garner herself a

few mom glares. "He likes them to play hard to get, huh? That's *so* last century."

I sigh as a kid runs past me toward the Switchback slide, shoving his little sister so that she stumbles. "I don't know."

"Well, you know what I know? Working with an ex has to suck. Especially when he's got seniority. You know what you need? A little bit of sneaky revenge." Sonnet clicks her tongue, glancing around. "Let's give him something to liven up his afternoon. See those kids over there? Friends of my little sister's. They will do *anything* for ice cream. How about we fake a little swimmer's cramp and force Sawyer to jump into the pool? That guy never gets wet."

"He did once."

"Oh, yeah. So he could manhandle your wet butt." Sonnet looks at me as if doubting our breakup. "From what I recall, he had his hands all over your cute little behind."

"It was only a lifeguard thing."

Sonnet winks at me. "Sure it was. No matter what, he deserves to get soaked. It is really hot today."

Before I can stop her—not that it's feasible—Sonnet heads over to a group of girls, who huddle around her like a cheerleading squad. Not five minutes after Sawyer climbs back to his post, the girls enter the Lazy River without their tubes. Soon there's a bunch of scared screeching, followed by Sawyer's dramatic jump into the pool, followed by a bunch of squealing laughter. I bite my lip as I watch the girls listening not so seriously to a patented this-is-not-funny Sawyer Holms lecture.

Maybe a little workplace revenge *is* the answer.

```
Dear Miss Swoon:
When is it ethical to seek revenge at
work? What if your boss is your ex-
husband? Quitting is not an option since
we co-own the company. But I need to do
something to maintain my sanity.
—Ethics Or Sanity

Dear Ethics:
Sell your share in the company before
you sell your soul.
—Miss Swoon
```

Not Shakespeare's Sonnet!

Blond count: 1.5 (Thank you, guy-at-party, dude.)

Random Acts of EX-Revenge (inspired by my summer reading list—yeah, I know: dorky):

Is it best to hook up with lots of girls/guys? Did R.S. really feel better after dating half the water polo team after T.M. dumped her? Or did she just spend a lot of money on antibiotics? (See Gonorrhea and a Pack of Gum here.)

The self-improvement plan? You go, guy, Max Reams! We all cheered when you ditched the 104-pound biatch. And we really noticed when you ditched a few lbs. after joining the track team instead of chasing that unappreciative horror of a GF.

Rumors? Yeah, it's like Basic Breakup 101. Spread a nasty rumor. (For a particularly meaty example, see Polly Martin Revs Another Engine here.) Bonus question: does the rumor have to be true?

Tell me your favorite revenge stories. I'm kinda missing *The Count of Monte Cristo* after sucking down all 1,321 pages. I need more revenge stories. Now! Feed me!

Chapter Nine

Payday! Normal girls—like Sonnet Silverman—head to the mall, buy cute little tank tops, nail polish, a snack at the food court, tickets to the blockbuster movie. What did I do? I headed to the bank and put half my money in savings. I spent the other half on nail polish, sunscreen, and, you know, carrots, lettuce, tomatoes, apples, oranges, and other members of the plant kingdom. While unloading groceries, I reach in to grab an apple that's rolled to the back of my trunk when I hear wheels skid to a stop next to me. Skateboard wheels.

Xander reaches into my car, saying, "I can get that." He holds the apple out to me, and I'm suddenly having a flashback to a Sunday school lesson—back to those few weeks when my parents thought that churchgoing might save their relationship. Apples = temptation. One side of Xander's mouth curves into a smile. He's enjoying this way too much. And then he takes a bite out of *my* apple. Juice drips down his lip. He catches it with his tongue. Xander = temptation.

"Okay. Well, um, thanks, but not really, since you're eating my apple—and that, you know, cost me like three and a half minutes in that stinking Lazy River, but whatever. Consider it a gift." I slam the trunk.

He takes another bite. "Let me pay you back."

Way too smooth for a guy who used to dip his Tater Tots in chocolate pudding.

"I think it's about fifty cents." I stare at the ripped-up stickers on the bottom of his skateboard: skulls, swearwords, and other evil stuff, like, um, lips and tongues.

"That's not exactly what I meant, but okay." He reaches into his pocket, shifts through some coins on his open palm—it's so pale, pink compared to his dark skin. "I only have thirty-five cents. Maybe we should share it?" He hands me the apple.

"No, that's okay." I tuck a strand of hair behind my ear. "Besides, I was only, you know, joking."

"Next time watch your word choice." He snaps off another chunk of apple. "The best jokes are short and sweet. It's all about timing."

He grins while chewing, and it really should be completely gross. But it isn't.

I shift the bag of groceries to my other hip, trying to think of something cute but not too cute to say about word choice, but I'm stuck on the word *timing*. Instead I blurt out, "You're right! You're completely right. It is about timing. And now is not the time. Thank you. The apple is all yours. Now, if you'll excuse me, I've got to go make dinner. See you another *time*."

I square my shoulders, quite satisfied with myself. I pick up the other bag of groceries, turn on my heel, and head toward the house. I expect to hear Xander's skateboard clacking down the driveway. Instead I hear him say, "Oh, we'll be spending plenty of *time* together."

I turn. "What?"

"You heard me."

My face heats up like the flame sticker on the bottom of his skateboard.

"See you tomorrow," he says. "How about we sleep in, though? Since it's Saturday. Nine o'clock?"

I nearly drop my groceries, and I'm forced to catch a bag by lifting up my thigh in a most-definitely-not-cute move. "Um, I don't know what you're talking about."

Xander laughs, but at least he clangs his skateboard onto

the pavement. I watch for a second—just long enough to see him stop, pull that little notebook out of his pocket, and write something down. The guy gives me the creeps! Well, at least I *wish* he gave me the creeps. He should. I'm going to work on that. Maybe I'll read one of those rabid feminist magazines Mom bought after the divorce; I'm sure they're still stuffed under her bed.

The house seems empty when I open the door. Grace must be off somewhere with Amy. I've gotten the feeling that Amy's parents don't approve of how much Mom has been working lately. Join the club! The door to my room—Grandma's room—is ajar. I could use a good dose of Miss Swoon sensibility. A guy like Xander shouldn't turn me into a tongue-tied, blushing, grocery-dropping mess. I peek inside, expecting to see Grandma clacking away at her keyboard, but instead she's lying on my bed, eyes closed, snoring softly. It's only five o'clock in the afternoon. Poor Grandma; she's been working so hard on her book deadline.

I head to the kitchen. I'm dicing and slicing, popping carrot rounds into my mouth like they're candy; their crisp vegetableness tastes so refreshing. Dark green lettuce leaves fluff together in the salad bowl. Next to me on the counter I have Sawyer's Incident Management Plan. Number one: work on assertiveness. Telling Xander that he owed me for the apple was assertive, right? Not flirty. Number two is to memorize the pool rules. I can't quite imagine yelling, "Stop. Do not enter the water with that open sore." I'm not about to look at anyone closely enough to notice something like *that*. If Wild Waves wants to keep the water clean, they need to ban children.

I'm looking out the kitchen window, peeling a cucumber into the sink, when Mom's car pulls into the driveway. She's still wearing her Hamburger Heaven halo, as if she's completely surrendered her last shred of dignity. She climbs out of the car, looking stiff and tired. And then she reaches into the back seat for those familiar white and gold Hamburger Heaven bags. Not again! I notice that her stretchy white uniform pants have grown snug this week.

Mom puts the To Go bags on the kitchen counter. "Your angel has arrived from heaven with a Chinese Chicken wrap that should have been a Chipotle Chicken wrap and some other goodies." Mom lifts a lettuce leaf out of the bowl. "What is this strange lifelike substance?"

I toss diced cucumbers into the salad bowl. "I thought we could, you know, eat a little lower on the food pyramid."

"You mean I've been getting it backwards? Focusing on the fried food group?"

"It's not funny, Mom."

Mom picks up a jagged tomato slice. "Who had it in for this poor tomato? You cut them not step on them."

"Maybe if our knives weren't so ancient."

Mom laughs. "Yeah, well, I'm holding on to them so I can sell them on *Antiques Roadshow*." And then she riffs on her paring knife being worth thousands of dollars.

I don't laugh.

"I need a more enthusiastic audience. Where's Grandma?"

"Sleeping."

Mom glances back toward my room. "Really? I hope she's not coming down with something."

Grandma swings into the kitchen, with freshly applied lipstick shining on her lips. "No need to worry about me! I was simply storing up some creative energy. I've decided to add a chapter called 'Quick Quips'."

"That's a great idea, Grandma! You have so many great old columns to quote." I nod at Mom as if to say, *Look, here's a good example of how to use your skills, your brain.* "I'd sure love to read them again."

"You don't need to read them in a book. You've got *me*." Grandma peeks into the To Go bags. "Oh, I love that Chinese Chicken wrap. I get first dibs."

Part of me wishes that she noticed my salad, but maybe she's just trying to make Mom feel good, and everything. That's kind of like her job, right? "Hey, Grandma. Maybe we could talk sometime?"

"No time like the present!" Grandma pops a cold french fry into her mouth, and I try really hard not to think about all the columns she writes about treating your body with respect.

"I'll finish up with dinner prep," Mom says. "Grace is having a sleepover at Amy's."

"Again? Mom she's practically living over there this summer."

"I thought you'd like to have some time to yourself."

"Yeah, kind of, but . . ." What I really want is a deep, share-your-inner-secrets friendship without, you know, the danger of actually sharing your deep inner secrets. I met Jane for a frappuccino on Wednesday night, but all she wanted to do was talk about different ways to run into Rowdy accidentally. She hardly said a word about starting her new journalism class. When she wanted me to analyze what went wrong with my past relationships, I pretended to receive an emergency text message from Mom and got out of there quick.

Jane hasn't called since. Thus, I'm left without weekend plans.

"Don't frown, dear," Grandma says. "You don't want to create wrinkles." Grandma stretches her eyes wide and pats her face as if she can press out the fine lines. "Let's talk about what's bothering you." I follow Grandma into the living room.

Where to start? "Jane. She's changing so much! She's practically obsessed with this guy, and he's not even her type. Jane's serious and studious, and this guy is a total goof." I think back to the other night. "The kind of guy who prides himself on catching popcorn in his mouth."

"Oh, honey. You're jealous because Jane's got a new beau?"

I try to relax my body and not look jealous. "No. I want to help her avoid making a huge mistake."

"Love is about balance. A serious girl like Jane may need a silly boy. It creates harmony of the heart." Grandma crosses her hands over her heart, splaying her jewel-studded fingers and does the patented Miss Swoon swoon. She mostly does it when she's interviewed on the local news and morning talk shows.

I crinkle my forehead, thinking that not only is she doing her theatrical swoon, she's repeating word for word what she wrote in a recent column.

Grandma presses her fingers to my creased forehead. "No grumpy faces allowed."

"I don't know, Grandma. Don't people need to have stuff in common? That's what you wrote to Birds of a Feather."

"Naw! Sometimes it's about natural attraction. Like Jerry and me."

"You divorced."

"Aw." Grandma flaps her hand. "We had some good times. You can't deny that opposites attract; it's simple chemistry."

"Physics. But maybe you have a point. Today Sawyer flirted with Sonnet like a living example of the good guy going for the bad girl cliché!"

"It can be a lot of fun, if you know what I mean."

"Yeah, well, he's certainly thinking with his reproductive organs not his brain, if you know what I mean."

"Don't knock reproduction. If your father hadn't found my flighty daughter so irresistible, I wouldn't have you and Gracie Pie."

"That's sweet, Grandma. But Sonnet's just trying to collect encounters with blond boys this summer—she's even blogging about it."

"Sounds better than all the baldies I've been collecting lately. Really. I'm finding that a man with more than six strands of hair turns me on."

"Ew. Grandma."

"Although with my luxurious auburn locks, maybe I do need to give those baldies a break. There's that cutie over at the bookstore." Grandma giggles. "He could be night to my day, spring to my fall, north to my south."

I hold up my hand. "Okay, Grandma. Enough."

And then it hits me: if I am going to avoid hooking up with apple-stealing skateboarders who flaunt toned obliques, maybe I'm going to have to become a bad girl, too.

Maybe I *will* take Sonnet up on her offer to hang out this weekend.

```
Dear Miss Swoon:
I'm a straight-A student and totally fo-
cused on my future. So why am I falling
for the class clown? Shouldn't I be go-
ing for the valedictorian instead? What's
wrong with me?
—Unfocused

Dear Unfocused:
Love is about balance. A serious girl
often needs a silly boy. It creates har-
```

mony of the heart. Go with the flow. Give
it a try!
—Miss Swoon

*Looking straight into my eyes, bold as a blast of winter, she
blushed the color of autumn leaves.*

—X.C.

Chapter Ten

We're headed up to some amazing party at a house that looks more like a hotel sprawling along the mountain ridge. Even from this distance I can tell that ten of my house could fit inside it. The street curves above the sparkling town lights.

Sonnet takes the last corner too fast, not downshifting, not acknowledging the stop sign, speed limit, or the whole driving-on-the-right-side-of-the-road thing. I'm trying not to think about her brakes sounding like they can use a tune-up. Bad girls don't worry about auto maintenance. Bad girls drive fast to get to parties.

The breaks grind as Sonnet slams to a stop, barely missing the bumper of the car in front of us. As she yanks the key from the ignition, I realize that this counts as parking. We're sticking out into the street at an acute angle, but that doesn't seem to matter. My cell phone rings and a goofy picture of Jane flashes across the screen, but I ignore the call. Just like I ignored her text this morning about a *Matrix* marathon at Rowdy's house. Bad girls don't go to movie nights with the yearbook staff. I will focus on my friendship with Jane at a later date.

Tonight I'm Sonnet's "pardner in crime." All the way here we've been making fun of Sawyer's stupid sayings and inventing new ones that are kind of, um, X-rated, but hey, it's all in fun. Sonnet has brought a whole new meaning to Sawyer's twenty-yard-line reference.

"Okay." Sonnet applies a thick coat of lip-gloss. "Rules?"

"No running by the pool. No communicable diseases. Appropriate swimwear only."

Sonnet laughs. "I love hanging out with you. You're hilarious!" She adjusts her top, creating more cleavage. I do the same. Bad girls = boobs. "So, rule number one: no going for the same guy. Rule number two: no letting each other go for a total loser guy. If you have information, share it. Rule number three: we go home together. Unless we've found true love. Oh, and I've got a midnight curfew—a total double standard. My brother, who, I might add, is only a sophomore, does not have one, but since he can't get pregnant . . . Whatever." Sonnet rolls her eyes. "Now, let's make a memorable entrance."

"Like a back flip off the high dive."

"I'm loving you, Pol." She reaches over and tugs *my* top down! "That's better."

Sonnet stumbles through the front door, pulling me along after her, laughing like she's been sucking on a helium balloon. Several guys look our way. So do the girls. And let me just say, it's a good thing that looks can't—how do you say it?—kill. Sonnet insisted on coming over an hour early to get me "party ready." I'm wearing really snug jeans, a skimpy tank, strappy sandals, and enough eye makeup to star in a soap opera.

The house is crowded with people; I recognize a few kids from school, but it's not exactly the AP credit–collecting crowd I usually hang out with. I spot a guy from my French class, who looks at me like I've just used three adverbs in a single sentence. Not that he would know an adverb from a noun in any language, but whatever. So what if I don't usually show up at these kinds of parties?

Sonnet wiggles through the crowd, keeping the beat with the techno dance music blaring from the surround-sound speakers. All the furniture has been pushed to the edges of the room. A plasma-screen TV mounted above the fireplace plays *The Matrix*. I stop and stare for a moment.

"I thought that's what you were trying to avoid," Sonnet says, yanking my arm so hard, I stumble and turn an ankle.

"Just contemplating the irony," I say.

"Rule number four: no four-syllable words."

I follow her into the kitchen. She starts talking to a football player who's eating Lucky Charms right out of the box. "Hey, there," she says. "You know you're supposed to drink milk with those, right?"

Not exactly a great line, but the guy's not exactly listening to her words; he's far more interested in what her boobs are saying. I cross my arms over my own chest. It *is* kind of cold in here, in spite, of the, you know, body heat, leering gazes, and sweaty football players.

Lucky Charms says, "You could get me some milk."

Sonnet dips a cup into a large bowl filled with pink mystery punch. The kind every drug awareness pamphlet warns against. "Mmm," Sonnet says. "This is way better than milk."

I search the countertop for a plastic cup that looks less, um, *used*. Smudgy lipstick marks most of them. I find one that might be clean, stuck to the bottom of another cup.

"Watch this!" Lucky Charms tosses a handful of cereal into his mouth.

"My turn!" Sonnet opens her mouth wide. Lucky Charms tosses a whole handful of cereal at Sonnet, most of which lands in the punch bowl, adding a little too much—what would you call it?—texture. I set my cup down. Maybe I can just take a few baby steps toward bad-girldom?

Sonnet, picking a few pieces of cereal from her cleavage, changes the subject to the various marshmallow shapes. "Oh, I think the pink hearts are my favorite."

"What about the green clovers?" Lucky Charms asks.

Suddenly discussing the physics of the Matrix seems like a far more appealing way to spend an evening, even if I would have to watch Rowdy snuggle up with Jane all night. I sneak a peek at my cell phone. No calls. Sonnet and Lucky Charms have moved on to the topic of cold cereals in general.

I wander over to the French doors leading to the backyard. Outside, people mill around in the dark, talking in small groups near the glimmering, lit swimming pool. In the shadows I think I see a familiar tall, slender someone. He glances through the glass at me.

Oh no! This is exactly what I'm avoiding. He's not part of the jock crowd. How can he be here? Well, about a thousand people are here, but whatever. I turn and leave the kitchen. Mainly to comply with Rule number two: he's a total loser, right? In seventh-grade cooking class he poured water on his crotch and walked around pretending that he'd peed his pants. So what if he's suddenly grown all tall, dark, and handsome? Now he flirts too aggressively, eats other people's apples, carries that weird little notebook around, and looks way too good without his shirt.

I follow a group of girls down a carpeted stairway. Girls = safe. The girls crowd into the small downstairs bathroom, talking about lip-gloss flavors. What *is* the collective IQ at this party? I've been so nervous that I've licked the cherry (a total cliché, apparently) sheen off my lips. The posh basement is a gamer's paradise. Several guys lounge around on supersized beanbags, playing video games on a huge TV. There's also air hockey, a pool table, pinball machines, and a couple of vintage arcade games. Oh, crap: Donkey Kong!

I glance around the room. No one's looking. Just a quick fix. I've got the little man, leaping barrels, jumping up and down—and I'm totally in the zone, watching my score click higher and higher. *I'm so good.*

"Hey, if it isn't P.M. Polly Martin. Looking good." And something about his voice suggests he's not referencing my impressive score. I spin around, ignoring the angry yell from the little ape. I swear the little primate's saying, "Don't do it, Polly," in his mechanical voice, but whatever. Ex to the fourth power, Jack, holds a bottle of beer by the neck, takes a swig, and smiles at me out of the corner of his mouth. "Haven't seen you around this summer."

"Yeah, well, I've been working, you know, outside. Sunshine verses fluorescent lights."

Still holding the cold beer bottle, he rubs a finger along my shoulder. "It shows. Nice tan, P.M." I'm *not* noticing how the tips of his callused fingers feel ticklish; I concentrate on the fact that in this dim light *everyone* looks tan. *Don't fall for it!* The game makes a dying sound.

"Wanna start a new game?" Jack puts an arm around me and presses the start button. The little ape jumps up and down. Argh!

"You know, I'm here with a friend. I really should—"

"Afraid I'll beat your score?"

"As if you *could*." I turn and smirk at Jack. We're standing way too close, but Jack doesn't move a muscle. "I completely dominate that little simian."

Jack's eyebrows knit in confusion.

I dumb it down. "That little monkey totally loves me."

Xander Cooper ambles down the stairs, with a girl following him—a tall Asian girl who rests her hand comfortably on his shoulder. Wasn't she the prom queen, like, my freshman year? And wasn't he the kid who didn't receive a single valentine from a girl in fourth grade? Prom Queen giggles, crushing her hand through Xander's kinky-curly hair. "I challenge you to the next round of Guitar Hero," she says.

Xander sees me and stops walking. I look away as half the

blood in my circulatory system rushes to my cheeks. Why does he look all shocked to see me here? He's the one who's been flying under the social radar—until like now. I *know* people here, like French class guy, and, um, Jack.

"Aw, come on, P.M." Jack puts his hand on my cheek, in a way too familiar way. "You know I can beat your score."

"Okay, let's do it." I immediately regret my word choice, but Jack's not exactly one to catch on to innuendo. He pushes the restart button, standing behind me, again in an overly familiar way, but whatever. Bad girls let guys stand too close. I glance over my shoulder, briefly catching Xander's eye. Mature Prom Queen pulls his arm to make him join her on a squishy beanbag chair. He's still looking at me, so I lean back against Jack. Just for show.

Jack whispers, "What are you going to do for me if I win?"

"What makes you think that's even possible?" I take the beer out of his hand and take a swig. Fizzy. Bitter. Yuck. I drink a little more.

And I win.

I push his shoulder playfully. "Told you."

"Give me a kiss to change my luck?" He leans toward me, softly touching his lips to mine. It's more like a peck, really. Nothing hot and heavy. He loses again, but this time I think it's on purpose. Still, I kiss him again. Longer. No big deal. He's a good kisser.

"I demand a rematch," Jack says, snatching another kiss. "Lemme go grab us another beer first."

I stand at the machine, watching the little ape jump up and down screaming at me. "Yeah, so maybe I'm making some not-so-great choices, but what do you know? You're a passé video game character, a mediocre graphic," I say aloud.

Part of me wonders if I should go find Sonnet—it's almost midnight, not that the party is slowing down. More and more people crowd into the basement. Xander plays Guitar Hero, and he's good. *Not* that I'm noticing. Another girl comes down a few minutes later. (Where *is* Jack?) Some guy says something about Xander scoring big—and, yeah, he might be talking about the video game, or whatever, but he might not be, so that's what I'm going to focus on. Xander = bad boy. Polly = bad girl. Bad boy + bad girl ≠ love, according to Miss Swoon.

Jack finally comes back down, high-fiving a group of guys about seeing Sonnet skinny-dipping in the pool with a bunch of guys. She's obviously not overly concerned about her midnight curfew. Jack hands me a beer, but I shake my head.

"Do you think you maybe could give me a ride home instead?"

Jack tilts his head. "Yeah, okay." He hands the unopened beers to a guy watching Xander's girl make a lame attempt with Guitar Hero. She may be tall and gorgeous and a former prom queen and all, but she lacks hand-eye coordination. Xander jumps up to help her. A bunch of guys make crude comments as they stand *way* close.

"Come on." Jack puts an arm around me. As we walk upstairs, I look back to see if Xander's watching, but he's too busy playing with his prom queen.

The house has emptied out upstairs, except for plastic cups and other debris. I can't find Sonnet anywhere, so Jack drives me home. He laughs and makes video game sound effects as we curve down the hill, and that makes me laugh, too. I like the way he doesn't take things too seriously.

My house is completely dark as Jack pulls into the driveway. I sit there for a moment, not sure what to say. I feel bad about leaving Sonnet, or did she leave me? And Xander? What's with the complete metamorphosis? And why do I care? I've *never* liked him, not since he called me a Polly bear during our Arctic mammals unit in second grade—and got a better grade on his diorama.

Jack turns off the ignition. "So, Polly, I've been thinking about you lately."

Oh no.

"Just because I still rule at Donkey Kong."

"No, before tonight."

Double oh no.

"Yeah, right." I playfully bump his shoulder. "You say that to all the girls."

Jack reaches over and plays with one of my curls, wrapping his finger around it. "You see, I'm going to this graphic-design camp thing in a couple of weeks, and my parents are going on a cruise, and they want to board Buster, and I don't know—"

"Ah, poor little Buster." I can't help it; it's a reflex. I discovered early in our relationship that Jack only dated girls who showed adoration for his squishy-faced, wrinkly, tough-looking, snuffly bulldog.

"I knew you'd understand." Jack lets his finger wander from my hair to my lips, and I stop listening because I think he's going to kiss me again, and this time no one's around, and it's really dark, and . . . I close my eyes.

"So you think you could maybe watch him while I'm gone?"

"What?" I snap my eyes open. "Oh. Yeah. Um, sure."

Jack takes my hands in his. "Thank you so much. Buster always did like you."

The dog liked me. Not the boy. The dog. The squishy-faced, wrinkly, bad-boy, snuffly dog. At least it's dark and Jack can't see my face turn as red as a dog's rabies tag. How embarrassing to be all foaming at the mouth for another kiss. The guy broke up with *me*—eons ago!

"Yeah, sure." I open the car door. "Look, Jack. I'd better get going." I slam the door hard, wanting to smack myself upside the head to knock loose the brain blockage I'm obviously suffering. The window zooms down.

Jack calls out to me, "I'll bring Buster by on Wednesday. Thanks, Polly! And by the way I let you win those last couple of games."

"You're a total dog!" I say.

I'm absolutely serious, but he laughs. "Good one. Thanks again, P.M."

```
Dear Miss Swoon:
When I broke up with my ex, we decided
to share custody of our dog. Now my ex
is moving out of state and wants to take
the dog with him. I can't live without
this dog!
—Not Without Him
```

Dear Without:

Let the dog move on! Go to your local animal shelter and fall in love all over again.

—Miss Swoon.

Not Shakespeare's Sonnet

Blond count: 5.5 (Now we're talking.)

So, yeah, the rumors are true. (Read <u>Where's The @ction's blog</u> here.) I'd show you proof, but I promised the parentals that I'd never post naked pictures of myself on the Internet. Whatever! I'll just say that my girl Polly and I had a really good time at R.J.'s party. And thanks to you blond boys, too! Now back to bed. Not feeling so hot. More later unless something better happens first.

Her body leans into his, but her eyes watch mine. Like the stray kitten Kyra found outside the Iceberg. Wide eyes watching, hiding under the dank Dumpster, tail puffed up. So afraid.
—X.C.

Chapter Eleven

I wake early on Sunday morning to the sound of Grandma's keyboard clacking away. I wade through the stuffed animals strewn over the floor. Grace, of course, is having another sleepover with Amy. I give a stuffed dog a swift kick across the room.

Last night after Jack left all happy about finding a dogsitter and practicing his, um, kissing skills, I sort of threw a—how do you say it?—tantrum. Grandma tapped on the door to suggest we meet in the morning over coffee to have a wee chat. It's not like I was *that* out of control, screaming *that* loud, and the neighbor turned on his lights only to let his cat out, probably. At least Mom hadn't been home; she now worked the closing shift at Hamburger Heaven. Big promotion, apparently. Better tips.

I knock on Grandma's door, feeling a little weird about asking permission to enter my own room. "Hey, Grandma?"

Grandma flings the door open. "Come on in. I've been up for hours! I woke in the middle of the night and had a complete breakthrough on my book. Thanks to you!"

I'm not sure if I should be flattered or frightened.

"Good." I sit down on my bed, feeling a bit wistful about my previously more private, less stuffed-animal-inundated existence. "Glad to be of service."

"Your little shenanigans reminded me of the power of positivity. I'm going to do a whole chapter on affirmations!" Grandma clicks away on her laptop, wrapped in her puffy blue bathrobe, mumbling something about the universe blessing her with love. Her hair sticks out in all directions, exposing the gray roots. Grandma keeps typing, and I realize that she's probably forgotten all about our scheduled chat.

"Well, I guess I'd better, you know, get ready for another urine-soaked, skin-cancerous, ex-boyfriend-filled day."

Grandma spins around in her chair. "Now, that's not very positive!"

I pick at a loose string on my pajamas. "But it's true."

"Honey, do you want to talk about last night?"

"Naw, that's okay. You're having a breakthrough, and I've got to get ready for work."

"Come on. Who better to advise the lovelorn than Miss Swoon?"

"I'm not lovelorn, Grandma. I'm an overly hormonal idiot." Tired of keeping the entire situation to myself—except when I'm screaming about it to the, um, whole neighborhood or taking it out on Grace's stuffed animals—I decide to talk. "I ended up at the wrong party, kissed the wrong ex-boyfriend, and now I'm baby-sitting the wrong bulldog."

"Well, it doesn't sound like you've done irreparable damage. We've all kissed an ex, and you like dogs, right?"

I flop back against the bed. "Grandma, I don't know what I like."

"What about that Nature Club you joined? You sent me a postcard listing all the flowers you saw in that National Park—"

"Gareth. I joined the Nature Club because of a cute guy."

"Well, that's why I signed up for my new book club, but, hey, the books look almost as good as the fella, so why not? You like doing outdoorsy stuff, right?"

"Not really. I don't know. I think I just liked Gareth, and if that meant memorizing Great Basin wildflowers, so what?"

"What about your involvement in student government?"

"Hayden."

"Well, honey. What do you like? Maybe start there."

"Nothing. Now that I've given up on the male half of the species."

Grandma purses her lips. She watches me with her wide-set eyes until I grow uncomfortable. Suddenly Grandma spins around and scrolls through the text on her computer screen. "Sounds like you could use some affirmations! Friends. Love. Relationships." *Click. Click. Click.*

She acts as if solving problems is as easy as ordering office supplies online like she did last week. Boxes and boxes of things have been arriving. Grandma is on a first-name basis with the express delivery guy and has a coffee date scheduled with him. But whatever. At least she's not baby-sitting the dude's bulldog.

I crush a pillow over my face; it smells like Grandma's perfume. "Maybe you could convince Mom to maroon me on a deserted island or somewhere where I can evolve into a smarter human being, without the temptations of—"

I sit up, distracted by the sound of Xander's skateboard curving down the street outside the window. *Don't look.* I cross my feet together to lock my body into a sitting position. Grandma jumps up and peeks through the curtains. "You've got to see this dreamboat, honey. The other day he was skateboarding, talking on the phone, *and* drinking coffee. Today he's dressed up. For church, maybe. Oh, if I were your age! Hubba-hubba."

"Oh, Grandma!"

Betrayed by my autonomic nervous system, I race to the window. Sure enough, Xander's wearing a powder blue button-down shirt—and, yeah, snug khaki pants. Without turning to look, he waves over the top of his head. "Oh. My. God," I whisper. "Just lock me up and throw away the key."

"No, no, no. Positivity. Affirmations. Write these down. Let's start with a basic."

I decide to forgo a piece of paper and instead write the affirmations on my arm with a Sharpie. Body ink = edgy. I'm too afraid of infection to get a real tattoo. Probably a good thing: at this point my arm would've looked like an old grocery list with a bunch of guy's names crossed off. Using three different colors, I pen the affirmations onto my skin.

```
1. I deserve harmonious relationships
   with myself and others.
2. I deserve happiness.
3. I deserve loving and supportive
   friends.
```

Grandma returns to her laptop. "Now, just repeat these affirmations ten to twenty times a day and you will transform your life like magic." She snaps her fingers.

"I hope so," I say. "Thanks, Grandma Swoon." I kiss the top of her head to get harmonious relationship vibes going. On the way out of the room I scrawl one more affirmation on my arm. *Number four: I deserve a life free from male contamination.* My ink-covered arm looks as if I donated it to a preschool art project, but whatever.

Before heading to work, I e-mail Jane a long, self-deprecating apology full of *Matrix* references, along with an invitation to go get our nails done at the mall after I finish my Wild Waves shift. I also rearrange Grace's stuffed animals into chatting groups of appropriately distributed species.

I can do this!

I silently repeat affirmation number four, the one about boys, as Sawyer mediates an argument between Acne Model and another guy. They both want to work the Switchback slide. Not because dealing with kids zooming through tunnels, knocking each other off inner tubes, and getting stuck in various eddies is fun—but because it's my assignment. Sonnet apparently blogged about the party, divulging plenty of details about her evening, mentioning that I'd joined her escapades—*not* mentioning that I didn't join the most titillating ones. What do these doofus boys think? That I'm going to whip my clothes off in the middle of my shift? Really! But then Acne Kid says, "You know, I kick ass at Donkey Kong."

Oh, crap. Obviously Sonnet isn't the only one with gossip-inducing escapades. *I deserve a life free from male contamination. I deserve . . .* The damn affirmation is too long. *No boys. I'm a no-boy zone. I do not attract guys.*

"Okay, enough. I'll work with Pollywog. You guys tackle the Lazy River." Sawyer scribbles on his clipboard. "Hit it out of the park, team."

The guys walk off grumbling. I overhear one of them saying, "He did too date her. I read about it in Sonnet's archived entries." The sad thing: I have no idea to whom he is referring. I take a deep breath, reaffirming, *I do* not *attract guys.*

"Having a good weekend?" Sawyer asks as we head over to the Switchback.

"Like you don't know."

"Whoa!" Sawyer puts his hand up. "Time out, cowgirl. I'm just asking as a friend."

"Yeah, right." But then I catch sight of the inky messages on my forearm. Happiness. Friends. "Sawyer, I'm having a dandy weekend, thank you. How about you?"

"I've been helping my parents with our garden, thinking about how nurturing nature is so *nurturing*, you know?"

"Must be why they call her Mom."

"You are so right, Pollywog. I hadn't thought about that." Sawyer stares off in thought. "Thanks for sharing your insightfulness." He says it so earnestly.

I'm almost relieved when kids zoom through the tunnels, smashing their inner tubes into my legs before demanding that I help push them out of the waterfall eddy. Whoever designed this slide must have failed their college engineering classes. Every *single* tube gets stuck. It's the most popular ride at Wild Waves, so I'm keeping busy. Sawyer's working the entrance, so pretty much everyone obeys the rules: only one person per tube, no trains more than three tubes long, no coming down with a sexy smile on your face, dark skin glistening in the sunlight . . . Xander Cooper violates yet another rule.

His tube spins backwards, and I'm not sure he's even seen me, but before I know it, he's smashed into my legs, and my feet fly out from under me. So I, um, end up in his lap. Our combined weight zips us *through* the waterfall—I scream as the water drenches me—and the tube slips down the next section, ricocheting off the walls. But I'm not thinking about physics—well, not for more than a second or two—because Xander's laughter reverberates through me, making my whole body ticklish, and soon I'm laughing. Our guffaws echo off the walls of the tunnel we're passing through. Right before the big drop at the end Xander wraps his arms around me, still laughing. I can't stop laughing and screaming, either. I can barely breathe. The tube tips over the edge of the steep slide, and we fly down it, catching air—floating for a moment—before crashing into the deep water at the bottom. Xander doesn't let go of me, and my whole body feels like it's smiling. What a rush!

After we break the surface, Xander whispers in my ear, "Feels good to let go, doesn't it?"

But he hasn't let go.

I nod, not even turning to look at him. He's still standing behind me, his fingers playing with mine. He traces the words written on my arm. I should feel totally embarrassed, but I'm not—must be all the endorphins rushing my system, from riding really fast and everything. Kids should be splashing into the pool behind us, but we're still standing there alone. I am aware of every single cell in my body.

A whistle starts blowing. Sawyer runs down the steps, talking on his walkie-talkie. "What are you doing? The whole system is jammed! Tubes are stuck in the eddy. You left your post! What the—?"

I should explain that the whole thing happened accidentally. I know this is the time to get serious, but I just start laughing, letting all those good, vibrating feelings escape.

"Polly, you must seriously be serious!" Sawyer blows his whistle again. He looks ridiculous, standing in his little cowboy swim trunks with a red bandana around his neck, freaking out about a poorly designed waterslide. I can't stop chortling. I'm not trying to be mean; I just can't help it.

"Relax, dude." Xander takes a deep breath, and I realize that we are standing *very* close. "This is a water park. A beautiful Sunday in June. No one is drowning."

"You!" Sawyer blows his whistle. "Out! You've violated the one-person-on-a-tube rule."

"This is nothing!" I say. "Nothing."

Sawyer points to me. "You better get back to work or you're fired."

I'm still glaring at Sawyer as Xander walks out of the pool without turning back. Kids finally start splashing down into the deep pool, and a moment later I'm questioning my sanity, wondering if any of that actually happened. Or maybe I'm just coming down with heat stroke.

Sawyer continues lecturing me, but I'm not paying attention. I watch Xander walk up the stairs as if *nothing* happened. I follow, feeling more confused than ever. Sawyer says something about strikes or penalties, but I think he's mostly pissed because I don't seem to care.

Finally I turn to him and say, "It was an accident, Sawyer. Get over it. Won't happen again."

But I hope that isn't true.

Dear Miss Swoon:
How many guys do you have to be with before you are considered a slut?
—More Than Three Boys

Dear More Than Three:
You can't win an Olympic medal for sex. Slow down.
—Miss Swoon

Our bodies hummed with laughter. I held her, our fingers knit together, felt her breathe and relax. And then NOTHING. NO thing. NOT hing. NOTH ing. Meaningless?
—X.C.

Chapter Twelve

The sun peeks over the mountains, adding a soft pink glow to the clouds gathering across the valley. Buster stops to sniff yet another invisible something. I figured since I was up anyway, I might as well walk the dog.

I've had trouble sleeping for the last few nights; I keep thinking about affirmations, advice, and the way Xander said it feels good to let go, with his arms, um, wrapped around me. I've analyzed those few words with more scrutiny than I gave the Emily Dickinson poem I dissected for my AP English final. I got an A on the English essay—not doing so well with the Xander Cooper thing.

Buster snuffles forward a few paces, lifting his leg on an ornamental shrub. The two of us are practically outcasts. In three days Buster has managed to alienate the entire family by chewing up stuffed animals, barking during Grandma's precious writing hours, and regurgitating Hamburger Heaven leftovers on Mom's shoes. Frankly I felt *that* statement deserved more study.

The affirmations written on my arm are getting plenty of analysis. Damn permanent ink! Sonnet told me that Sawyer tried to get me fired for violating the rule about excessive body art. She's come up with all means of revenge. The girl may not do great in school, but she's got one helluva creative mind. I'm still considering the soap bubbles thing.

Anyway, these affirmations may be making Grandma happy as she types away on her book, but they've done nothing for me.

Buster noses a stinky glob of muck in the gutter. "Dude, have *some* standards."

And that's the moment I hear the skateboard. It's too early! I'm wearing my pajamas and the Shrek slippers Jane gave me as a joke. I yank Buster's leash, prepared to race home, but Buster isn't a jogging kind of dog. He plants his wrinkly butt on the sidewalk and makes a low rumble in his throat. So I'm leaning down, pleading with a scrunch-faced bulldog—promising treats, belly rubs, offering up any of Grace's stuffed animals as chew toys—when Xander skids to a stop.

"So, you're the one who got stuck with Buster."

This is not the cryptic message I'm expecting. "What?"

Buster stretches on the sidewalk with all four legs splayed out like a girl trying to get a tan.

Xander tips his skateboard into his hand. "Jack asked everyone at that party to take care of Buster. Maybe if he'd offered to stick his tongue down my throat."

I turn away. Buster looks up at me with his watery eyes as if waiting for me to come up with a clever response. "That was nothing."

Xander nods. "You seem to have a lot of nothing going on."

"That's not what I said. I mean, it is what I said, but it's not what I *mean*."

"That seems to happen a lot, too." He's not smiling.

My heart beats faster, like I *have* been jogging. "Now, that's just *mean*, if you know what I mean." *God, I sound like Sawyer.*

"Don't try to be clever." Xander frowns, shaking his head. "Doesn't do much for me."

"Who says I'm trying to do anything for you?" I nudge Buster with my foot, hoping to make him stand up. "And what's wrong with dog-sitting for a friend?"

"It's just that Jack played you better than Guitar Hero."

I cringe. "Donkey Kong."

"Don't let guys do that to you. You're too smart for that."

"Oh, gee, thanks, Miss Swoon." I yank hard on Buster's leash. Nothing. Ha-ha.

Xander sets his skateboard back down but holds it steady with his foot. "No need for sarcasm. I know you can do better than that."

"What? Because we were in the same fourth-grade class? You don't even know me anymore!"

"Does anyone?" Xander steps onto his board and slips down the street, curving gracefully.

"No one knows you, either!" I scream. "You're the one who completely changed!" I sit down on the curb, resting my face in my hands. *Do not let a guy like that bother you!* You deserve harmonious relationships. You deserve happiness. Your friends are loving and supportive. Affirmations are a load of dog crap.

Buster finally inches his way up from the sidewalk, nuzzles me, slobbers on my arm, and when we get back to my lawn, promptly releases a pile of feces. I decide not to pick it up. Sure, I may step in it later, but that would only serve as a reminder of what my life has become.

I open the front door to the cacophony of Mom and Grandma arguing in the kitchen. Buster marches inside, tugging the leash; all that lounging around mocking me has apparently made him hungry. "No, wait." I listen for a minute at the doorway, waiting for Mom to crack a joke or something.

Buster whines.

"You said you would be contributing to household expenses!" Mom clangs the silverware door shut. "I'm barely hanging on. With Polly turning eighteen next year, I will be down an entire child support payment each month. I've got to save money this summer—one hamburger order at a time."

"Let's try and stay positive here."

"Where's the positive in having the electricity cut off during the hottest month of the summer?"

"We could start our own Bikram yoga studio?"

"That's just not funny, Mother."

"Well, why don't you and I find us a couple of millionaires to marry? And then I'll become a best-selling author, and we'll move to our own private island."

Mom blows out an exasperated sigh. "What about your book deal?"

"Well, it's not really anything formal. Since my old editor up and retired on me, and market conditions changed, and that edgy young Sassy thing is taking over. You should read about *her* book deal! Well, so my book—it's really something I'm doing for myself at this point. I have so much to say."

I peek around the corner. Mom leans against the counter for support. "So, there isn't any book money?" When Mom tips her head, I can see *her* gray roots. Can no one around here afford hair care anymore?

"Not yet, but with these affirmations . . . Look how well they're working for Polly; she's practically tattooed herself with them. Maybe I can include rub-on tattoos with the book? In the teen edition. Oh, I'd better go write that down, right away, before I forget. We can finish our chat a wee bit later."

As Grandma sweeps out of the kitchen, wearing her bathrobe, I make a show of returning from my walk, clearing my throat, and kicking my slippers off. Buster's so hungry that he eagerly gets in on the act, yanking me into the kitchen.

Mom smiles when she sees me. "I bet you're looking for cold cheese fries for breakfast," she says. "Too bad Grandma just ate them all."

"Very funny. Not."

Mom laughs. "Don't try to steal my material. I don't have much, but I've got that." She starts singing that old show tune about "plenty of nothing." But it has never seemed less funny.

Not after what Xander just said to me. Not after what Grandma just revealed. Not the way Mom struggles to pay the bills. I take my time getting a bowl of cereal for myself.

"You look like you need some cheering up," Mom says. "I've got just the thing."

"Chocolate? Bath oils? My own room back?"

"No, a joke, silly. One of my students came into the restaurant last night and told me this one—I think he expected extra credit or something. I gave him extra fries. Okay, ready?"

"I'm sure that I'm not."

"What do you get when you cross a french fry with a frog?"

"Mom, I really don't want to know."

"A potatoad. Get it? Isn't that cute? I told it to several customers last night and I think I got better tips. I'm going to work on a whole routine of hamburger and fry jokes. Break out of this town, go on the road, maybe score big bucks in my own Vegas show. What do you think?"

"I think I saw another stack of bills sitting on the coffee table."

"Just decorating, dah-ling." Mom swats my butt. "You'd better run along and get ready for a luxurious day in the sun."

"Hardly."

"You're becoming a bronze sun goddess."

I smirk. "Right."

"Okay, you're more of a porcelain shade goddess, but you're still my beautiful Polly Marie Martin."

"Whatever, Mom."

On the way to the shower I peek in on Grandma busily typing on her computer. Maybe Mom should give her break; she's obviously working hard on this book. I'm sure it *will* sell millions of copies. At least Grandma thinks big and takes chances that can create big results. Mom's schlepping burgers like a teenager. Before she met Dad, she wanted to be an international journalist, but she gave up that dream to teach fifth grade and take golf vacations. I don't think she's used her passport since college.

Grace pushes past me, screaming at Buster. "He's killing Peanuts! Bad, bad dog!"

Buster stops in front of me, jaws clenched around Grace's stuffed elephant, shaking his head, and sending clouds of stuffing into the air.

Maybe going to work won't be so bad. It's Thursday. Xander almost never shows up on Thursdays, not that I'm keeping track of his schedule or anything.

Dear Miss Swoon:

My mother just doesn't understand me. It's like we're different species! She's a cave dweller, always staying home and watching television. I want to fly—go out to parties, movies, shopping with my friends. What can I do to convince her that I'm old enough to go out?

—Trapped In The Cave

Dear Trapped:

Prove to your mother that you're responsible enough to have a more evolved social life. Offering to clean the cave every now and then couldn't hurt.

—Miss Swoon

Clouds
Pink as an open palm
An invitation.
—X.C.

Chapter Thirteen

I'm standing in a discarded pile of skirts, shorts, skorts, minis, T-shirts, tank tops, tube tops, and even stuff from the Career Woman department.

Jane peers over her shoulder at her reflection in the mirror. "I'm beyond help. I need a complete butt makeover."

The cropped pants strain and bunch across her thighs. "I think you look cute in those, but like I said about ten miniskirts ago, you've got great legs," I say. "Play up the legs."

"But Rowdy's a butt man."

"Okay, I *so* didn't need to know that. And I don't even want to know how you know that." I flip through a few skirts still on hangers while Jane strips off the pants.

"*Matrix* Marathon."

"Why didn't you tell me? I would've picked up a few robes and Gor-tex body suits for you to try on."

Jane shakes her head. "Stop being funny."

I push aside a pile of tops in various shades of blue-green, Rowdy's favorite color—because, you know, he made a comment during *The Lord of the Rings*. I perch on the little dressing room bench. Jane is beyond saving. And frankly, if things weren't so tense at home, I would be there instead of at the mall on a Friday night. Attending Grace and Amy's stuffed-animal picnic sounds appealing at this point.

"Don't let me forget to buy that Webimal."

Jane looks at me. "You've reminded me a million times. Now, what do you think? Hide the butt with a blousy top or wear this?" Jane holds up a superlong, flowing skirt that looks like it belongs in a 1960s documentary.

"Jane, my dear, we're living in the twenty-first century."

"Maybe my butt isn't. Maybe my butt belongs back in the eighteen hundreds or something. It's like a vestibule organ or something."

"It's a vestigial organ."

"Whatever." Jane slips the skirt over her hips. "You know people hate it when you do that, don't you? Correct them all the time. Sawyer once told me it makes him feel stupid, before you broke up."

"God, Jane! What a thing to say. I hardly *ever* corrected

him. Only when I absolutely couldn't help it. What are you going to tell me next? That I had a booger hanging out my nose three weeks ago? There's nothing I can do about it now."

"You could stop correcting people all the time. That's something, isn't it?"

"So what, I'm supposed to let people go around sounding stupid?"

"So, I sound stupid, huh?" Jane frowns and takes off the skirt.

I toss a sparkly green top at her. "Try this one; it'll totally show off your you know." I motion toward her chest.

"And you always do that, too!"

"What? Recommend fashion combinations? I thought that's what I was here for." I fold a few T-shirts into neat squares, feeling nervous. Why is she attacking me? I'm the one giving up *my* Friday night to help her shop for her big amusement park date with Rowdy and ten thousand other yearbook people. It's not like it's even a real date. It's more like a field trip, and those kinds of group excursions totally don't count. Even though at the time I thought the spring break Nature Club trip with Gareth counted. Maybe it didn't.

Jane holds up the top, making a face. "I don't want to come on too strong." She tosses the shirt onto my lap. "Polly, you're always changing the subject when I try to talk about something real."

"Real? So talking about clothes equals 'not real' but talking about my apparently numerous flaws is 'real'?" I decide to hang blouses back on hangers. That way I can't see Jane grimacing at me in the dressing room mirror.

"I'm only talking to you like a friend," Jane says.

I lean down and pick up a see-through blouse thing. "I don't know why you even deigned to take this one off the hanger."

"See, you're doing it right now." Jane shimmies into a pair of snug white jeans.

"Oh, so I can't talk about the clothes at all. That's going to make it pretty difficult for me to offer advice, you know. Maybe we can work up some kind of code. That five-four-six looks good with the seven-four-three. Is that better?"

"Grr." She growls, but she's not even looking in the mirror, so she might be growling at me. "Polly. Sometimes I want a confidante, someone to talk to about serious stuff."

"Yeah, so? I've been a totally good listener. I'm even supporting your misguided decision to pursue Rowdy."

"Yeah. That's real supportive." Jane finally glances in the mirror, tugging at the fabric clinging to her thighs. "The thing about being a good listener is that you need to be a good talker, too."

That's so not grammatically correct, but I don't say anything. See, I *am* learning.

Jane pulls off a navy blue T-shirt and exchanges it for a powder blue one. She tilts her head in the mirror. "What do you think?"

"I think it's a finalist."

"Me, too." She quickly disrobes and adds it to the meager maybe pile. I think about sneaking a quick peek at my cell phone to check the time, but that doesn't seem very friendlike so I don't. Besides, I'm just going to return home to a dinner of rejected hamburgers, a stuffed-animal party, and a grandmother who refuses to talk to my mother. Where's the positivity in that?

"And the nominees are . . ." I hold up the three outfits that have made it through the incredibly boring selection process.

"I think I'll get all three. That way I can change my mind tomorrow morning if I want. And if the weather—"

"Hot and sunny. That's the weather. You just want to be hot, right? So go with the"—I make a drumroll sound on my thighs—"supershort mini."

"I've got my mom's credit card, so . . ." Jane picks up the clothes without even looking at the price tags.

"Hey, you might as well get a couple of the reject outfits, too, in that case."

Jane eyes one of the reject blouses. "It's not like I can spend *that* much."

I peek at the price on the jeans: worth about fourteen hours of Lazy River duty. "Hey, if you've got it, spend it, right?"

"You should get something, too, Polly. What about that blue top? It totally makes your eyes pop."

"It's kind of scratchy." Jane convinced me to bring a few items into the dressing room, so I did, just to be in the spirit of things. But if there's one thing all the home-front awkwardness has proven, we're having serious financial issues. I'm pretty much saving all my money, except for a few bags of groceries now and then. Jane would never consider buying groceries with her own money; she doesn't even pay for her own gas.

"Plus, I'm trying really hard not to attract guys, you know. So I think if I'm going to purchase something, it had better be this." I hold up a really ugly, orange stretchy top that I'd picked up just to be funny. I talk in a gravelly smoker's voice. "Hey there, fellas. Wanna party?"

"See, there you go again. I was trying to be serious."

Oh no. I did not want to return to the subject of me. And my personality flaws. "Ten minutes ago you thought this shirt was totally funny. That's what you said. I'm just referring to an earlier joke. It's not like I'm condemning the future of our friendship. Have a sense of humor, Jane."

"I do. But here's the thing. Why should I always be the one sharing my secrets? Sometimes I want to hear yours, too. It's like equity or something."

Equitable. The word is equitable. But I don't say anything. I pluck a green T-shirt off the discard pile, put it on my head, and lurch toward the mirror, growling. Jane sighs, but then I make her laugh.

She slides the T-shirt off my head. "I kind of liked that one. I think I'll get it, too."

We finally leave the dressing room, and Jane goes to pay for her clothes. She spends more than what I make in a month working at Wild Waves. And then she wants to head over to the shoe department. But first she stops at the cologne counter to "catch a whiff of Rowdy's scent." He hardly seems like a signature scent kind of guy, but I can't say anything because Jane has endured many stops at this same counter so I could smell various ex-ex-ex-ex-ex aromas.

"Come on, Polly." Jane waves a cologne sample in front of her nose. "You love doing this."

"Not tonight." I play with the shoulder strap on my purse,

wishing I had a shopping bag to hold. "No need to go letting my olfactory complex trigger any scent-related memories."

Jane giggles. "You are such a doofus! You accuse me of hanging out with a bunch of dweebs when you're the biggest one of all—always spouting off with your big vocabulary and all."

"I am not! I'm totally channeling my inner bad girl. After work I purposely dropped an armload of kickboards just so that I could catch a glimpse of Sexy Lifeguard's crack when he bent down to help me."

She smirks. "That's, like, so junior high, Polly. A real bad girl would've had her hands all over that boy's—"

"Hey, it's a start. I'm trying."

She breaks into major guffaws, but I'm sure she's just high off sniffing too much Rowdy cologne.

Jane drops me off early, saying she needs get her "so-called beauty sleep," but really I saw her checking her text messages and getting that syrupy, reserved-for-Rowdy smile on her face.

"Have fun tomorrow!" I shout. "But don't fall in love; it will only lead to your downfall."

"Very funny."

I wasn't trying to be funny.

The house looks normal from the outside, but it's all chaos when I step through the door. Amy and Grace chase Buster around the living room, screaming about murder. Buster stops and shakes his head—a killer whale flopping in his mouth, tufts of white fluff on his wrinkled lips.

"You did this!" Grace yells. "You owe me a new killer whale plus interest." She learned that last part listening to Mom and Grandma arguing about money.

I toss the crinkly pink plastic bag with the new Webimal inside to Grace and make an attempt to trap Buster. He jigs to the left, kind of impressive, really, and races past, leaving a trail of unstuffed white whale guts. And Grace's tears. Amy moves in to comfort her. I'm disgusted with myself for allowing yet another male to leave me in the dust.

I follow the sound of teeth shredding fabric to Grandma's room. I half expect to see her typing away, but the room is empty. I frown at the dark computer screen. I had hoped to talk to her about Jane. The whole I-deserve-loving-and-supportive-friends affirmation just isn't cutting it. I need something more substantial.

Grace and Amy run into our room, slamming the door. I sit down at Grandma's desk, twisting in her new ergonomic office chair. I can't stop thinking about what Jane said about me always using humor to avoid talking about things. There's nothing wrong with being funny, right? Friends are supposed to laugh with each other. But she's right about me not telling her stuff. I haven't mentioned Xander; I haven't talked about Mom's feud with Grandma; I haven't told her that my dad hasn't invited me to the cabin for even a long weekend this summer. The last time Dad called, we spent ten minutes talking about the weather. Our temperature zones—we're only talking about thirty miles here—differed by two degrees Fahrenheit, not taking in relative humidity. I almost envied Grace's stuffed-animal-based conversation.

Jane with her happy little family, I'm sure, doesn't want to hear about all the drama in mine. Plus, it's completely embarrassing. Whose dad doesn't want to see her? That makes me a total reject, right? Plus, Jane will only try to make some pseudo psychological connection between Dad and Kurt. Unfortunately I made the mistake of breaking up with Kurt three days after she turned in her psychology essay on Freud. She only got a B minus, but that didn't dissuade her from diagnosing me.

"Do you think you maybe went for a car-obsessed guy since your dad, like, abandoned you after buying you a car? Like maybe you associate cars with father figures?" Jane's eyes had grown wide. "It's, like, so Freudian or something."

"Um, no. I went for Kurt because he revved my engine, if you know what I mean."

"Polly, you really should talk about this. I can tell you're upset."

"Not really. If there's one thing I've learned, relationships crash and burn like stock cars. Just look at my parents. And my grandma. She gets *paid* to give people marital advice, but she can't stay married."

"My parents have been together since like college."

"So go study them. They're the freaks of nature. Not me." But then I made the mistake of bursting into a humiliating display of emotion. I had tried so hard to make Kurt like me. Her reactions to my other breakups got exponentially more analytical, so that I didn't even tell her about Hayden until I'd recovered enough to turn it into one big joke. I told Jane he'd vetoed me. She didn't laugh. But at least I didn't cry. Much.

I flick on Grandma's computer, thinking that maybe reading a section of her book might give me some direction. I open the word processing program and click on the recent documents list. I find only Miss Swoon columns. Reading about people whining about boyfriends isn't going to help. I open a few more documents—affirmations, quick quips, chapter ideas—but I can't find her actual book anywhere.

Eventually I click on the Internet browser. It opens to a site called Golden Oldies. Ick! The stuff Grandma has to read for research. She did tell me the other day that she'd thought about doing a special series of columns about senior citizens. "Uh, gross. No," I said. "Besides shouldn't old people have it all figured out or just forget about it?"

Grandma laughed. "Oh, honey, if I had life figured out, I certainly wouldn't be living in my granddaughter's bedroom. I'd be on an island somewhere with my own personal hunk of a masseur. Did I tell you that I'm thinking of signing up for a massage class? Might help me find a man with good hands, if you know what I mean."

"I don't even want to know what you mean." I'd gotten out of there pretty fast, before Grandma had a chance to add any vivid descriptions—only to find myself overtaken by a fantasy involving Xander's ink-stained fingers.

Do not think about him! I'm just about to check my e-mail, not that I'm expecting anything, when an instant message pops up from "Graygander": *Hey, Swansong! Checked out that movie. Loved it. What do you recommend next?*

Grandma IMs these people? I click on the edge of the message to make it disappear and go to the "my profile" icon. *Swansong: age 68 years young! Looking for love, adventure, a man who knows his culture but also knows how to laugh.* She's even posted photos!

This seems to be going a little beyond research for geriatric-themed columns. Up in the corner next to Grandma's name is a little number beside "minutes logged in." I'd need my scientific calculator to figure out the number of days Grandma has spent cruising around looking for Golden Oldies. Is she even *writing* a book?

Buster finishes masticating the stuffed whale and stands by the door whining to go out. As I swing the door open, I see a note taped to the door.

```
Dear Miss Swoon:
My sister had a bad boyfriend and
that bad boyfriend had a bad dog
and that bad dog ate my stuffed
whale. I hate her. Help!!!!!!!!!!!
—Good Girl
```

I rip down the note, and scrawl:

```
Dear Good Girl:
Survival of the fittest! That whale
should have stayed out of the dog's
way. If you know what's good for
```

you, you will stay out of your sister's way.

—Miss Won't Ever Swoon Again!

P.S. And when you're old enough, avoid boys! Especially the desk-licking losers.

Chapter Fourteen

$\mathcal{A}$ late afternoon thunderstorm moves across the valley, dropping fat raindrops onto the hot pavement. Moms scream at kids to get out of the water, but the novelty of rain falling into the pool whips the kids into a splashing frenzy. The waterslides have been closed since Sawyer first spotted lightning in the distance, but kids still float in the Lazy River. Not wanting to get electrocuted, I walk along the edge, forcing kids to swim to the sides so I can pull them out of the water.

Within minutes the whole park has been cleared. I'm standing by the entrance gate, handing out Rainy Day Return coupons when Xander comes by with the kids. He flashes his eyebrows, and a surge of electricity shoots through *me*, but I'm sure it's just something in the air—like the heavy scent of rain on hot pavement, maybe random electrons. I'm almost glad when a woman starts complaining that she had to drive two and a half hours to get here and she wants a full refund, et cetera, et cetera. By the time I've directed her to the manager's office, Xander is long gone.

Sawyer walks over to me, shaking the water from his hair. "Go ahead and sprint to home plate, Pollywog."

Part of me wants to stay because I could really use the money, but another clap of thunder crashes above me, and my car seems like the safest place to be. I race across the parking lot past a few moms packing children into their minivans. I climb into my front seat. It's soaked. I'd left my window cracked open so that the car wouldn't get too hot in the sun. I stick my key in the ignition, sitting there for a moment *not* thinking about Xander's eyebrows. I turn the key, and my car makes a sound like Buster hacking up a chunk of stuffed animal. Next to the check-engine light a yellow symbol flashes. I try again. *Hack. Hack.* Nothing. Rain pelts me from the open window.

I hit the steering wheel. "Come on, car, not today. I know I should've gotten you an oil change, but I got distracted. Just start for me, and I'll take you to the doctor first thing tomorrow. Please."

"I don't think it's listening." Xander leans down and

peeks through the window. "Sounds like your alternator has gone out."

"You couldn't possibly know that. It's just flooded." I turn the key again, even though I know that the engine is most definitely not flooded and that, yeah, the little yellow light probably does have something to do with the alternator. But I just don't want to give him the satisfaction. Besides, guys who know about cars are bad news. I've learned that much!

Xander smiles. "Look, you can sit here all night if you want to, or you can let me give you a ride home."

"On your skateboard? Yeah, that's really tempting."

He laughs and jingles his keys. "I meant a car ride." He nods toward an old Subaru station wagon.

I search through my bag for my cell phone. "That's okay. I'll just make a quick call." The damn thing is dead. "Arrr! I forgot to charge it."

"Come on," he says. "You can trust me. You've known me since, what, second grade?"

"I'm not sure that's much of a recommendation." Yeah, I've known him for most of my life. Except he used to be a chubby, desk-licking freak; now he's hanging around at jock parties and skateboarding around without a shirt on *that* body. I'm not sure I can trust *myself*, not with his hair curling wet around his cheeks, his eyebrows flashing up and down, his full lips, that smile, those big brown eyes, that water-soaked shirt. Plus, the other night at the mall I fought the urge to price skateboards. Not a good sign.

"Make up your mind, because I can't leave the kids in the car alone. They keep changing the presets on my radio."

Kids = safe.

"Okay, but just because I don't want to get hit by lightning." I grab my bag and my useless cell phone.

"I'll take that as a compliment," Xander says.

"Well, don't."

Xander hands me a towel as I slide into the front seat of his car. The towel smells like Boy. The car smells like a million McDonald's Happy Meals. I concentrate on that odor. Xander introduces me to the kids as he buckles them into their car seats. His niece, Kyra, whose hair is beaded with three shades of pink beads, grins, and says, "Is the pollywog coming for french fries?"

"Pollywog?" I should just walk.

"We're just giving her a ride home because her car is broken."

His nephew, Dex, pouts. "But what about the french fries, Uncle X? You promised!"

Xander looks at me. "Maybe we could all use a snack?"

The little black notebook Xander has tossed onto the dashboard distracts me. What's in that thing? I stare at the rumpled pages.

"Polly?" He starts the car. "Okay if we make a quick run through the drive-thru? My treat?" A blast of air conditioning textures my arms with goose bumps. It's *not* the way he gazes at me.

"Come on, Pollywog! French fries! French fries!" the kids chime in from the back seat.

"Yeah, okay. But call me Polly. Please."

"But Soggy calls you Pollywog."

"Soggy?"

"I think she means Sawyer." Xander puts the car in reverse, looking over his shoulder, resting his hand on my seat. *Not* that I'm noticing his slender dark fingers, inky pink fingertips. "Sawyer yells your name a lot. The kids have kind of picked up on it."

"Great. But where did they get Soggy?"

"I kind of started that." A mischievous grin flickers across his face. "I could tell you didn't like the whole Pollywog thing."

"I don't." I fold my arms across my chest. "But I can handle it myself."

He looks at me, but I can't read his expression. Then he says, "Who wants fries?"

"We do! We do! We do!"

I don't say much on the way down to the Iceberg drive-thru. Rain falls on the windshield, and Xander's wipers squeak. I focus on the sounds. The sky turns darker. Lightning flashes right above us. I just want to be home. Everything about this situation resembles a scene in a horror movie—before things go terribly wrong. I'm half surprised there isn't ominous music playing. Xander leans forward and turns on the radio; that Raffi song about baby Beluga blares from the speakers.

His cheeks darken and he mumbles, "It's not my car."

Am I making him blush? I'm so disconcerted by this whole unexpected situation that I blurt out, "I used to love this song."

The kids start singing along, and the next thing I know, we're all singing the lyrics about a little lost whale all alone.

"Do it jazzy style," Kyra says. "Come on, Uncle X!"

Xander glances at me quick, but then embellishes the next stanza with a bunch of doo-wops and sound effects. For a moment I flash back to the weird humming noises he made in elementary school, but we're all laughing as he pulls up to the drive-thru window.

The girl, a JV cheerleader I sorta recognize, leans through the window, squeezing her cleavage together. "Let me guess," she says. "Three orders of fries. Extra fry sauce?"

"Make it four."

The girl pulls back, noticing me for the first time. "O-kay." She says it real slow, as if already mentally composing the text message she's going to blast to all of her friends.

"Can we get shakes, Uncle X? If we promise not to tell Mom?"

Xander flashes his eyebrows up and down at the kids in the rearview mirror. See? It's something he does to everyone. He's a big flirt. "Three chocolate shakes and one"—he looks at me—"strawberry?"

Instead of answering with words, my cheeks flush the color of a strawberry.

The girl at the counter acts put out. "It may be a while. I'll have to get another batch of berries ready."

I make a *never-mind* motion with my hand, but Xander says, "You go ahead and do that."

We sit there waiting, kiddie tunes blasting on the radio, windows steaming up with our breath, and I'm starting to freak out. Why am I in this car? How does he know that I like strawberry shakes? Is he a total stalker or what? Was he watching me yesterday when Sonnet shoved me into Sexy Lifeguard, spilling strawberry shake down my chest?

"You better help her wipe that off," Sonnet had said.

Sexy Lifeguard rolled his eyes. "I think she can handle it."

Sonnet nudged me hard, prompting me to say something bad-girl-worthy. "I can handle a lot of things," I practically purred. Sexy Lifeguard shook his head and walked away. The whole bad-girl-repelling-bad-boy thing obviously worked on him. But did Xander write it all down in his little notebook like some sort of sicko spy?

I reach for the notebook, but Xander grabs it first. "What's in that thing, anyway?"

"Nothing."

"Oh? I thought you hated that word."

He shoves the notebook under his thigh. Facing the take-out window, he practically whispers, "I just like to capture small moments. That's all."

"Oh-kay."

He doesn't say anything, but he nudges the notebook farther under his leg.

"Like having strawberry shake spilled all over me? Is that in there?"

Xander shrugs, still not looking at me. The guy is seriously strange. Capturing moments? Bizarre. I turn around and watch the kids make Itsy Bitsy Spider motions with their hands, content in their car seats.

I finally say, "Beats blasting crap all over the Internet, I guess."

No response from Xander. What's his problem? *I'm* the one who's sick of being everyone's essay topic.

"Here are the fries." The girl shoves the bag at him. "I'm still figuring out the shakes."

"It's not astrophysics," he mutters, and I can't help smiling.

I try to think of a witty remark, something to lighten the mood, but I'm distracted by the way Xander opens a small tub of fry sauce and places it in the middle of each little carton. I'm having a total flashback to my dad. He used to take me to the Iceberg, this exact location, after my ballet lessons back when I was seven or eight. Just the two of us. Grace was still a baby. We'd eat in the car and talk. He'd really listen. No distractions, no arguing with Mom, no baby screaming. Just the two of us. Sometimes the windows would steam up, just like now, and I'd draw pictures with my finger. The memory floods me with emotion. I bite my lip and turn my head. But I can't stop myself from trailing a finger through the film on the glass.

"Pollywog!" Kyra calls out. "Now draw a frog."

Tears fuzz my vision. Dad used to call me Pollywog. How could I forget something like that? A small shudder ripples through me. I just want to go home. Turn on some music really loud. Forget about this.

"Come on, do a frog!"

"I want you to make a kitty," Dex says.

But I'm sitting there as frozen as the shake Xander has just handed me. Thick pink ice cream spills over the top of the clear plastic lid, dripping onto my fingers. Xander wraps a napkin around my hand, takes the shake from me, and says, "Let me help you with that."

And I just look at him, through my blurry eyes. He doesn't ask me what's wrong, what I'm thinking about, or even make a joke about messing up the car. He just dips his spoon into my shake, taking a few big bites so that it no longer spills over the lid, while his chocolate shake melts over its lid in his lap. He hands my shake back to me, and I take a few bites, but the sweetness tastes wrong in my mouth; the ice cream barely makes it past the lump in my throat.

"Can Pollywog come over and play?" Kyra asks.

"Maybe another time, K.K. Better eat your shake before you turn into a chocolate monster."

I glance back at the chocolate beard smearing Krya's chin, thinking it's too late.

She grins. "I'm a chocolate monster and I'm going to eat

you up, Uncle X!" She stretches her messy fingers toward Xander's shoulder, leaving smudgy fingerprints on his shirt, but he simply smiles as he pulls the car into the street.

He doesn't say anything as he drives me home, but when the "Wheels on the Bus" starts playing, he quickly turns the radio to the pop music station. The kids protest. I'm actually relieved to hear a love song, even if it is the one Sawyer always said reminded him of me. I climb out of the car, careful to remember to leave Xander's towel behind.

"Um, thanks." I hold up the shake, and I'm about to make a joke about owing him fries or something, but I stop because his big brown eyes look at me so earnestly.

"I don't just write about you; I write about lots of things. If that's what's bothering you."

I tip my shake, spilling melted pink ice cream on my shorts. "Clumsy, me! Hey, no worries." My voice falters, so I turn away. "Yeah, so thanks again, for the, um, shake and stuff." I point to my leg. "Guess I've got some laundry to do."

"Hey, Polly. Take care," he says, except it doesn't sound like a throwaway line. It sounds like he means it.

And that scares me.

I run to my front door, so incredibly grateful that Grandma forgot to lock it again. Once inside, I slam the door shut, lean against it as if barricading myself from—what? I'm shaking. Just because I'm cold—because I'm wet, ate a milkshake, the air conditioning is on . . .

It's so quiet that I can hear the sound of Xander's wheels pulling on to the wet pavement. I focus on that sound until it disappears. Then I switch to thinking about the slight hum of the air conditioner. The weird grinding sound coming from the dishwasher. Anything but the thoughts wanting to push themselves into my head.

```
Dear Miss Swoon:
My boyfriend is perfect in every way.
The only thing we ever argue about is
music. I can't stand his music and he
can't stand mine. How can we create a
little more harmony?
—Messed-Up Melody

Dear Melody:
If you're making beautiful music to-
gether as a couple, it doesn't matter
what's playing on the radio. Learn to
love each other's differences.
—Miss Swoon
```

Not Shakespeare's Sonnet

Blond count: 6 (slow week!)

Welcome to my new series: Attention Grabbers!
A shout-out to Polly Martin for the inspiration.
Picture strawberry shake on ample cleavage and
the letchy look on a certain Sexy Lifeguard's
face. (See Random Locker Room Fantasies here.)
You're a naughty girl, P.M.!

So, yeah, ladies: put your boobs front and center. Invest in a good bra. That goes for everyone:
big, small, saggy (hey there, Mom!). Think color,
lace, and SUPPORT. I know what you pay for your
makeup, but trust me, no one is going to notice
a blemish if your girls are perky!

Oh, and to make things interesting: a mall gift
card to the best boob-related comment—but
keep it PG-13. (Parents demanded my new pass-
word. Hey there, Mom! This goes for you, too,
don't you agree, Dad?)

*A smile turns upside down as a finger traces foggy glass. Dark
clouds hover. Rain falls. Outside. Inside. Summer strawberries
taste too sweet.*

—X.C.

Chapter Fifteen

I'm so late for work. I slept in because Grace unplugged my clock again and I didn't hear Xander's skateboard zip past my window. Grace also failed to rise for her usual dawn cartoon marathon. Too many late nights with Amy.

I run into the kitchen, grab the only box of cereal left in the cupboard. All that's left are dusty bits of ground flakes on the bottom because no one has bothered to enter a grocery store for several days. Does Mom honestly expect us to eat leftover burgers for breakfast, too? Whatever. I need to eat *something*. The sink overflows with crusty dishes. I can't find a single bowl in the cupboard, so I grab a handful of chalky-tasting cereal and cram it into my mouth. While I'm searching for some sort of vessel to hold milk—never mind, it expired three days ago—Grandma wanders into the kitchen wearing her fluffy blue robe.

"What time is the dishwasher man coming?" she asks.

I stick my head under the faucet and wash down the stale cereal with lukewarm water. Yummy. "Um, I'm not a calendar."

"No need to get snarky."

Buster wanders into the kitchen and stands by his bowl whining. Instead of searching for dog food, I pour the rest of the cereal into his bowl. Even he won't eat it. Buster looks at me with watery eyes. "What?"

"Oh, that reminds me," Grandma says. "Buster's young man, Jack? Called last night. I wrote it down." Grandma sifts through a pile of newspapers, magazines, bills, and, you know, hamburger wrappers, looking for the message. "He wanted to arrange to pick up Buster. I said that he could meet you at Wild Waves this morning."

"What? That can't happen."

"Well, you'd better take it up with Jack. Is that his name?"

"Yes, it's Jack. But I can't take a dog to work. That's like one of the most basic pool rules. No animals. Not that the kids don't completely resemble wild animals, but whatever. Grandma, I can't take him. You'll have to find that message, call Jack, and tell him to pick Buster up *here*."

"I thought that it would be convenient. Plus, I have a lunch date."

"But Grandma, I cannot take that dog with me."

The doorbell rings, sending Buster into a barking frenzy. Grandma runs back to her bedroom to "put on her face and something decent." I glance at the clock on the microwave. It's blinking. No one has bothered to reset it since the power flashed off during that thunderstorm *eight* days ago! I follow Buster to the front door.

The dishwasher repairman stands on the porch. "Can you please put the dog outside?" he asks. "I have a no-dog policy. Bad experience." He shows me an ugly scar on his ankle.

Buster growls deep in his throat.

"Yeah, so do I. But it isn't working."

The guy wrinkles his forehead at me. "You have a broken dishwasher?"

"Yeah, that isn't working, either. Not much *is* working."

The repairman finally enters the house after I convince him that Buster only bites stuffed animals. Grandma sweeps into the room in a cloud of perfume; her hair still sticks out all over the place, but she's put on a silky blouse and some black pants. The effect is far more mental patient than glamour-girl, but whatever. I'm *really* late for work. I search through my purse for my keys while Grandma shows the repairman into the kitchen.

"We're just a house full of women," she says. "We can't fix a thang." I swear she's thrown a bit of Southern twang into her speech. "That's a mighty big toolbox you've got there."

"Omigod, Grandma! Where did you put my keys?" She borrowed my car last night—fresh out of the repair shop—for her so-called book club meeting last night, even though I'm fairly certain the only reading she did involved some septuagenarian's online profile. "Grandma! I'm late."

Grandma rolls her eyes at the dishwasher guy. "Teenagers."

Buster follows me to the kitchen, still hiding behind my legs, growling low in his throat. But he's just a big chicken. "I really need my keys."

Grandma searches through her purse, dumping out receipts, used tissues, a tin of mints, a hairbrush, and several movie ticket stubs on the counter. How many movies has she seen this summer? She hands me the keys to my car and Buster's leash. "Don't forget this."

"I can't believe this. This is ridiculous. And I'm completely fired. I hope you realize that. Cancel your lunch date, please?"

"Don't be too dramatic, sweetheart. Think of your affirmations." She turns to the dishwasher guy leaning against the counter. "Do you use affirmations?"

I can't believe it! I hook Buster's leash to his collar. "By the way, Grandma, there are *no* affirmations for taking your ex-boyfriend's dog to work."

"Forgiving regrets past brings future happiness."

"That barely makes sense!" I fling my purse over my shoulder and drag Buster, who has suddenly become interested in the repairman's shoes, toward the front door.

"That's profound, ma'am," the repairman says.

"Oh, don't you dare 'ma'am' me," Grandma says. "I'm almost younger than you are."

The repairman laughs.

I scream, sending Buster shooting between my legs to hide.

The repairman's van blocks my car in the driveway. I storm back into the house, Buster protesting because he wants to pee on the bushes out front. "You need to move the van! I mean could you please move your van, sir?"

I arrive at work thirty-two minutes late. With a bulldog. Sawyer's all over me like I'm doing cannonballs, naked, off the Lazy River's bridge.

"Polly! You're in the penalty box for sure. Strike two." He shakes his blond hair at me. "And what's—" He looks down at Buster. "Rule number five, Polly? That's a pretty big violation."

"Yeah, well. I'm feeling pretty violated myself, Sawyer."

His face softens, all concerned. He lowers his voice. "So you feel like you need a guard dog?"

"No!" I yank Buster away from a kid's Baggie of crackers. "That's not what I meant. I used the wrong word."

Sawyer's eyes widen. "Really?" A smug smile flickers at the corners of his mouth.

"Don't look so pleased. Look, there was a total misunderstanding, and so I'm stuck with this beast until his owner gets here. I know it's a rule violation, but I thought I could just keep him, you know, tied up away from the water, and—"

Sawyer shakes his head. "I could lose my managerial statute."

"Stature." I can't help it; it's a habit. Like, what's the big deal?

Sawyer's mouth hardens into a frown. "No dogs allowed."

I've blown it. Quick, I move into a flirtatious stance, letting my swimsuit slip down a little. Tossing my hair—which honestly would be far more effective had I, you know, bathed— I step close enough to smell his piña-colada-scented sunscreen. "Can't we work something out, hmm?"

Sawyer steps back. "I don't know."

"Come on. You're totally good at thinking of solutions to

problems," I say. "I'm stuck here. Can't you help me out? Just this once."

Sawyer glances across the O.K. Corral to the lifeguard chair by the Splash Pasture. On the other side of the shallow pool filled with life-size cows and a jungle gym shaped like a barn, Kipper Carlyle's examining her nails, not paying much attention to the kids crawling all over the place, splashing, fighting, nearly drowning.

"You're aware of Kipper, right?"

"Um, yeah. I've worked here for nearly four weeks. I think I'm aware of Kipper."

"You're, like, a girl, right?"

"Yes, thank you. I do possess a uterus."

Kipper leans back in the lifeguard chair, face catching the sun, holding her arms out like she's tanning. And *I'm* the one getting in trouble at work.

"Okay, Sawyer, so we've established my femininity. Do we need to establish your masculinity?"

He smoothes back his hair. "Very funny, ha, ha, ha."

"Hey, I was just trying to, you know, lighten the mood."

"Maybe I'm not in the mood for your moods, huh, Polly? Be serious for once."

"Okay, but only this once."

He just looks at me. "Never mind. Just take the dog home. You can pick up your final check on Friday."

I reach out and grab his wrist. "I'll do it. Whatever you want. Just give me one more chance." I'm completely compromising myself for the cash. Paying for car repairs wasn't exactly in my summer savings plan, but I'm too nervous to approach Dad with a financial request. Even Mom suggested I pay for the repairs myself, so that means she must be fighting with Dad about money again.

Sawyer bites his lip, thinking. And I swear you can watch the wheels in his brain turn like the big old fake water wheel churning next to the Lazy River. "You promise? No jokes?"

"No jokes." Buster flops on the pavement, all his limbs stretched out. He resembles Kipper Carlyle; well, she's not quite that wrinkly, but after a few more decades of tanning . . . Whatever. "What do you want with Kipper? You want me to teach her to read?"

"You—"

I hold up my hands. "Sorry!"

"Well, I kinda"—Sawyer looks away, turning the color of a third-degree sunburn—"want to ask her out."

I fling my hand out like a game show hostess. "Go for it. You guys will make a real cute couple, all blond and everything."

"You think so?" He's serious. "It's just that I, well, I was kind of hoping you could talk to her first. You know, see if she likes me."

"You've got to be kidding me. You want me to be your dating service?" Even Buster raises his head as if he expects more from me. But then Sawyer stares down at my animal violation, so I relent. "Yeah, sure. No problem. I'll talk to her."

Sawyer returns to a normal color. "Thanks so much. You're a great pal, Pollywog. Hey, get it? Now you're my Pallywog."

I *don't* get it. I don't get *me*. The last thing I want to do is set up my ex-boyfriend with a totally inferior specimen like her.

"I really don't want you to call me Pallywog."

Sawyer ignores me and reaches down and scratches behind Buster's ears. "The dog can hang out in the break room, okay?"

I nod, tugging on Buster's leash, but he looks completely disgusted with me. He shakes his head as if he's trying to erase all memory of this stupid deal I've made with Sawyer. I'd like to do the same. Except I've got a date—ha-ha—to chat up Kipper Carlyle.

Sawyer makes me a "roving deputy" so I'll have plenty of time for my little talk with Kipper. I decide to get it over with quick—ripping my dignity away with one quick stroke, like removing a Band-Aid.

Kipper's texting when I walk up to the lifeguard chair. Never mind that she's violating a major rule, one that's probably more dangerous than bringing dogs to work. Dogs like to save people. They bark as a warning. Text messages simply distract.

"Hey there, Kipper," I say. "You on break?"

"No. What does it look like? I'm working."

It looks like she's on break, but whatever.

"But I would totally love a break, deputy," she says. "Wanna swap spots?"

"I'm kind of assigned to rove."

She rolls her eyes. "I'm *so* sick of certain people playing favorites. You get all the easy jobs. I'd love to rove myself over to the snack bar, maybe the break room, maybe someplace where I get decent cell reception." She checks her phone. "I'm expecting an important call."

"Boyfriend?"

"No! My sister's having her baby. Any minute now."

"Oh? Does Sawyer know? I'm sure he'd be totally cool with you taking, you know, an extra break or something to check calls. He might even let you leave early." I remember the purpose of this interaction. "Sawyer's a real sweetheart about things like that." Bringing the ex-boyfriend's dog to work, not so much.

"Yeah, if it's *you*!" Kipper bites her lip, as if worried about my reaction.

I take a deep breath. "Not anymore. That's over. Way over."

"Doesn't seem like it. Have you read Sonnet's blog lately?"

"Well, Kipper, give your sunglasses a good polish, because it's so over—like two boyfriends ago over."

She shrugs. "Rebounds."

The last thing I want, need, or can even remotely handle is Kipper Carlyle analyzing my love life. "Kipper, dear. Sawyer likes you. He wants me to see if you're into *him*. That's why I'm the roving deputy today."

"Omigosh!" she squeals. "Really? But he's a senior! I mean, I know I'm going to be a junior now, but—Omigosh." She grins down at me. "His hair is, like, so blond."

"Yup. And his eyes are green."

"So green!"

"Okay, well, why don't you mosey on over to the corral there and ask to call your sister, and you can maybe chat a bit, and who knows?" I tilt my head to indicate the future flirting, dating, making out, wedding plans, whatever, maybe 2.1 disgusting kids.

"Polly, you're the best. No matter what everyone says. I can't believe he likes *me*."

My stomach lurches as if I've eaten a stack of day-old rejected hamburgers heaped with extra humiliation. "I'll take your spot while you're gone."

Kipper flips open her phone as she jumps from the lifeguard chair. "Guess what? Oh? That's great! It's a boy? Fabulous. Amazing! Guess what?"

Yeah, she's as deep as the puddle I'm standing in. Maybe it was just another one of Sawyer's malapropisms. He didn't mean *deep;* he meant *dumb*. I wasn't dumb enough to be his girlfriend.

I'm standing in the middle of Splash Pasture, blowing my whistle every few seconds, surrounded by squealing kids having a huge water gun fight, and feeling really, um, lonely.

Over by the Lazy River Sawyer flirts with Kipper. Xander gives me rides but ignores me. And I don't want to like him. I can't! Especially since skateboarding has started to look like an appealing form of transportation (no gas, no pricey repairs, no Dad issues). Jane's officially going out with Rowdy, if hanging out in the basement counts. Mom works a ton of extra shifts at Hamburger Heaven. Grace has practically moved in with Amy. Dad hasn't answered my e-mail about the cabin. And by the time I return home Grandma will probably be dating the dishwasher guy. I'm going to hand wash all my dishes as a matter of principle!

Why won't all the noise push the thoughts from my mind? I'm not finding the positivity.

Somehow, being surrounded by so much laughter, joking around, happiness, just makes me feel that much worse. It's as if everyone else in the world has figured out how to enjoy life, even the smallest toddlers who giggle as they splash around in the shallow water together. All the moms sit around in groups of friends. No one wants to be my friend. Jane acts completely sick of me. Sawyer just used me to get close to Kipper.

"Ugh! I can't believe I did that!" I blow my whistle just to tell my thoughts to stop! *Warning to self: you're violating all of your rules!*

I look at a Band-Aid stuck to the bottom of the pool and wonder what kind of wound has been left gaping open. I look up to see Jack ambling toward me holding Buster's leash, and a girl's hand.

"Hey, Pol. Buster looks great. Thanks. You're a sweetheart."

The girl smiles at me in a way that shows that I'm not the least bit threatening to her. Buster wades over to me in the pool. Several kids shriek, "Puppy!" I know I'm violating several health department codes and Sawyer's going to explode if he ever stops gazing into Kipper's vacant blue eyes, but I can't help but wonder why *this* girl didn't watch the dog.

Buster splashes back to Jack's actual girlfriend. "I would've loved to baby-sit little Buster-wuster." She pouts, patting Buster's head. "But my mom is so anal about her floors. I'm, like, really."

"Yeah, really."

"So, P.M., think you could drop Buster's stuff off at my place tonight? We're going out," Jack says.

"My dad's company picnic." The girl sighs dramatically. "Like, really."

"Really." I'm like one of those scratched DVDs we watch in science lab. Stuck. "I'm actually—"

"A total pal. Thanks." Jack smiles.

I'm not anyone's pal! If he thinks I'm going to deliver his dog's slobbery dishes, stinky food, and stained pillow to his house while he's off with his girlfriend, he's killed too many brain cells playing video games! Does *she* even know how he enticed me to dog-sit by using his . . . his lips?

Sawyer's whistle blows, and he charges over like a rodeo steer. "Dog! That dog! You said—"

Jack tosses out an easy smile. "Relax, Sawman. It's all my fault."

"Out!" Sawyer leans over, catching his breath, panting, pointing to the exit. He looks at me with a mixture of surprise and disgust. "You're in—"

"The doghouse?"

He just looks at me. "Yeah." He holds his fingers an inch apart. "You're this close to losing your job."

"What else is new?"

A kid behind me starts wailing. I have to bite my cheek hard to stop my own tears from flowing. I brace myself for Sawyer's patented question of concern, but he's already walking toward Kipper. I can't lose my job. I need the money more than ever. But I could never tell him that.

I'm standing alone in the middle of everyone, tears escaping from my eyes, but no one even notices.

```
Dear Miss Swoon:
How can I stop saying yes when I want to
say no?
—No Not Yes
```

Dear No Not Yes:

Tattoo it on your forehead and point!

—Miss Swoon

Not Shakespeare's Sonnet

Blond count: 7.5 (sick little twerp, sick!)

Listmania!!!

Things You Should Never Do for an Ex:

1. Fix them up with someone (P.M., No!!!!!)
2. Lend them money (Like, hello. B.B.?)
3. Loan them your car (Two words, R.J.: Driving Record!)
4. Baby-sit their bulldogs (Come on, P.M.! You're on this list twice)
5. Believe what they say when they break up with you (Everyone!)

Your turn, folks! Let's make this list comprehensive.

Chapter Sixteen

Despite new affirmations—more like specific instructions about not making stupid mistakes, now written less conspicuously on my ankles in Sharpie marker—I found myself making yet another stupefying decision. It's those foolish affirmations. If I have loving and supportive friends, then I should go along with their plans, right? And if I have loving and supportive friends, then I should love and support them, even if that means hanging out with their doofus boyfriend late at night in an empty strip mall parking lot.

I should've gone to the bonfire party with Sonnet. So what if Xander Cooper told her about it? He hangs out with the hardcore partiers now, too? Sonnet made way too big a deal about how he'd asked her to tell me.

"He's so into you," Sonnet said. "Do you see the way he

stares? And he's always writing stuff in that little notebook. Probably odes to his Fair Polly."

"I'm sure it's just a grocery list or something. I think he uses a lot of hair product."

"You think you're so funny, but the guy seriously has his rhyme and meter going for you."

I rolled my eyes. "You make it sound so dirty."

"Oh, do I? Or is that the way *your* mind is going?" Sonnet flipped her hair. "What if I write a few sample Xander love odes for my blog?"

"What if I convinced every blond guy within a thousand metric miles to die his hair puke green?"

"Green makes me horny."

I pushed her off the Lazy River bridge in a totally illegal, bad-girl move.

Sonnet bobbed out of the water, cleavage quite exposed. "You could've just said no."

"No!" I'd screamed. "A thousand times no."

But now here I am standing under the yellow glow of the parking lot lights with my arms crossed. We've removed our shoes to create a slalom course for a grocery cart race. Why did I wear my newish sandals? The nerd patrol has rounded up two carts. One guy even went shopping with his mom so he could hide the cart behind a Dumpster. That's the level of quality I'm dealing with. *Loving and supportive friends*, I chant to myself, ignoring the fact that Jane has barely acknowledged my presence. She's all over Rowdy, running up and down the shoe course in her bare feet, giggling as she rearranges our footwear. Really she's acting like she's been infected with some viral brain disorder.

We've divided into teams. As one of only two female specimens, I get to be a team captain. I only picked guys who would never in a geologic era appeal to me. One of the guys—he was in my AP Physics class—struts up to me. He reminds me of Buster, except without the, you know, musculature. "So, Martin," he says. He's trying way too hard. "We've got to work on achieving maximum velocity, don't you think?"

"Well, Akim—"

"Call me Razor—like Occam's Razor, Akim's Razor. Get it?"

"Okay. Whatever. Actually, um, Razor, I think we should focus on trajectory more than velocity."

Akim nods, all serious. One of my other teammates starts arguing with him, but I hear Akim whisper, "Yeah, but dude, I know she doesn't look like it or act like it, but she breaks the class curve every single time."

I roll my eyes, wondering how this guy knows anything about my grades. I keep that stuff low profile, but whatever. "It's just a grocery cart race, right?"

"It's pride, man." They do an awkward chest bumps. Works better with drunk football players than with sober members of the academic team. "And loser pays at Hamburger Heaven!"

"Oh. No. That's okay. Pride is just fine." I'm not showing up at Hamburger Hell with these lower life forms! Not on a Friday night. And then there's the whole Mom situation. I will not let the other team win! I will lie about my curfew!

"Okay." Jane bounces over to me with far too much enthusiasm.

"The course is ready. What do you think, Polly?"

I glance at the random placement of shoes streaming between the bookstore on the south end and the craft store at the north. "Let's just get this over with."

Jane's face falls.

"I've got to get home early."

She puts her hand on her hip. "But you're spending the night?"

"Oh. Yeah. Right." I really need to donate my brain to science, possibly as soon as tomorrow, so someone can figure out what went wrong. "Joking."

Jane shrugs her shoulders. "That was lame, even for you."

"I'm just trying to throw you off your game so we can dominate. Right, guys?"

We high-five each other, and I climb in the cart with Akim the Mighty Razor. I don't want to rehash the calculations based on weight distribution that went into *that* decision. Let's just say that I won't be fantasizing about any of these guys early in the morning. Not that I do that about *anyone* anymore. Not since Xander's skateboard passed my window this morning, anyway. So? It's a difficult habit to break! *No male contamination. No male contamination. No male—*

"Ready, Polyamide?"

We all have new nicknames. So what if Helium (don't ask) wants to insult me by insinuating that I'm synthetic, as in "fake"? This is the first time we've ever spent more than a class period together. So what if I sometimes ask stupid questions or pretend to get a bad grade now and then? Guys love to explain things, not have them explained. After enduring a Polynomial versus Polyamide debate, I've also decided to name my future kids—not that I plan to mate with anyone—after an unpronounceable symbol.

Razor and I distribute our weight for maximum velocity. Helium and Sulu stand behind, ready to push. Jane sits in the other cart with Rowdy; you can bet that decision was hardly based on a scientific formula. More like a hokey love potion. I'm totally not into this whole endeavor, but as long as I'm here, we might as well win.

"Go!" Campos screams. (These guys spend way too much time watching those *Fast and Furious* movies.)

My whole body jiggles as the grocery cart careens around the shoes, nearly tipping over. I'm thrown against Akim. "Distribute! Distribute!" he yells.

I start laughing. Jane and Rowdy's cart catches up with us. They aren't distributing anything except their hands all over each other! My boobs bounce all around, but Razor's too busy screaming instructions to notice. "Veer to the left. The left!"

Jane and Rowdy overtake us around a tight turn, tipping precariously to the side, which slows them down. Our cart shoots ahead following a straight trajectory.

We win!

Sulu, Razor, and Helium immediately call out Hamburger Heaven menu items—along the lines of "I'm getting like two shakes, dude, and cheese fries and a Devilish Bacon Burger."

I'm still feeling all light and giggly from the ride. "Let's do best two out of three." I grin at Jane. "You up for a rematch?"

"You're on!" Rowdy comes over and bumps his fist against mine. "Should we rearrange the course?"

I look over at my shoe, flattened by a speeding cart's wheel. Well, the sandals are kind of oldish. And it's not like I'm out to impress anyone. Ever again. "Only if you want to move my sandals away from the finish line."

Razor says, "No, the course stays the same to maintain the integrity of the scoring."

"You're quite right," I say. "We don't want anyone to invalidate our results." I sort of enjoy hanging out with these guys who've mastered their SAT prep words, scientific notation, and, you know, *Star Trek* characters. Apparently I'm smiling a little too much because Akim slings his arm around my shoulders.

I shrug him off. "We shouldn't mix business with pleasure, there, Occam's Razor. We've got a race to win."

He clasps his hands behind his back. "Oh, right. Right."

Yes. I'm in complete control. We climb into the carts again. As we start the second race, sirens blare and lights flash: the mall security truck rounds the corner, heading toward the far parking lot entrance.

"Cops!" Sulu just lets go of the cart, sending me and Akim careening toward the curb. Wham! The cart lands on its side.

I hit the pavement. Hard. I sit up, dazed. Droplets of blood bubble on my arm, but the pain hasn't hit yet. I've got a big rip in my shorts.

Akim screams, "Run!"

"Get in the car!"

We all scramble toward Rowdy's van, picking up random shoes. I manage to grab one sandal before Jane screams at me to "Hurry! Hurry!" Razor takes my hand and pulls me into the van, onto his lap. We peel out of there just as the security guy pulls over to investigate. Everyone speculates about the potential chase that's about to ensue, but the security guy simply gets out, shakes his head at the stray shoes littering the pavement, and gets back into his car.

"Damn," says Akim. "There goes my opportunity for a decent story to tell the ladies."

"What ladies?" Sulu laughs. "You're going to need a lot more than that, my little Akim."

My arm throbs. Bad. I bite my lip. "Um, Akim? Could you maybe move your knee?" He jams his patella into my butt cheek. "Maybe not quite like that." I shift, groaning with pain.

"Ooh, Polyamide, that's quite a superficial scrape on your dermis." Akim's hand hovers above my arm before he changes his mind and puts it back on the armrest.

"You think? Serves me right for spending my evening acting like an uber dork."

Silence. The entire van goes silent.

"Polly," Jane whispers.

Now *I* feel like a lower life form. "I didn't mean it." I bite my lip, hoping that will keep my tears in check. My arm really hurts, almost as much as my lame social life. "Maybe I just have low blood sugar."

"Mmm," Akim murmurs, jamming his other bony knee into my butt, before going into a long explanation about glucose levels.

"Maybe we do need to stop at Hamburger Heaven," I say. "I really should eat something, I guess."

"But who pays?" Helium asks. "Since we didn't finish the rematch?"

"We'll all pay for ourselves," Jane says. She sounds way too happy for a girl who just lost a grocery cart race and got chased out of a mall parking lot by a rent-a-cop.

Cars crowd the Hamburger Heaven parking lot even though it's nearly 11:00 P.M. Don't these people have responsible parents who give them appropriate curfews? Not that I'm exactly on Mom's radar screen these days. Everyone leaps out of the van, but I'm still sitting on Akim's lap. We've parked between Mom's car—and Hayden's!

"I think I'll wait here." Do I really want to be seen on a Friday night with the geek squad? Not to mention that my mother will probably be my server, I may bleed to death before my order arrives, and Hayden might try to get me to sign a petition or something.

"You should wash your arm in the bathroom," Akim says, but I think he wants me to get off his lap. We *are* the only ones still sitting in the van.

"Oh, yeah. Right. Good idea, I guess."

My leg hurts as I limp out of the van. I've got another long cut on my upper thigh. When Rowdy opens the restaurant door, it sounds louder than a school assembly. Mom spots me right away and smiles enthusiastically. "Kids! I've got just the table for you."

"Hey, Mrs. Martin!" Rowdy says. "I didn't know you worked here."

"How else am I going to see my favorite students?"

"Aw, but you always made me stay for detention."

"Laugh and the class laughs with you, but you get detention alone."

Rowdy laughs. "I wish you taught high school."

Everyone slides into the big booth that's way too close to the door, the bathroom, the bar area—practically everyone in the restaurant has to pass by us.

Mom leans down, angel halo bobbing. "I'll give you all a discount, and let me just tell you that the chocolate shakes are particularly delicious tonight."

Jane grins. "Your mom is the best."

Akim's eyes widen. "Mrs. Martin is your mom?"

"Like, duh." I roll my eyes.

He looks me up and down. "I suppose I see some genetic similarities."

"Uh, thank you? I'm kind of recessive?"

He nods his head real slow. "Don't say it like it's a bad thing."

"She looks like her dad, stupid," Jane says.

I don't like where this discussion is heading. "Uh, okay. I'm going to the restroom."

As I scoot out of the booth, making Helium move, Jane finally notices my wounds. "Omigosh, Polly. Your arm. And your leg!"

I wince. "Anything for the team."

On the way to the bathroom, hobbling around in my one squashed sandal, I spot Hayden sitting with a bunch of student government types: girls who sport serious haircuts and wear preppy outfits to hamburger places on Friday nights. They never show up at parties because a single incriminating photo on the Internet could derail their future careers. I backtrack down the aisle and walk out of my way to avoid Hayden. A few kids sitting at tables greet me cheerfully before giving me funny looks when they notice my gaping—okay, bleeding—wounds.

In the bathroom I discover that florescent lighting doesn't do much for road rash. I look like I tried to run myself through the Hamburger Heaven meat grinder—not that they don't completely use frozen patties, but whatever. I soak a few paper towels and rest them on my injured arm and leg, and I try to brush some of the dirt stains off my shirt and shorts. I'm a mess.

Emmy Winters, our next class secretary, comes bounding into the bathroom. "Omigod, Pol. The whole restaurant is buzzing. What happened to you? Did you jump out of a moving car?" She drops her voice. "You're not back with Kurt again, are you? Because Sonnet Silverman wrote this totally mysterious poem about you on her blog."

"No, I'm not with Kurt." I gently remove the wet paper towels from my skin. The air stings. "And Sonnet apparently has a death wish."

Emmy's eyebrows rise above her eyeglass frames.

"Joking. Look, the whole thing's a silly—Whatever." I flap

my hand. "It's stupid, really. And since I'm kind of bleeding to death here, you know?"

"Fine. Fine." She holds her hands up. "But you've got to promise to tell me all about this sometime. I'll keep it a *top* student government secret."

I flash her a smile. "You betcha!" I catch my big cheesy grin in the mirror and blush. Polyamide. I *am* completely synthetic.

"Bye, Polly. Let's hang out sometime; we can start brainstorming prom themes."

I raise my arm. *Ow!* "What about prom horror movies?"

"You're, like, so funny! See ya, Pol." Laughing, Emmy leaves the bathroom.

After spending far too much time patching my wounds, I head back to our table. Mom's setting down platters of food. The guys gush, "Thanks again for the free wings and everything, Mrs. M!"

"Okay," Mom says. "Why did the student eat his homework?" Thankfully she doesn't give them time to guess. "His teacher told him it was a piece of cake."

Everyone laughs. I can't take this. I'm about to slide next to Jane, avoiding the whole Akim situation—I do not want to run the risk of physical contact again—when Rowdy calls out, "X-Man!"

I turn around, confused. Xander strides toward the table, smiling. "Guys! Thought you'd still be setting world speed records and generally—"

Xander sees me and stops talking mid-sentence. I hover, halfway sitting and standing, even though the gash on my leg hurts.

"Ouch!" That's so not what I wanted to say.

"Polly, your leg. It's bleeding pretty bad," Jane says. "And it's kind of getting on stuff." She uses my supposedly profuse bleeding as an excuse to climb into Rowdy's lap.

I stand up in a rickety-old-man kind of way. My leg throbs. My arm throbs. My heart does *not* throb! Xander stares at me, brown eyes wide, mouth turned down in a sympathetic-looking frown.

"Polly, you didn't?" Xander looks at Akim.

Akim nods. "Oh yeah. She did."

"Thought you were the bonfire party type," Xander says.

"Oh, she is," Akim says. "We completely stretched her capacity."

"What does *that* mean?" I watch blood seep through my shorts. "I'm the one who told you to go with trajectory."

"True. But you also made it clear that we were kind of lame."

I sigh.

Mom swings back around, holding a heavy tray of drinks. "Excuse me, X-Man," she says slipping behind Xander. She knows Xander Cooper? *She* calls him X-Man? "You kids going to be here tomorrow for academic team practice? I'll have the mozzarella sticks waiting."

"Sure thing, Mrs. M." Xander grins at her.

I'm standing there gaping: mouth, wounds, hole in my shorts, brain . . .

Mom finally grabs a clue and notices me. "Oh my goodness, Polly. What's happened to you? You look like you've been through the meat grinder—not that we have one, but you know what I mean. Sweetheart, you need to get home and clean up right away."

Across the room a server drops an entire tray full of dishes, sending a huge clatter echoing through the restaurant. Mom rushes over, halo bobbing, to help. Someone yells, "You go, girl, Mrs. M!"

The entire academic team digs into their greasy refreshments. Jane's not even looking at me because she's eating the french fries flapping out of, you know, Rowdy's mouth. Disgusting! She once lectured me about public displays of affection when Jack and I ate the opposite ends of a licorice stick at the movies. The double standard, the hypocrisy, the—hot guy staring at me, looking all concerned and doe-eyed like freaking Bambi or something.

"I can give you a ride," Xander says. "Not on my skateboard." He smiles.

"My friend"—I glare at Jane—"promised to give me a ride. Because I'm spending the night at her *house*." But Jane's moved from french fries to, um, French kissing right in the middle of Hamburger Heaven.

"Jane!"

She looks at me, lips puffy, a moronic grin spreading across her face. "Hmm?"

"I'm spending the night at your house?"

"You sure? You're so hurt and all, and—"

Rowdy's got his hands in her hair, leaving behind an oily residue, and, yeah, ruining my appetite for cheese fries, probably forever. A drop of blood tickles as it runs down my leg.

Xander hands me a paper napkin. "That looks kind of bad—might need medical attention."

"It's just a flesh wound," I say, doing my best *Monty Python*. Even though I'm channeling my inner geek tonight, that reference embarrasses me more than anything else I've done in front of Xander, but he just starts laughing. He and Akim then do a whole *Monty Python* riff. I should've known.

Mom comes by carrying a tray full of broken glasses and

wet rags. "Oh, honey, if you're going to bleed to death, maybe you should do it in the ER. I think you might need stitches, and I left my sewing kit at home, so—"

"I could take her, Mrs. M." Xander straightens his shoulders, acting like the teacher's pet he used to be.

"Um, Mom. Maybe I should just call Dad."

Mom shakes her head, almost imperceptibly. "Don't go there. Not tonight. Not here."

So, next thing I know, I'm lurching out of Hamburger Heaven, on one shoe, bloody napkins stuck to my leg. Xander holds my arm tenderly, *not* that I'm noticing the way his fingers feel on my skin, what with the blood gushing painfully from my leg and all. Really I'd probably be better off dying a slow, painful death in the restroom that was last cleaned by K.W. at 9:15 P.M. The only thing that makes my exit even kind of worth it is the look on Hayden's face—not to mention those of his little harem of Future Lawyers of America.

Dear Miss Swoon:
My friend has been accusing me of selling out just because I've started hanging out with some different, more popular
people. I say I'm just making some new

friends. How do you know when you're
hanging out with the wrong crowd?
—Wrong Crowd

Dear Wrong Crowd:
If you're happy, you're doing something
right.
—Miss Swoon

Not Shakespeare's Sonnet

Blond Count: 8 (might be 9, tho)
Fantasy Love Poems:
Ode to a Siren
by XCish
Water gushes through the tubes,
But I gush about you, fair one,
Dark curls cascade across cherubic cheeks,
And your other cheeks ain't so bad either.
I hide out watching,
Wanting to speed things up with you.
Get out your little black notebooks, folks.
New contest: supercool prize to the best love
poems!

Chapter Seventeen

Xander walks me over to a hard plastic chair in the Emergency Room waiting area. A few other people sit around in various states of bleeding, brokenness, and intoxication. Across from me a kid moans, clutching his arm. The air smells like rubbing alcohol.

"Wait here, and I'll check you in. Do you have your insurance card?"

I shake my head no. Where is Mom? She swore she'd rush right over here as soon as she got someone to cover for her at Hamburger Heaven—she's probably too busy joking around with Jane and Rowdy while I'm over here suffering. Xander shakes his hair back from his face as he strides toward the reception desk. I can't see his expression as he talks to the young receptionist woman; she smiles and bats her eyes as if she's at a desperate speed-dating thing like The Sassy Sage recommended in her column the other day.

Xander jogs over to me and crouches next to my chair. "Hey, they need consent, and your mom isn't answering her phone. Do you have another guardian, like maybe your dad?" He sounds awkward and hesitant.

"Um, yeah." I wince with pain as I stand. "I can call my dad. I'll just—"

He rests his hand on my shoulder. "Just sit. I'll take care of it."

"*You're* going to call my dad?"

"Sure, why not?"

Part of me thinks, *Yeah, why not?* Maybe having a strange boy calling him from the ER might kick Dad into gear, remind him he still actually has, you know, biological spawn, parenting responsibilities.

Xander watches my face. "It'll be okay. Trust me."

I don't trust anyone.

But my leg's throbbing, bleeding, dripping all over the plastic seat in a contaminating way, so I give him my dad's phone number. Xander walks back to the reception desk, dialing his cell phone. He talks for a few seconds and then hands the phone to the receptionist. Dad doesn't even ask to talk to me. Maybe he's rushing right over so I don't have to spend the night alone in the Emergency Room with the drunk freak, the kid with the broken arm, and the guy who makes my heart palpitate. With anxiety! Nothing else.

Xander walks back to me a few minutes later with a stack of magazines. "Okay, so the selection is quite limited. There's a *People* magazine from . . . ooh, last year. *Cosmopolitan*, but it looks like it's been heavily censored." He shows me the ripped-up magazine. *"Ladies' Home Journal, Road & Track, Field & Stream—"*

"Too many bad associations."

A smile flickers across his face. "Really? You have bad associations with trout?"

"More than one." I grab the magazine. "But I am going fishing with my dad next month, so . . ." Our fingers brush.

"Oh, is that right?" Xander grins. "I like thinking about you hooking—"

"Don't." My body feels fizzy, even though it's probably just blood loss.

"Don't what?" He flashes his eyebrows at me in a way that momentarily makes me forget my pain.

"Don't look at me like that."

"Okay." He bites his lower lip to squelch another smile.

"I'll sit over here, and you can read up on your fly-fishing techniques."

"I use bait."

"I'm sure you do."

Now I'm smiling. "Quit making it sound dirty."

"I'm not saying anything." He does that thing with his eyebrows again. "I can't help what you're thinking."

I quickly page through the magazine. "I'm thinking of a Slow-Poke jig." I hold up the photo of the lure on page 119.

"And you're accusing me of talking dirty."

I reach over to whack him on the knee with the magazine, but moving my leg makes me wince with pain. "Ooh." More blood seeps through the napkins, dribbles down my leg. Tears spring to my eyes. I tell myself that it's 100 percent caused by the pain, but I'm also feeling bad that Dad didn't even want to *talk* to me on the phone and that Mom is having too much fun hanging out, munching on cheese fries, with Jane and Rowdy. I could call Grandma, but she's probably whispering soapy nothings to Dishwasher Dude.

Xander jumps up and runs over to the receptionist, and I half expect to hear him yell about needing a doctor in some dramatic way like in the movies. Instead he starts flirting! The girl dissolves into smiles and giggles. And I'm thinking, *Great, not only have my parents abandoned me, the guy who's supposed to be keeping me company wants to score a date with a most definitely out-of-high-school ER receptionist.* I look down at the magazine, but my eyes have trouble focusing through the tears pooling in my eyes. From the pain. Only the pain. I look up to see Xander strutting toward me, a triumphant look on his face.

"You're up next."

"What?" I'm completely confused, not sure what he's talking about.

"I told her that you were bleeding quite a bit, so she moved you up on the schedule." He sits down next to me, leans over, and whispers, "Ahead of the broken arm, even." He tilts his head. "What's wrong?"

"I thought you were—" Suddenly I'm too embarrassed to say anything about flirting. "I mean, I thought I'd have to wait longer."

"Naw. I know how to work the system." He leans back, stretching his legs out wide. "Kyra has a lot of asthma attacks, so I've spent my share of time sitting here, and I've learned that you get further with sweet talk than screaming. My sister can be quite the screamer, so I'm used to smoothing things over." He nudges me with his elbow. "Thanks for not screaming."

"Yeah, okay. I guess." I go back to flipping through my magazine, but I can't concentrate, what with the pain, the close proximity of Xander's arm next to mine. Every now and then his bare skin brushes mine. Feels warm.

"So, why do you help bring Kyra to the ER?"

"My sister usually wants someone to tag along." Xander looks at me all seriously. "It's really a bitch being a single mom. So I try to help out when I can. Watch the kids. Keep her company. Let her have some kind of life."

"That's nice of you." Just like this is nice of him. Waiting with me. Just when I'm analyzing his potential character flaws—he's obviously a complete doormat like I am, and that's the last kind of person I need to hang out with—a nurse wearing purple scrubs pops out with a clipboard. "Polly Marie Martin."

"That's us!" Xander stands, holding his hand out to me. I hesitate. But he grabs my hand, using his other hand to support my back as I stand. The pain in my leg wallops me.

"Easy," he whispers. "I've got you."

And he's so gentle, so kind. A tearful sigh shudders through me. *Suck it up!*

"What did the nurse say when the vampire asked if he needed stitches?" I ask. "Oh, I'm positive. Get it?" I think I've mixed up the joke because he doesn't even smile.

He says, "It's okay. I'll stay with you. You're going to be just fine."

The way he's reading my mind truly freaks me out.

The nurse guides me to a small area separated by a thin curtain. "Can you get those shorts off?" she asks. "The doctor will want to see the entire scope of the injury."

"I'm not about to—"

"I won't look," Xander says.

"What kind of hospital is this? A burlesque show?"

The nurse glares at me as if I'm the one acting unreasonable. "Just slip the shorts off. I'm sure your boyfriend—"

"He's not my boyfriend. I don't have a boyfriend."

The nurse looks me up and down, assessing my mental stability. "Just get yourself into that hospital gown, okay?" She turns around and leaves. "The doctor will see you in a few minutes."

I stand there leaning against the narrow wheeled bed.

Xander takes a step back. "Look, I can leave."

"Thanks." I breathe through a wave of pain.

He steps behind the curtain, and I watch his tall shadow as I unzip my shorts. I'm reminded of the sound of his skateboard on the pavement and my ill-advised Xander-zipper fantasies. If only I had a concussion, then I'd be oblivious to this humiliation. And maybe *that* would be worth Dad tearing himself away from his girlfriend of the month to come see his oldest daughter in the Emergency Room. I edge the fabric down my hips. That's when I get stuck. I can't move the stiff denim over my wound. Hurts too much. I attempt to hop on my good leg, but I lose my balance and crash to the floor.

"Polly!" Xander twists through the curtain, pulling me up from the floor. My shorts puddle around my ankles. I'm wearing pink Wednesday underwear. It's Friday. Not that it's my main concern in this situation, but still.

"Let me help you onto the gurney, okay?" He scoops me off my feet in that foolishly romantic, bride-and-groom-crossing-the-threshold way. He sets me down gently. My leg hurts so much, and without my shorts staunching the flow, my bleeding increases. A deep gash carves through my upper thigh.

I hear the doctor flip through my chart as he comes over. "Prepare a suture kit," he says to the nurse before shifting into friendly-doctor mode. "Well, what do we have here?" No one wants to hear that cheerful voice at midnight, especially when the hot neighbor guy has just seen you in your pink undies.

Xander steps away from me. "I'll wait outside the curtain."

I reach out for his arm. "Um, don't?"

"You sure?"

I nod my head yes. The air in the room feels so cold. And I'm hurting so bad.

The nurse brings a tray of shiny silver tools that look like they belong in a museum of medieval torture or something. The doctor probes my wound, squeezing it, watching blood spurt. I gasp.

"It's a deep one. You said you were"—he looks at my chart—"riding in a grocery cart? Do you know how you got cut?"

I'm biting my lip so hard that I can't answer. I shake my head.

Xander takes my hand. "Squeeze as hard as you want to."

I feel completely self-conscious as the doctor rinses my leg with an orange iodine solution. But then he starts in with the needles. One to numb me. One with antibiotics. One to protect me from tetanus. He lifts a long needle into the light. I squeak. And I squeeze Xander's hand so hard that I might break some of his bones, but he doesn't say anything. Instead he brushes the hair from my sweaty forehead.

"You're going to be okay." He kisses my forehead.

I can't stop the tears from coming. My lip quivers. Big fat drops slide from my eyes. The thing is: I'm not feeling anything physically. I'm numb. But for the first time all summer the rest of me is most definitely *not* numb. I'm feeling everything.

And that's when I feel myself slipping into the fuzzy dark edges in my vision.

Dear Miss Swoon:

My ex-husband is great about paying child support but not so great at actually supporting our child. It didn't used to matter when my daughter was little. But now she's started asking me why her daddy doesn't come to her school programs, etc.

—Needing More Support

Dear Needing:

Time to call in reinforcements. Families are born, but they can also be created. Find a new and improved male role model.

—Miss Swoon

So many stories in an ER. Did the stoic kid break his arm while trying to skateboard to impress other kids? (No, that was me.) Why does the man in the filthy, tattered coat drink so much? (Is it because of his father?) Why did her hand grip mine so hard? (Not pain. Is it her father? Probably not me.)

—X.C.

Chapter Eighteen

$\mathcal{I}$ roll over, whimpering, in bed, blinking into the too-bright sunlight. I'm feeling muscles I never studied in Honors Bio. Gently I touch the bandage over my stitches. *Ooh.* The skin on my arm feels tight as a million little scabs form; I look like that guy who paints with the dots—what's-his-name, Seurat—has had his way with me. So, yeah, I guess last night *did* happen.

A strange rush of emotion twitters through me. Xander kissed me (on the forehead) and held my hand (out of pity). Xander also watched me bleed, cry, faint, and, um, wear my pink Wednesday panties on the wrong day of the week. Somehow fixating on that detail feels safer than contemplating other details like his sitting with me for the three hours after I passed out. Even after Mom arrived.

Thinking = Pain.

I inch my aching self out of bed and wander into the kitchen to find Grace and Grandma making Fourth of July pancakes: blueberries, strawberries, whipped cream.

"Hey, what do you know, something not on the Hamburger Heaven menu."

"Happy Birthday, America!" Grace squeals.

I pick at the thick bandage on my leg. "Just because you throw a birthday party doesn't mean you're going to get presents, you know."

Grace sticks her tongue out at me. "Does so! Grandma already bought me a Webimal: the patriotic bear! I named her Betsy because I played Betsy Ross in our fourth grade program. And she made the first flag." She plops whipped cream on her pancakes.

"Maybe Grandma could buy me a clue."

Grandma swipes a finger through Grace's whipped cream and slurps it into her mouth. "You doing, okay, sweetheart? Heard you had a spill. Let me look at you." Grandma makes a *tsk-tsk* sound as she examines my arm. "How did you manage this?"

"Well, I gave up on my pathetic attempt at channeling my inner bad girl. I thought that hanging out with a bunch of geeks would be, you know, safe and innocent. But I still ended up standing in front of Xander Cooper in my pink Wednesday undies. On a Friday."

Grace drops her fork.

"No big deal, Grace. The nurse made me do it. But promise me you'll never wear day-of-the-week underwear. It just complicates things."

She nods slowly. I'm completely warping the poor child.

"I'm sure he wasn't reading your underwear." Grandma grins. "Not with your tight little fanny."

"Yeah, I was real attractive bleeding all over the place."

"Maybe I should try the damsel-in-distress routine." Grandma puts a hand to her forehead. "Oh, dah-ling."

"I think you kind of did that already with the dishwasher," I say. "'Oh, I don't know a thang about washin' dishes,'" I imitate.

Grandma giggles. Very un-Swoon-like. "Some girls have all the luck. Hank's a cutie, but he's no skateboarding hunk."

I tear off a hunk—okay, wrong word—of pancake. "No one uses that word anymore."

"Your mom said he waited in the ER with you for three hours."

"It was only two hours and forty-seven minutes."

Grandma drops blueberries onto her pancake stack. "Honey, he is obviously smitten."

"He's just incredibly responsible. I'm sure he's got that do-gooder complex like Always Helping Out from last Tuesday's column."

Grandma smiles. "Maybe he's just a good boy?"

"You make him sound like a dog." I take a plate of pancakes to the table and flip through the paper to the Style section, purposely skipping the serious political news. Style is all about Fourth of July picnics.

"Hey, Grace. Dad called about the fireworks, right?"

She shakes her head. "I'm going with Amy. To the parade and the fireworks!"

"But Dad said—"

Mom walks in and, I swear, she's still got halo hair. She says, "I'm sure we'll find plenty of ways to keep you entertained. Maybe you can attempt to amputate your left arm tonight."

I'm not in the mood. "But Dad called, right?"

Grace shakes her head. I watch emotions flicker across Mom's face.

"I told him that I had to spend the day with you or I'd melt away." Mom makes a big show of melting into the floor.

Grace and Grandma laugh.

I can't even fake a smile. "But he didn't come to the ER. I haven't seen him in forty-three days."

"That's obsessively mathematical," Mom says. "Maybe I should hire you as my accountant?"

"You'd try to pay me in Hamburger Heaven leftovers."

"How did you know?"

Grace pops a strawberry into her mouth. "Dad sent me an e-mail with the cutest little puppies."

"Oh, send that one to me, Gracie Pie," Grandma says. "At least he's trying to stay in touch."

"You're saying I should feel all warm and fuzzy because he sent me and thirty-five other people a donation request for Triathlete Barbie's latest charity bike race?" My leg throbs.

Grandma laughs, sputtering coffee onto her robe. "She does look like a Barbie!"

"They all do," Mom and I say at the same time.

"Well, sorry, dear." Grandma pats Mom's arm. "If I'd known you needed to look like that, I would've dated a Ken doll, not a series of boy toys named Ken." Grandma guffaws at her own joke, and even Mom cracks a smile. But I catch her running a hand over her plump hips. The weird thing is Mom used to jog five days a week and enter the occasional 5K for charity, but she hasn't since the divorce. Did she do that only to keep in shape for Dad?

"So, Mom, I guess it's you, me, and Grandma for the fireworks."

"Actually"—Grandma raises her eyebrows—"I've been invited to Hank's house for an intimate barbecue."

"But, Grandma, you hardly know him!"

"Mother!" Mom looks shocked. "The Fourth of July is a family holiday."

Grandma strikes a pose. "Maybe I'm expanding my horizons."

Mom scoffs. "By the way, the Fourth comes three days after the first. The day the mortgage is due. Minor details."

"You always know how to rain on a parade," Grandma says. "I've got to freshen up. Make sure I'm wearing the right day-of the-week panties." She giggles.

"Grandma!"

She swats my butt on her way to refill her coffee mug. "Gracie, you've done a bang-up job on these flapjacks." She kisses Grace's forehead.

Grace grins.

Mom slams dishes into the sink, swearing when she chips a plate. So, yeah, it's shaping up to be a real great holiday. Part of me wants to call Dad, but I don't want to hear him make awkward excuses. I just wander back to my room and plan to lose myself in my summer reading list. *Anna Karenina.* My life isn't *that* bad, right?

I crawl back into bed with my book, but I'm having trouble concentrating on anything. It's that first line about happy families. I used to think we had a happy family. Maybe because I had all the stuffed animals I ever wanted. And then right after Mom and Dad divorced, it was like Christmas on steroids: they both tried to out-purchase each other to win our favoritism. Grace apparently still has her price. I look at the fluffy red, white, and blue bear sitting on her dresser.

"Knock, knock." Grandma peeks into my room. "I have a little something for you, too." She dangles a pair of red, white, and blue earrings in front of me. "Everyone needs some fireworks in her life, if you know what I mean."

"Thanks, Grandma. But what I could really use is some advice." I hold up *Anna Karenina*. "I'm not finding much here."

Grandma wraps an arm around me, carefully avoiding my road rash. "Come into my office, formerly known as your room. We can talk while I get ready for my big date."

My room looks like a department store during a one-day sale. I shove aside some clothing so I can sit on the bed. "I'm just so confused."

"Me, too. Do you think Hank would prefer the red blouse or the blue?"

"The blue. The red kind of clashes with your hair."

Grandma slips the blue blouse over her head. "Are you confused about having a crush on that skateboarder?"

"I don't have a crush. I'm just tempted to learn how to skateboard again. Even though I ended up looking like this"—I hold up my scabby arm—"the first time I tried to learn."

"Skirt or slacks?"

I smirk. "Why don't you show off *your* fanny in the pants?"

"My saggy rump looks great in these slacks, for your information." She shimmies the pants over her hips. "But now I'm confused. Why do you want to learn to skateboard?"

I groan. "Because *he* skateboards."

"Well, honey, Hank fixes dishwashers, but I'm not about to learn how to do that."

"Yeah, well, you have other stuff in common, probably."

Grandma shrugs, sorting through her jewelry box. "He makes me laugh."

"Well, then, you're doomed, because that's not enough. Look at all the stuff Mom did for Dad: golfing, jogging, piano lessons—at her age—oh, and, that French cooking class. Disaster! He still left her for Real Estate Barbie."

"Oh, honey. Like I told your mom after she tried to make me eat one of her soufflés, you've just got to be yourself."

Grandma holds up two pairs of earrings. I nod to the rhine-stones.

"What if you don't know who that is?" I peel away a corner of my bandage, peeking at the thick black stitches beneath.

Grandma twirls in front of the mirror. "Hmm?"

"Nothing. You look great. Hank's going to *swoon*."

"Very punny."

"Yeah, well, it's a good thing he makes you laugh. Because the rest of the family is completely humor-challenged."

"Your mother spends too much time with ten-year-olds."

"Tell me about it." My head aches. Body aches. Heart—I don't know. "I think I'm going to lie down for a bit."

"You do that, sweetie." She kisses my forehead. See? Grandmothers kiss foreheads, not guys! "I'll catch you in the morning, but not too early."

I hobble back to my room and snuggle under my covers. I admire the way Grandma keeps trying to find a relationship that works. Every new guy gets a fresh chance to prove his worthiness. I keep thinking about how Grandma said that maybe Xander is a good guy. And maybe she's right.

What if the problem is me? No one likes me when they really get to know me.

Not even my own father.

I don't usually let myself think about it much; but when I

do, that thought hurts worse than the gash in my leg. I roll over in bed, curling my legs to my chest, pulling my comforter over my head. I allow myself to cry hard for a few minutes. I miss my daddy. I don't care if he hates Mom. Or keeps busy with his girlfriend-of-the-month club. Why doesn't he want to spend time with *me*?

And no one wants to hear me talk about it, either. Not that I try that often. Grace doesn't get it. She was so little when our parents divorced that she doesn't remember that *Dad* used to make Fourth of July pancakes. We used to spend the entire day *together*. And we'd have ice cream sundaes after we got back from the big fireworks show at the park. Dad used to call me his Precious, Precocious Pollywog. I felt like the center of his world. And now he screens my phone calls like I'm one of his irritating clients. Yeah, I've kind of stopped calling, because nothing hurts worse than hearing the formal tone of his voice mail message, knowing that he probably recognized my number and chose not to answer.

I'm drifting into self-pity-induced sleep when I hear a light knock on the door. "Come in," I say. "And I don't know why you're bothering to knock at this stage of the game. It's not like anyone around here values privacy anymore."

The door opens a crack. "Sounds like you're feeling a bit better." Xander peeks into my room.

"Argh!" I pull my covers back over my face. "What are you doing here?"

A normal guy would leave if a girl talked to him like that. Not Xander Nightingale Cooper. "I brought something to cheer you up."

I pull the covers off my face; my hair zings with static electricity. But I'm not trying to impress anyone. He might as well see me at my worst. It will just save him time.

He walks over to the bottom bunk and kneels so that his head is exactly level with mine. "You've been crying. Does it still hurt that bad? Are you taking your pain medication?"

"Why do you *care*?" I'm acting like a trapped animal on a *National Geographic* special: snarling, scared, all teeth and claws.

He ignores my question. "You wanna see what I brought?"

"Knowing you, you're going to insist on it. You're as tenacious as black mold."

Xander laughs, still holding his hands behind his back. "Now, that's a line I haven't heard before."

I scoot up to a sitting position, kind of grimacing and grinning (I do pride myself on a good zinger). "Okay, what did you bring me?"

I expect flowers. I think they're a cliché. A stuffed animal. I detest them. Chocolates. Another total cliché. But he hands me a little square of paper folded into a crane.

"They're for good luck. My Thai grandma taught me to make them."

"Um, thanks." I hold the light pink crane in my hand. The paper is so thin, folded so delicately. I flush a little, because the paper reminds me of the soft way Xander's lips felt on my forehead. He didn't choose pink because of the underwear, did he? "You made this."

"Yeah." He rests his hand on my good arm. "Glad to see you're doing okay. You should've seen the doctor freaking out after you passed out. He thought you might have lost too much blood. And that's when your mom arrived and she started screaming—she puts my sister to shame—and they were all rushing around, getting IV fluids and everything. You missed out on quite a show."

"Trust me, I am more than happy to have missed it." I touch my finger to the tip of the crane's pointy head. "Besides, I was fine."

"I knew that."

I look over at him. Brown eyes level with mine. Leaning his elbows on my bed in a familiar way. Why is Mom even allowing a guy into my room? She barely let Kurt come into the *house*.

"You have this certain smile when things are okay. Kind of *Mona Lisa* mysterious, but serene like a Thomas Cole landscape."

I crinkle my mouth into a sarcastic grimace, but Xander puts his finger on my lips. "No, don't," he whispers. "That's not it." His fingers smell like maple syrup, and I wonder who makes his Fourth of July pancakes. And then he moves his finger, but I still feel his touch lingering on my lips. He leans over and kisses me on the lips, soft, delicate—like that paper crane.

I'm too surprised to respond.

"That's it," he whispers.

I open my mouth to speak, but Xander shakes his head, smiling with his lips closed, looking into my eyes. He stands up and leaves, closing the door quietly behind him. I hear him call out a goodbye to my mom. Grandma gushes about how much I appreciated his help last night. I'm about to jump out of bed to defend myself when I notice writing on the paper crane.

I unfold the fragile paper, careful to remember how to make the crane whole again. I read: *With a dancer's grace she curtsies, bending to pick up a crushed soda can.*

I look at the carefully printed words again, not understanding. It's hardly a love letter. Or even flirtatious. And it maybe sounds almost romantic, until the garbage is mentioned. The whole thing is weird, really. As inconsonant as the strange humming noises he used to make in fourth grade. I refold the crane, wishing I hadn't dissembled it in the first place. He obviously made it out of some kind of scrap paper. I feel kind of foolish, thinking he would have written a note to me. I'm not the kind of girl that guys send notes to. I'm the kind of girl they flirt with, joke around with, mess around with, maybe send a few e-mails or texts, before moving on to someone truly girlfriend-worthy. I think of Sawyer wanting me to help him snag Kipper Carlyle.

I'm tempted to crush the tiny crane in my hand. But I can't. Instead I set it on the windowsill above my bed, where the sound of Xander Cooper zipping open the pavement enters the room every morning.

That night Mom and I watch the fireworks, just the two of us, but we don't even bother driving down to the park. We watch the show from our backyard.

"Ooh! Look at that one!" Mom exclaims.

"Mom, I can barely see it." I squint. "I practically need a microscope."

"Enjoy the colors! That one looks like your new earrings."

"Except smaller."

"True." She hugs me close. "Maybe we should just run to

the store and get everything we need for red, white, and blue Fourth of July sundaes, huh? What do you think about that?"

"I think we've all been eating enough sweets and fried foods this summer."

Her hand moves to her hips. "Yeah, I suppose."

When we head back inside, I say, "I think I'm just going to go to sleep early," I ignore the sad look on Mom's face. Before climbing under my covers, I tuck the little crane behind the window shade. I don't want it to distract me, because I can't figure out what to do. Grandma tries, but how seriously can I take her advice? It's almost eleven and she's still not home. She will come home, right? She's too old for *that* kind of thing, isn't she? Not to mention that she would be going against practically every advice column she's written since 1977. Not that she seems particularly predisposed to taking her own advice, and she did wear her black bra.

Maybe I need to approach my life like a scientist. I stand up—ouch!—and search through the random junk piled on Grace's dresser and find my half-filled bio lab notebook. I'm going to map out a truly scientifically based theory. I will propose my scientific question: why does Polly Martin suck at relationships? Background research. Let's see: Kurt, Jack, Gareth, Sawyer, Hayden. So, now I need a hypothesis.

```
Polly   sucks   at   relationships   of
all  kinds  because  she  has  five  ex-
boyfriends, a father who never calls,
a  best  friend  who  barely  tolerates
her,  and  she  cannot  even  trust  her
mother  or  grandmother  (who  everyone
adores!).  Therefore,  Polly  would  be
much  happier  and  would  consequently
benefit  society  if  she  hereafter
avoided  relationships.
To  prove  my  hypothesis,  I  will  not
attempt  any  sort  of  relationship  be-
yond  the  acquaintance  stage  with
Xander  Cooper.  Paper  cranes  are  not
indications  of  relationship  status.
```

Just to prove my point I toss the little pink crane into the trash can. But five minutes later I retrieve it: it really is cute. I stick it in my underwear drawer. *Not* thinking about my pink Wednesday underwear. Because they are in the wash.

Oh, and that kiss. Like a brother, not that I have a brother, but I'm sure it was a purely platonic, I-care-about-you-like-a-brother-who-waited-all-night-in-the-ER kiss. It didn't make me feel tingly. That was the pain medication. I'm sure ibuprofen can do that.

Underneath the chart for my new scientific experiment I make a few notes.

```
One:   I   will   not   let   boys   dis-
tract me.
Two: I'm going to save money.
Three: I'm going to study hard and
get into a good school and find a
laboratory-based profession, work-
ing with microscopic life forms or
maybe rats—safe from humans—to make
the next Nobel Prize-winning discov-
ery. That I can one day turn into an
anti-love potion.
```

That's my new summer plan.

And I totally do not hear Xander's skateboard zipping down the pavement. I *don't*! Where's he going way past midnight? Who has a curfew this late? Guitar-Hero-playing, past prom queens, that's who.

See? He's totally not interested.

Dear Miss Swoon:

I live at home with my parents. We get along great, but they never let my boyfriend stay the night. I'm plenty old enough to make those decisions for myself. Besides, we both work a lot and we like to spend a few nights a week together. How can I convince my parents that they are the ones being unreasonable.

—Old Enough For Sleepovers

Dear Old Enough:

Buy your own home, pay your own rent. As long as you live at home, you play by your parents' rules.

—Miss Swoon

Two cats: one jogs over to greet me, rolls on the sidewalk, exposing its underbelly for a rub. The other runs, hides under a parked car, watching with round eyes. Girls are so like cats!

—X.C.

Chapter Nineteen

Wild Waves is closing early for a campaign fundraiser for a stodgy school board candidate. Since I've missed a few days of work due to my, um, accident, I've signed up for overtime. Padding the old bank account with some college funds. Sawyer assigned me to be the liaison, since I can't be on water duty, what with my stitched-up leg wound and excessively scabby arm. More than one bratty kid has asked me what happened. I've been varying my answer between "I got in a fight with the Tooth Fairy" to "I disobeyed my mother." Either makes a kid scurry over to Mommy.

I start telling one little girl the truth. "Never get into a grocery cart with a boy."

"Not even my brother?" The girl furrows her forehead in utter confusion.

"Nope."

I glance over at Sonnet, hand cocked on her hip, frowning. Okay, bring back the bad-girl. I shake my head, almost disgusted with myself. "All right, I'll tell you what really happened."

"What? What?"

"I got caught sneaking into Santa's workshop, and let me tell you, those elves are mean! Do not ask for a doll this Christmas. That's all I'm saying."

Sonnet giggles as the girl turns and runs. "I still like the Tooth Fairy's arsenal best," she says.

I shrug. But then I see the little girl's mother marching over to Sawyer. He nods, making notes on his clipboard. That's the problem with channeling my inner bad girl: I hate getting into trouble. Next thing I know, Sawyer's sticking to me like chewing gum on hot pavement.

"Pollywog, we have an honor code to honor here at Wild Waves."

I put up my hand. "No need to give me patented lecture fifty-three, Sawdust. I was just having a little fun. Maybe our patrons need to have a sense of humor."

"Yeah, Sawyer." Sonnet thrusts her chest forward. "The kid overreacted. Like, really the world does not need another pint-sized interrogator. It was practically self-defense for our poor little Pollywog."

Kipper bounces over. "Oh, are you guys talking about the extra hours? I could, like, really—"

"Use a night off? That's so sweet of you because I could really use the hours." Sonnet steps in, and it's almost like battle of the cleavage or something, but Sonnet scores the hours. Sawyer doesn't like to play favorites. But then he falls all over himself, promising to take Kipper somewhere special, when she goes into a dramatic "we need to talk about my feelings" routine.

I've just never done that. I have to remember that for my study. Refusal to discuss feelings definitely helps in the avoiding guys department.

An hour later Sonnet and I are setting little cellophane-wrapped party favors next to paper plates in the Buffalo Bill Pavilion.

"Alternate red, white, and blue," The bossy woman wears a hideous red T-shirt that says "Do It The Waxman Way" across her boobs. "I see two red ones next to each other on table four."

"Quel horror!" Sonnet whispers.

"I'd better get that fixed before the earth stops rotating around its axis." I walk over and make a dramatic show of fixing the favors. "So, you must have hit the post Fourth of July sales," I say to Bossy Lady. "All the red, white, and blue, huh?"

"I've had these prepared since the second week of June," she says. "The key to any winning campaign is preparation."

"Preparation H," I whisper to Sonnet, making her laugh. When Bossy Lady turns her back, Sonnet switches several blue ones with red ones, creating a crazy pattern. Then she decides to sneak all the white ones onto Table Six.

Bossy Lady rushes off to supervise the guys starting up the barbecue.

"I don't want to get in trouble. I need the, you know—" I stop myself from saying the M word: money. It's turned into a swear word at home.

"Aggravation?"

I run with it. "Yeah, I totally need aggravation because I'm not, you know, dating anyone right now. So I've got to find my daily dose of drama at work and stuff." I laugh. "My family is trying, but you know." I tilt my head and roll my eyes.

"Polly Martin not dating anyone? That's a good one. I heard Xander Cooper carried you out of Hamburger Heaven after you got stuck in the meat grinder or something." She gestures toward my scabby arm. "I thought it was an exaggeration, but now—"

"That's not how it happened. I mean, really, if you believe everything you read, I've got a space alien for you to date." One of Mom's stupid Uranus jokes pops to my head, but I have the sense not to repeat it.

"But you were with Xander Cooper?"

"Technically."

Sonnet pops a party favor into her pocket. "Ooh, that sounds kinky."

I feel my face reddening like the barbecue flames shooting into the air near Bossy Lady. "It's really nothing."

"Oh, really? The guy's been stalking you all summer, writing love odes and all, and then he rescues you from being mangled by a meat grinder, and you call that nothing? I'm lucky if I can get a guy to hold my hair back while I vomit."

"That's a pleasant image."

Sonnet laughs. "Yeah, right. Well, that bonfire party got a little crazy the other night. Hey, where were you? I watched for you, for a while, anyway. Until Travis showed up. But that's a long story."

"Do tell. I love long stories, especially when I'm stuck working for a pattern-obsessed political volunteer." I make a big show of putting two red party favors next to each other. Sonnet starts gabbing about the party, and I'm more than happy to avoid the whole Xander Cooper topic. So what if people have started rumors? I've lived through that plenty of times before—five times, to be exact.

Just as the fundraiser is about to start, Bossy Lady walks over and hands us each a "Do It the Waxman Way" T-shirt. "I'd like each of you to wear one of these for the party. If you want to keep them, I'll need a minimum twenty-five-dollar donation."

Sonnet scrunches her mouth into a look of disgust. "They're so baggy!"

"Um, yeah," I say. "We kind of have our Wild Waves uniform code and all."

The woman looks me up and down like one of the lecherous old dads Sonnet recently blogged about. "I think something with a bit more coverage might be more becoming to this austere occasion."

"I don't think we're allowed." Sonnet stands up tall so that her suit dips even lower. "Oyster occasion or not."

Bossy Lady huffs. "The word is austere."

I roll my eyes, like, really does she not think we know our SAT vocabulary? Sonnet takes AP English, too.

"I'm sorry," I say, "but due to company policy Waxman will not be able to have his way with me."

That sends Sonnet into a fit of un-austere giggles. And I realize that I've made the whole thing sound dirty.

"Must be the latent bad girl in me," I say with a smirk as Bossy Lady strides over to switch party favors around.

"Latent?" Sonnet whispers. "I'd say it's manifesting. I heard you and Xander made out in the ER."

I roll my eyes. "I bled so much that I passed out."

"In Xander's muscular arms."

"Not exactly."

"But sort of?"

"Just don't blog about it, okay? I'm starting to look like a slut."

Sonnet shrugs. "Just makes you interesting."

Bossy Lady aims her red, white, and blue fingernail at table six. "Fix that—I see several conspicuous errors! I'm going to supervise the caterer."

"We'll fix the conspiring errors for this oyster occasion," I say, grinning at Sonnet.

The woman shakes her head, seeming to realize that we've been making fun of her. But then she narrows her eyes, gives us a quick nod, and stomps off, holding the bright red "Waxman Way" T-shirts.

A few minutes later Sawyer lopes up to us carrying those hideous red T-shirts.

"Hey, guys. I really appreciate that you're following the rules and everything. But since this is a private party you can privately wear the party T-shirt."

"What if we don't want to?" Sonnet pops her hip out. "It's, like, way baggy, not to mention the ugliest shade of red ever invented."

"We're trying to keep the customer happy here, so . . ." Sawyer shakes his hair out of his eyes.

"So we can sell out our ideals for—what?" I put my hand on my hip. "I mean, do we even know what this Waxman person stands for? What if he wants to curb our civil liberties, take away our freedoms?"

Sawyer looks at me. "You're one who wanted the overtime."

"You're the one who respects big ideas and depth of character."

He glances at Sonnet, who looks like she's already composing her next blog post in her mind: ex-lovers have a poolside spat. If he dares put his hand on my arm, she'll probably write that we had sex in the tube slide.

"This isn't the timeliest time for this, Pollywog."

"Right. Now's the time to be the happy little pool girl." I tilt my head and speak in a sultry voice. "Coffee, tea, or me, Mr. Waxman? We're a full-service facility here at Wild Waves."

Sonnet guffaws. "Oh God. Polly. You're too much!"

"Please. Just cooperate, okay?" Sawyer puts his hand on my shoulder. "We can discuss this later."

I cross my arms across my chest, bumping his arm off but giving my bust a boost. "I'm not into talking, remember?"

Sawyer blushes, not quite the otherworldly color of the T-shirts but it looks like 83 percent of his blood has rushed to his face, giving him an instant sunburned look. Sonnet's eyes bug out, and I can tell I'm back in her blog again. Already. "Just wear the shirt," he says quietly and leaves.

Sonnet and I decide that we'll wear the shirts, all right, in the form of halter-tops. With the knot in the middle I fold my T-shirt to read DO WAN WAY. I start laughing. "It's like we're being paid to be personal billboards by some nerd's mother to help him lose his virginity so he'll move out of the house or something."

Sonnet doubles over, cackling like a cartoon hyena. "I wish I had my camera. This is too funny! And so bloggable!"

"Sonnet, I'm beginning to think you have a problem. Maybe you should check into Bloggers Anonymous or something."

"I know, right? I'm still blogging about you and the Sawdust, though. Can't hurt to make Xander a little jealous, right?"

"Sonnet." I sigh.

• • •

Finally, the political fundraiser is in full swing. Sonnet and I run around fetching beverages and a variety of barbecued meats. Some people in the crowd wear swimwear while others wear business suits, making the party look like a set up for a bad joke. Waxman talks loudly about his plans for "our blessed community" while waving a bottle of water around and occasionally mopping his forehead with a blue paper napkin that's leaving grayish smudges on his sweaty forehead. Mrs. Waxman stands at his side smiling. Her face doesn't change even when Waxman starts talking about poverty. And sure, she looks pretty and her dress probably costs more than I've spent on clothes over the last three years, but she seems so vacant. I'm tempted to ask her a real question—maybe whether she'd prefer a burger or a hot dog. Just to see if her mind functions on its own.

I'm about to conduct my mini-experiment when someone rests a hand on my shoulder. "Polly, I didn't know you were involved in the Waxman campaign!"

I spin around. Hayden smiles at me, wearing the same hideous red T-shirt with a pair of khaki pants. "Hey, is it okay if I put a bumper sticker on your car?"

"I'm, um—" Not expecting to see him.

"Great." He flaps a stack of bumper stickers. "Knew you'd come around. He's going to make a big difference. Bring back the moral authority in the schools, clean things up morally, reverse the moral decay."

Hayden sounds like he's memorized the guy's apparently redundant campaign brochure. I stop listening. I'm too focused on the wife: the way she just stands there not talking to anyone, not seeming to listen, not engaged in her life at all. What would she rather be doing? Does her husband even know? Does he even care? He treats her like a prop, touching her arm to make a point about "preserving families" or slinging an arm around her waist as he goes on about motherhood being "the most important profession." Her smile never changes.

"His wife," I say, not bothering to answer whatever question Hayden just posed.

"Oh, she's terrific. Two-time Mother of the Year."

"She looks so . . ."

"Elegant? I know. She's like the perfect example of a political wife. Looks great, supports the right causes—"

"But isn't all that stuff just on the surface? Like, what is she *thinking* right now?"

His forehead crinkles. "What do you mean?"

"Nothing."

He starts in on something about libraries, but I excuse myself as Sonnet holds up her tray, looking a little sweaty and frazzled. "I'd better get back to work."

"That's all it takes, a little hard work," Hayden says, again sounding like a campaign slogan. He still doesn't seem to realize that I'm actually working at the party. Stupid T-shirt! I spend the rest of the evening refreshing drinks, clearing plates, and serving slices of cake frosted with that same unnatural shade of red. The whole time I keep an eye on Mrs. Waxman.

Only after everyone has left and I'm searching for garbage in the dark does it occur to me that sometimes I act as superficial as Mrs. Waxman: smiling when I don't feel like it, not speaking up when I disagree, letting others take charge. Did I say yes to a bumper sticker?

I push the thoughts away like the paper plates I'm shoving into my garbage sack, but they keep floating to the surface like the plastic cups bobbing in the Lazy River. At this point I'm feeling pretty certain that the Waxman Way does not include strong environmental policies. Maybe I'd make a great political wife, delivering funny one-liners and looking cute in my little outfits. Is that why Hayden found me attractive? Does he like women like that? But she looks so . . . empty.

The way I've been feeling lately.

I spot one more massive dumping spot with paper plates piled on another picnic table. It's right near a trash can, but whatever. As I'm clearing the table, I think about how Mom's probably doing the same exact thing at Hamburger Heaven. I'm sure she's joking with the customers, making her teenage coworkers laugh. Don't they see that it's all an act? No one works so they can see their favorite students. They work because their ex-husband is going to stop sending child support in six months and there's a stack of unpaid bills taking over the kitchen counter like a fungus.

Grandma's the same way. She's full of wisdom when she does interviews and stuff. She always says something quick and snappy in her columns, but at home she's pretending to write a book while she's really trolling for men online. Plus, she's had a few of those mystery callers that I've come to recognize as people wanting their money. Could Grandma be having money trouble, too? Is that why she's not paying Mom? But she's so famous!

I look over at the moon shining on the wide Watering Hole pool, a mirror image of the sky. You can't see the hidden depths. And the moon and the water look so beautiful, so perfect. Why would anyone want to see what's underneath? It's all old Band-Aids, chewed-up gum, dead bugs.

```
Dear Sassy Sage:
My boyfriend reads a lot of men's maga-
zines and wants me to wear sexy lingerie
almost every time we're together. I'm
worried that he has expectations that I
won't be able to meet.
—Needs Another Bustier

Dear Needs:
Maybe you need to be reading the same
magazines. You can learn a lot! And all
of it will help in the satisfaction de-
partment. Go for it, girl!
—Sassy, and don't forget Sage!
```

Not Shakespeare's Sonnet

Blond count: 8 (Or is it 9?)

EX-change of Information:

Polly Martin—where to start? Sawyer Holms can barely keep his hands off you, even when his new fling is around. Kipper, girl, are you worried? I overheard Sawyer waxing on about having his way with sexy little Poll. Wouldn't be her first ex hookup this summer. (See <u>Ex-change of Saliva</u> here.)

Brandon S.—No news is good news, right? Maybe she is thinking about you!

Winner!!!!! (drumroll) The best love poem goes to Razorblade09. You've got a twisted mind & I like it. Are you blond?

Chapter Twenty

$\mathcal{M}$y alarm goes off way too soon. I'm not even close to getting those medically advised eight hours of sleep or the respite I need from Wild Waves. I wander into the kitchen for a bowl of cereal, only to find Grace and Grandma hunched over the newspaper. Grandma is explaining various lingerie items to Grace, and I'm thinking that things with Hank the Wonder Repairman have gone way too far.

"Grandma, isn't Grace a little too—"

Grandma looks at me, raising her eyes to the ceiling. "Sassy Sage," she says in a too-cheerful voice. "I wonder if they realize what hip and edgy are doing to breakfast table conversation?"

"So, why do people want to wear those again?" asks Grace.

"Honey," Grandma says, smoothing Grace's bed head. "I don't know, because they pinch like the devil."

"Yuck! They should fire that Sage person, Grandma. You're much better."

Grandma kisses the top of Grace's head. "You're a sweetheart, but I'm just an old dinosaur. It's all about sex, sex, sex nowadays."

Grace looks at Grandma with wide eyes. Grandma smiles, looking sad. "That's another conversation, sweetie." Grandma pushes away her empty cereal bowl. "I'll need a more substantial meal to take on that one."

"Tonight, at dinner! Promise?" Grace runs off to phone Amy, because they haven't talked in a whole twelve hours.

"You know, that candidate who was at the political fundraiser I worked last night talked a lot about that kind of thing: improving our community morals."

"We could do that by banning politicians."

"Yeah, well, I'd like to ban political fundraisers. Those guys acted like pigs, leaving their trash all over the place." I pour cereal flakes into my bowl. Again I'm stuck with the dusty dregs—and I bought this box!

"Most politicians are pigs, that's for sure."

"Hayden thinks this guy's okay."

"You've got to think for yourself," she says, again sounding too much like a Miss Swoon column. "Don't let a man make your decisions."

"Grandma, have you even been listening to me this summer? I'm completely through with guys."

She stands and scoots her chair back under the table with too much force. "No need for the attitude! I was just offering friendly advice."

I call out to her retreating back. "I *like* your advice!" I let my spoon sink into my cereal bowl. "It's just that sometimes I want to have an actual back-and-forth thing. What do you call them? Conversations!"

Grace slides through the room. "Talking to yourself means you're crazy, you know."

"Then I guess you should be worried. You never know what I might do to your stuffed animals while you sleep!"

Grace runs out of the room. "Mom! Polly is going to hurt my stuffed animals! Mom!"

I glance at my clock. I've got fifteen minutes to get to work. I grab my keys and holler goodbye, but no one answers.

At work Sawyer assigns himself to Kipper's station. Sonnet gets Sexy Lifeguard. I'm stuck on garbage duty; apparently Sawyer thinks I could have been more committed to my task last night. The job is far more disgusting this morning. Ketchup has congealed with mustard, birds have strewn dew-soaked buns across the O.K. Corral, and napkins dot the grass like poppies. The early moms have plenty to say about Wild Waves hygiene as they step around the trash. Surveying the wind-blown garbage, I realize I could really use a rake.

And speaking of rakes, Xander arrives with Kyra and Dex. The kids run over and ask if I'll go out for ice cream after swimming. Uncle X promised them a treat if they didn't fight once, and they're not going to fight because they have a plan to not swim near each other all day. I can't help but smile. They're so cute!

"Good luck, guys! I'm sure you'll earn that ice cream." I pick up a plate with a smooshed piece of cake and shove it into my garbage bag.

Xander wanders over to me with a pair of soda cans in his hands. "You can come for ice cream if you want. As long as you don't fight with anyone today." He smiles.

"I'm not sure I can manage that. Some of these ladies look like they're itching for a rumble." I make fists and jab at the air. A smile plays in his eyes. I feel completely silly, and my cheeks warm, despite the morning breeze. I reach for the cans that Xander holds out to me. "Thanks for helping out my cause and everything." When my fingers brush against his, I fumble and drop the cans. So I bend down in a curtsey like I've been doing since I first took ballet in preschool.

Oh! The words written inside the swan.

Holding the dripping soda cans, I stand up to see Xander's amused expression. "That *was* about me," I whisper.

He raises his eyebrows in response. And I'm equally speechless. We stand looking at each other in a quiet way, and I don't move a muscle until warm soda drips from the cans onto my toes.

I break his gaze and tuck the soda cans into the recycling bag. "Okay, well, I'd, um, better get back to, you know, work." I turn around and head toward a paper plate stuck against a forsythia bush. I hate the way he makes me feel so awkward. The way I can't think of anything to say. The way his fingers feel so warm. The way he looks at me like he can see inside my thoughts. *Is* he writing about me in that little notebook?

"Don't forget about the ice cream," Xander says. "My treat."

Finally something I can joke about. "Maybe—I'm not sure I can stay out of trouble." I nod toward a lady kicking at a balled-up paper napkin with the toe of her sandal.

"I'll keep an eye on you."

Again I get all flustered. "Um, yeah, well. See you. I mean, yeah, I'll just be over here."

He laughs. When I look back a few minutes later, he's writing something in his little black notebook.

• • •

By lunchtime I'm more than ready to escape from the heat and eat my meager rations. Seriously, if a neighbor hadn't brought over some tomatoes, cucumbers, and lettuce from her garden, I'd be stuck with the crackers left over from Mom's end-of-school potluck and a few slices of American cheese that Grace threw into the cart during a rare visit to the grocery store.

I push open the door to the staff room to find Kipper locking her legs, arms, and lips around Sawyer in a way that looks way too much like an implausible movie scene. An icky jealousy creeps into my stomach. My throat tightens. *I'm over him. I'm over him. I'm avoiding all males.* But why her? She's not smart. She can't be that deep—except for her tongue reaching down his throat! Yuck! I take a step back, hoping to escape unnoticed, but Kipper breaks from him long enough to glare at me. "Excuse me," she says.

"Sorry, didn't know we were casting for *Days of Our Lives* here at Wild Waves."

Sawyer's body straightens at the sound of my voice. He wipes his mouth with his hand. "Oh yes, so Kipper, we need to, uh, discuss—"

"Looks like you're discussing things just fine—in French, no less."

Sonnet pushes her way past me. "Oh. My. God. A little decency, maybe?" Sonnet gives me a dramatic pout of sympathy. "I know you're trying to do it with the whole student body, Sawyer, but do we all have to watch?"

"We didn't do it," I say. "Your blog kind of misrepresented that."

"Who else *have* you dated?" Kipper asks him. "I knew about Pollywog." She says my nickname as if it tastes slimy in her mouth. "But who else?"

Sawyer looks like he's searching through his entire head for a single brain cell that can help him out of this situation. I've seen enough. Forget lunch. My stomach suddenly feels so twisted that I might never want to consume food again. I turn around, biting my lip to prevent the lump in my throat from coming out as an ugly froglike croak followed by swampy tears. Sonnet starts listing Sawyer's various post-Polly hookups. Really I'm surprised the Hollywood tabloids haven't hired her. But I've heard enough. Had enough.

I head straight for the exit. I'm just going to drive home. Who cares if I get fired? No one should have to suffer this much for minimum wage and prematurely aged skin. Sawyer asked me to hook him up with Kipper, but I didn't expect him to flaunt it like this. Does he think I'm a robot? Jack did it, too, showing up with his girlfriend—the one who *didn't* have to spend two weeks with his bulldog—like I wouldn't have any feelings. I reach my car, parked in the blistering sun on the far side of the lot. I'm looking forward to the burning hot seat against my legs, the rush of heated air smothering my lungs. Anything to stop feeling . . . *this*. I yank on the door handle. Crap! I left my keys in my locker. But I'm not going back there.

I want to hurt him! Make him hurt like he hurt me. But he doesn't care. That's why I hooked up with Gareth during the spring break hiking trip. To hurt Sawyer. And yeah, he found out all about it (thanks, Sonnet), but he didn't care. Because he'd moved on. From me. With apparently three other girls. Whatever. He actually stopped me in the halls one day to say, "You make a real cute couple." Gareth and I had already broken up. Not that we'd ever technically been official or anything, but he hadn't called me since I'd been too busy to pick up trash along the wetlands trail. Now that's all I do: pick up trash.

And feel like trash. Disposable. I keep trying to recycle myself, but it's just getting desperate, and my reputation looks as mottled as that really cheap paper Mom started buying for Grandma's printer. I cringe thinking about the stuff Hayden said that night about political wives. Apparently I'm not even appropriate material for a student council member's girlfriend.

I garner a few strange looks from the ladies arriving for the afternoon Wild Waves rush. I do kind of look like I'm trying to break into my car. I pound my car on the hood—and scream out. My fist really hurts. Not as much as my heart. The sweat on my forehead drips sunscreen into my eyes—that's why I'm crying—as I walk back toward the water park. I put my hand over my mouth to stop my lips from quivering, but now my shoulders shake. Keep it together!

I can't let anyone see me like this, so I sit under a tree by the entrance. One by one I pluck blades of grass out of the ground. I try out an affirmation just out of habit, not to mention, you know, desperation. *I deserve loving and supportive friends.* I'm thinking of Sonnet. A supportive friend would follow you out to your car. Offer to help you drown your feelings in ice cream or something. That's what happens in those idiotic romantic comedy movies, anyway.

Maybe I should call Jane. But then I'd just be doing the same old thing: calling her when I have a problem. She's been so in love with Rowdy lately that she's barely called me. And I haven't called her because listening to her gush about Rowdy reminds me how much I suck at relationships.

I'm a terrible friend.

Sawyer's whistle rings through the air, and I realize that I've probably taken too long for my non-lunch break. I brush the grass off my knees, stand up, straighten my shoulders, plaster a fake smile on my face, and stride back to the O.K. Corral to pick up the lunch mess. I'm almost looking forward to stabbing things with my little garbage poker stick. Stab. Stab. Stab.

A few times I catch Xander's eye, but I look away quick. He returns to writing something in his notebook. I don't deserve his kindness, which is completely misplaced and confounding. I should send him a link to Sonnet's blog so he can read all about me and move on before he wastes any more of those smiles, eyebrow flashes, soulful gazes, and ice cream offers.

Late in the afternoon practically the whole staff rushes over to help manage a big water fight in the Splash Pasture—older kids are hurdling over the plastic farm animals—but I take the opportunity to run into the locker room and grab my keys. I'm out of here the minute the clock strikes five, pardner. For the rest of my shift I avoid Xander. Right as the closing whistles ring out, I slip out the gate and run to my car. Throwing my car into reverse, I peel out of the parking lot like I'm trying to win a NASCAR race.

Dear Miss Swoon:
How soon is it okay to start dating af-

ter a breakup? My ex already has a new girlfriend—and it's been less than a week!

—Too Soon, Right?

Dear Too Soon:

I'm betting that your ex is a good basketball player—because he sure knows how to rebound! You cannot control your ex, but you can control yourself. Take a time-out from love. Stick to the sidelines for a while.

—Miss Swoon

Used napkins dot the grass like white poppies, almost beautiful, if you ignore the truth.

—X.C.

Chapter Twenty-one

I don't go straight home. I can't help it. I drive by Jane's house first because I *do* need to talk. Grandma's out doing research, and I don't even want to know what that means. A matinee with the express delivery guy? I don't want Mom to try to joke me out of my hurt feelings, not that she's home, either. I figure Jane won't act angry if I show up in person. Her car isn't in the driveway, but I wait for a few minutes until I'm convinced that she's off doing something amazing with Rowdy. Plus, her neighbor keeps peeking through the curtains. Why is everyone looking at me as if I'm a demented criminal today?

I feel more tears pricking my eyes—damn sunscreen—as I drive home, way under the speed limit. I drive past my house because I'm distracted by the fact that, um, Xander is sitting on my front steps. Like a complete fool I back the car into the driveway, trying to act like I'd driven past my house on purpose. I sit in my car for a minute, attempting to channel cheerfulness.

"Hey!" I say with way more enthusiasm than I feel. Xander hands me an ice cream cone. Double scoop. Two different kinds of chocolate.

"I didn't know which one you'd like better, so I got both. You made it just in time, it was threatening to melt all over my hands." He tilts his head so his curly hair brushes his shoulder. "I only had to lick it once. Okay, twice."

I bite my lip. Why am I such an emotional mess? I can't even manage a flirty thank-you.

"You'd better give it a quick lick yourself," he says.

I twist the cone with my wrist, coating my tongue with both kinds of chocolate. My body relaxes. I close my eyes, letting the flavor soothe me. I take a bite of the top scoop.

"You're welcome," he says.

"Oh, yeah, thanks. Sorry, I just—" I feel scolded like a little kid who has to be reminded to be polite.

"I didn't mean it like that. Your shoulders said thank you—and that was enough."

I shimmy my shoulders as if trying to get them to shut up. I'm suddenly way too conscious of my body language. I don't know where to put my hands, feet. I keep crossing my ankles.

"Sit down." Xander says it like an invitation.

I sit one step down from him, but he moves next to me. "I figured you deserved some ice cream even though I saw you fighting with your car. I hadn't really made a ruling on inanimate objects so . . ."

"You saw that?"

"Happened to be in the parking lot getting Krya's floaty." He opens his eyes wide, and again it feels like an invitation.

"Yeah, well, I forgot my keys, and . . ."

"And that made it hard to make a quick getaway?"

I crinkle my forehead. "I guess."

"Sonnet has a big mouth, and she updates her blog with record speed."

"You read—?" Somehow keeping up on the high school gossip doesn't mesh with the skateboarding, baby-sitting, and academic team. This guy is more complicated than the thousand-piece jigsaw puzzle Grace and Amy have started.

"I'm not just an academic team stud."

"Isn't that a contradiction in terms? An oxymoron?"

Xander laughs. "I love the way you use SAT words in conversation, appropriately."

"I usually try not to." My cheeks flush, so I lick my ice cream cone again.

He nudges me with his elbow. "You're saying that I'm lucky?"

I shrug my shoulders, taking a huge bite out of my cone, smearing ice cream onto my chin.

"I'd better help you with that." Xander leans over and takes a bite, and then he licks my chin!

I start laughing. "I can't believe you just did that! I can't believe I just *said* that."

Xander takes the cone out of my hand and tosses it into the bushes, and I crack up. "Enough of the ice cream, and the embarrassing chin licking."

"You used to lick your desk in fourth grade: Kool-Aid."

His cheeks go dusky. "I don't do that anymore."

"What do you do now?"

He leans over and kisses me, cold lips brushing mine. I kiss him back, harder. My head swirls with the smell of chocolate, the warm feeling of Xander's lips, his sticky fingers intertwining with mine. We stop when Mom's car pulls into the driveway. Xander rushes to help Mom with her *grocery bags*, and I start to wonder if I've entered some kind of time warp or alternate universe.

I'm still tingling from the kissing. As I heft a bag of groceries, Xander puts his hand on my back. I love the way it feels, but this is just a little rebound thing—just because of Sawyer, you know. I'm not really buying into the whole situation, but I'm too distracted to stop Mom from inviting him to stay for dinner. He accepts!

What am I going to do with him for the next two hours? Besides *that*!

```
Dear Miss Swoon:
My boyfriend says that a guy can be in-
jured down there from not going all the
way after too much kissing. Should I let
him have his way?
—Truth?

Dear Truth:
You're not going to hurt anyone but
yourself by letting your boyfriend have
his way with you. Resist!
—Miss Swoon.
```

Not Shakespeare's Sonnet

Listmania!!!! Biggest Ex Offenses

1. Making out (PG-13 or more extreme) with new gf/bf in front of an ex.

Your turn now. I'm kind of stuck on seeing Sawdust drifting all over the female student body. Bodies. (For those HOOK-UPdates, see here, here, and here.) Winner gets a free Wild Waves pass. (Yeah, I know it's made of lame.)

Chapter Twenty-two

I'm ready to drip under the table like the milk Grace spilled—on Xander's leg—when Grandma asks for "a man's perspective."

"You don't have to." I touch his wet leg and then immediately take my hand away, because it's too . . . too intimate. He's just a friend, after all. He brought me ice cream like a good friend. That other stuff? A hormonal lapse.

Xander advises Grandma on Hank the Dishwasher Repair Hunk versus Roger the Bookstore guy versus Friendly Supermarket Checker (has she even *gone* to a grocery store?). She keeps listing men!

When Grandma mentions a "hottie" who works down at the coffee shop on Main Street and adds that "age may be an issue," Xander says, "I think you've moved beyond my level of expertise with that one."

"What about that Guitar-Hero-playing prom queen? She's way older than you!" I clap my hand over my mouth. "I mean, it's your business. You look really cute together and everything."

Everyone is completely silent, except Xander, who starts laughing—a little too loud and a little too crazy. "We've always looked cute together, even back when our moms made us wear matching outfits."

"You've been together since—back then?"

"Oh, we go way back."

Mom and Grandma laugh; they get the joke. But my face must reflect the confusion storming through my brain because Xander puts his hand on my cheek, leans toward me, and whispers for everyone to hear, "She's my cousin."

Grandma swoons and Mom starts making swoon jokes, but my forehead crinkles. "What?"

He kisses me between my eyes—right in front of everyone!

Grandma says, "Aaah. To be young and in love."

"Grandma! We're just friends. I mean, yeah, like mere acquaintances or something."

Now everyone's laughing. At me! Like I've said something untrue. I'm feeling confused. Embarrassed. "Stop it!" I push away from the table, but Xander catches my hand.

"I heard a rumor—okay, I read a certain blogger's post about how you'd be at that party." He tilts his head. "So I called my cousin, since I don't really hang out with the jock crowd." He shrugs. "Being on the academic team and all."

"And I was . . ." I blush, thinking about Jack.

Xander leans close and whispers, "My cousin wanted to make you jealous. Did it work?"

"You went to the party just for Polly?" Grandma gazes at him with the kind of lust she usually only shows over-the-hill repairguys. "You're a real catch!"

"I'm not catching anything," I mutter.

"Oh, let's play catch!" Grace shouts, happy to finally understand something, I guess. "I'll get my squishy ball and we can go outside."

I grimace. The poor kid is completely starved for fatherly attention and she doesn't even know it. She bought that stupid squishy ball with her own money after watching some sappy old movie about dads and baseball with Grandma one night.

"I'm very good at catch." Xander answers Grace, but he looks at me. I know there's a sea of hidden meaning under his words, but I'm not about to go diving in to find out. Somehow I've let things get completely out of control: first the ice cream, then the, um, kissing, but a family dinner? What was I thinking? Of course they all adore him. This family is so man-starved that anyone who comes into the house sporting male anatomy ends up with a date!

"You go ahead," I say. "I'm going to help with the dishes. I'm not sure anyone around here remembers how to load a dishwasher."

"Just a dishwasher repairman," Mom jokes.

"Not funny." Grandma swats Mom on the butt—in front of Xander—and laughs. "If only he were a little more loaded. That's my new financial plan. I'm going to marry my retirement account."

The mirth drains from Mom's face. "Mother. Just write your book."

Grace bobs back into the room with her squishy ball. "Let's go."

Xander looks at me and tilts his head toward the door. "See you in a minute?"

I nod, afraid to say anything. What is happening here? I don't like the way my heart pounds too fast. The way his smile makes me feel. The way he flashes his eyebrows at me. Like we share a secret or something. I'm apparently the only one not in on the secret!

I stack the dinner plates on top of each other, focusing on the busywork of dishes.

"I may not be very good," Grace says. "I haven't had much

time to practice. My dad said he'd come over, but he works superhard all the time, and so I haven't learned how to catch very well."

The front door slams shut as Xander says, "I know all about busy dads."

And I realize that I know nothing about this guy. I've made assumptions, based way too much on elementary school. What was I like in third and fourth grade? I try to think back—but I mostly remember crying into my pillow at night after Dad moved out. And I might have been obsessed with my own stuffed animal collection . . .

I carry the dishes into the kitchen, watching Xander toss the ball to Grace outside on the front lawn. Grace keeps missing, but she's laughing. "It's really pathetic that Grace has to search for a father figure in the random boys that show up for dinner."

"He's not exactly a random boy, honey. He's been hanging around here all summer."

"Just because he lives up the street and can't help riding by on his skateboard, or whatever."

Mom takes a dish from me and puts it in the dishwasher. "I think it's because he likes you."

"Well, that's too bad. I've given up that kind of thing."

"What kind of thing?"

"Love, dating, the inevitable ensuing heartbreak."

Mom laughs. "Correct me if I'm wrong, but you two seemed a little cozy on the porch when I pulled into the driveway. I thought I might have to use pliers to pry you apart."

"God, Mom. Do you have to turn everything into a joke?" I plunk a dish into the top rack of the dishwasher with a little too much force. "If anyone around here bothered to spend three minutes listening to me, you'd know that I've given up guys. Forever. I'm focusing on myself, my education—not that anyone is going to pay for it—and—" Mom puts her arm around me, but I shrug her off. "Don't."

"What's happened? To make you so guarded? So angry? Is this about your father?"

"No! It's about Kurt, and Jack and his bulldog, and Sawyer, and that thing with Gareth, and Hayden, who's, like, whatever. None of them wanted me once they got to know me. I'm completely unlovable."

"That's not true. I love you, Grandma loves you, Grace loves you—in her own way. Maybe if you could stuff yourself, grow some pink hair on your body . . ."

"That's so far from funny." I wrap a piece of foil, an artifact from Mom's actual cooking days, over the leftovers. "And you didn't even mention Dad, hmm?"

Mom frowns. "I knew this was about him. Look, our divorce is about him and me, not you, except he doesn't seem to realize it. This whole thing with the child support has me so angry."

I hold my hand up. "Please, don't. I don't want to know."

"Polly, problems get better if you face them head-on."

"Oh, really? First of all, you sound like Miss Swoon." I nod my head toward Grandma's room; she's preparing for a late-night movie date with some random Internet stranger. "And she's not exactly one to take her own advice. And second, what are you facing head-on, huh? The stacks of unpaid bills? The fact that you have to waitress to pay the mortgage? The way you're not taking care of your own health?"

"I'm doing the best I can," Mom whispers. "I'm doing the best I can."

"Well, maybe I am, too. I know what I'm doing. And not doing."

Mom shrugs at me.

Outside, Xander throws the ball to Grace. She catches it nearly every time now. A big smile stretches across her face each time the ball makes contact with her hand—like that's all it takes: a little attention. They've been out there for what? Twenty-five minutes. And Dad says he's too busy. Look what he's missing. That smile!

I don't think about myself—that place inside me feels too

tender. The sky is growing dark. I slip outside to sit on the front steps where I can hear Xander and Grace's laughter.

"Okay, try this move. Behind the back." Xander curves the ball around his slender body.

Grace giggles. "How do you do that?"

He notices me. "Let's save that one for next time, okay?"

"Like tomorrow? You can come over anytime, you know."

"Tomorrow sounds great."

I start to say something, but Grace runs past me to "call Amy and tell her how you can play catch as good as *her* dad."

I expect that word—a loaded word in my household—to freak Xander out, but he says, "Don't start a fight, Gracie. Dad pride is serious business."

"Okay, but you totally are better!"

Xander laughs as he sits next to me, leaning into me a little. "She's such a cutie. Like her sister." He slips his hand around my back.

I'm glad it's dark, because I don't want to see his expression—let those eyes get to me. I've got to put a stop to this before things go too far—not that they haven't gone far enough already, but whatever. I'm not going to end up making mistake after mistake after mistake like Mom or Grandma. I'm not going to get hurt again.

"Thanks for inviting me to dinner," Xander says.

"My mom invited you."

"But you didn't freak out. Verbally, anyway." He bumps his knee against mine. "But it worked out okay, didn't it?"

I don't answer.

This is not going how I expected. I scoot away from the warmth of his body; it *is* still hot out. But he wraps me close to him in a side hug, quick, before releasing me. "How about I say good night?"

He stands up, pulling me to my feet. I nearly stumble, but he catches me. "You take that speech you're working on in your head and go write it down, okay?"

"I'm not—" Then I realize that my chance to fix this situation is escaping like the embarrassingly loud heartbeats in my chest. "It's just that, I think you've gotten the wrong impression, and we're better off—And I'm not going to start writing stuff down just because that's what *you* do, okay? And I've vowed never to learn how to skateboard."

The corners of his mouth curve into a smile, and before I can stop myself, I'm jumping up a step so that my face is level with his. I lean in to kiss him, not in a quick good-night way, either. I break from him. "Now that—"

He quickly steps down from the porch. "Good night, Polly."

I stomp my foot in frustration. "You can't keep kissing me like that!"

He pops his skateboard into his hand, and I watch him walk away in the moonlight. I swear from the way his shoulders are shaking that he's laughing. "You kissed *me*," he calls over his shoulder.

Oh yeah, right. I did.

Dear Sassy Sage:
How do you know if you're a slut? Is it
two guys in one night? Three?
—Unrestrained

Dear Unrestrained:
It's not about the numbers; it's about
the way you feel about yourself. If
you're okay with it, then that's okay.
—Sassy

Melting chocolate ice cream slips across her tongue. Our lips
touch. Her breath catches. Our sticky fingers intertwine.
—X.C.

Chapter Twenty-three

Grace and I are sitting in a little café near Dad's office, waiting for him to meet us for lunch. I took a personal day at Wild Waves, once again humiliating myself in front of Sawyer, who needed to know why. He's so nosy. People complain about Sonnet's blog, but at least she's open about wanting to know everyone's business, even if she is prone to exaggeration. Sawyer pretends like he has to know every detail of my life so he can record it in the Wild Waves personnel files or something.

"Look, I'm kind of sick of the lack of privacy in my life. I'm just not going to be here tomorrow, okay?"

Sawyer had tapped his clipboard. "You know Wild Waves frowns upon this kind of thing."

"Well, you go ahead and put your—" I try to think of a scientific name for facial muscles, but those terms escaped my brain mere seconds after the final exam. "Just deal with it, okay?"

I've read the menu several times, and Dad's more than a half hour late. The server brings Grace another strawberry lemonade. "Maybe we got the wrong restaurant. And he's waiting for us?" she says. "And we'll waste the whole time—"

"He's just late."

She puckers her mouth, but it might be the lemonade.

Fifteen minutes later Dad walks in talking on his cell phone. He squeezes Grace's shoulder and ruffles my hair as if I'm seven, not seventeen. He finishes up his phone call, saying, "Give me an hour to make some calls and I'll check back with you." He slips the phone into his pocket. "So, how are my favorite girls?"

Neglected because you're dating a bicycling, blond bank teller. "Fine," I mumble.

Grace gushes about how she and Amy have planned a big picnic for their stuffed animals. "We even get to make brownies."

"You still working?" Dad asks, as if the financial aspect of my life interests him most. I'm sure Banking Barbie's financial life interests him the *least*.

"Five days a week."

"Not spending too much time at the mall, are you?"

I shake my head, wishing I had the guts to say something about saving money for groceries since he's going to stop sending child support in six months. Not to mention the fact that my career aspirations require an education beyond high school biology.

"Good. Good." Dad peruses the menu quickly, shutting it with a snap and motioning to the server. "You ready to order?" He looks at his watch again. "I've got to get back to the office for a conference call."

Even Grace frowns, using all those facial muscles I can't remember, when he says that.

"Thanks for taking time out of your busy schedule to see us," I say.

"Sure thing." He doesn't catch the sarcasm. "So, have you guys been to see any new movies?"

"Amy's mom takes us to the movies every Tuesday, and she even buys us popcorn!"

Dad checks his cell phone for e-mails again. "That sounds nice, really nice. What about you, Polly? Any of your boyfriends take you to the movies?"

"I don't have a boyfriend."

Grace looks at me, perplexed. "What about—?"

I shake my head. Just because Xander's been coming over

every night to play catch with her doesn't mean he's *my* boy-friend. I expect Dad to pick up on Grace's confusion and start asking questions, but his phone rings and he leaves the table because he's "gotta take this call."

Grace whispers, "Why didn't you tell him about Xander?"

"Because he's more your friend than mine. We're more like acquaintances."

"Doesn't seem like it." She puckers her lips and sends me an air kiss.

"Just shut up." I whack her in the arm. "Dad doesn't want to hear about it, anyway."

She nods a few times, as if mentally adding Xander to the list of subjects called Things We Never Discuss with Dad: Mom, money, bad grades, money, Grandma, money, emotions, money, school clothes, money, anything negative, and, of course, money.

Dad comes back as the food arrives, providing us with several safe topics of conversation. Yes, those are onions. I'm not sure, but I think it is Swiss cheese. Yes, the croutons are flavorful. Yes, the french fries are crispy.

"But I like the french fries at Hamburger Heaven best. Mom—" Grace looks at me like she's been caught uttering a bad word.

"So, Dad I've been getting ready for our trip to the cabin. Just two weeks, right?"

Now he looks at me like I've let loose a string of expletives. "This has already been discussed." He sounds angry. "I told her that I wouldn't be available. Didn't you get the message?" He speaks to me in the same tone he used with the person on his business call.

"Message? I guess I should fire my secretary."

Tears well in Grace's eyes; I fight the prickly feeling in my throat and blink my watery eyes.

"Oh, this is just great. She didn't tell you? I told her to tell you. That woman—"

Fat tears roll down Grace's cheeks, but she doesn't wipe them away. Dad looks around the restaurant, as if we're embarrassing him. Sharp retorts fly through my brain. *Maybe she was too busy working her ass off at Hamburger Heaven to deliver your messages. Maybe you should deliver your own damn messages. Maybe you should have included it with one of your e-mail forwards.*

But I'm too scared to say anything.

Dad gets up to take another phone call, so Grace and I just sit there; neither of us eats another bite. The server brings over dessert menus. "You dad said to order whatever you want. He had to rush back to the office."

Grace stands up quickly; her chair falls over, creating a huge clattering sound. Everyone in the restaurant stares as she cries out, "He wouldn't leave without saying goodbye!"

The server looks at us with pity, and I can't stand it. I ball my hands into fists and a surge of adrenaline rushes through my body as my fight-or-flight instinct kicks into gear.

I don't even open the little leather menu. "We'll take one of everything, please. To go."

"Excellent choice." She takes the menu from me.

I'm feeling fairly satisfied, until I catch the look on Grace's face reflected in the window. She looks like she's adding this moment to some kind of mental list, too. It's the same look she gave me when I threatened to rip every one of Hayden's precious bumper stickers off his car.

But I'm too angry to care. She still lives in the soft world of stuffed animals and simple friendships. In other words, she hasn't really started to deal with the male portion of the species yet. Dad's the one teaching her that husbands and fathers can just up and leave and go on and find themselves better lives filled with nice apartments, sports cars, interchangeable blond women, and business trips to exotic places. He doesn't miss us at all. We're more of an inconvenience than anything. A drain on his vacation fund.

The server comes over carrying three plastic bags packed to

the top with Styrofoam containers; the dessert menu is apparently a little longer than I'd imagined.

"There are quite a few flavors of ice cream in here so I'd get these home right away," she says.

"Thanks!" I manage a bright smile that I don't feel. For a moment I imagine driving into the city to deliver the desserts to homeless people, or taking them to kids in the park, or even back to the Wild Waves staff room . . . But when I walk outside, the hot air, bright sunshine, and clear blue skies provide such a stark contrast to my mood that I have to suck in a big sob of a breath.

I just need to get home quick.

I pile the desserts around Grace in the back seat, but she scoots away from them as if they're filled with poison, like Snow White's apple or something. I mentally scold myself for thinking about that stupid movie; Xander talked about watching it with his niece and nephew. This is about Dad! Leaving us in the middle of lunch. Canceling our cabin trip. Not knowing how to talk to us. Fighting with Mom about money. Hurting Grace, again!

Hurting me.

I drive home too fast, cornering like I'm in the Indie 500. Grace doesn't say a word, sitting in the back seat, gripping the door handle, as Styrofoam dessert boxes tumble around, slipping out of the plastic, falling onto the floor. Rattling too loud. Part of me wants to get pulled over by the police—I want to get in trouble. Real bad-girl trouble. Just to spite him. Maybe he didn't show up at the ER, but he'd have to show up at jail, right?

Unless he had an important call. Unless it cost him money. Unless it involved *me*.

I slam the car into the driveway. Grace jumps out and runs into the house before I cut the engine. I sit there for a moment, letting the day's heat overtake the air conditioning, trying to feel every molecule change in the air. Pretty soon the car is heat stroke hot, and I think about how little things can stack up in life, little by little, until you don't realize that everything is ruined.

I need to be in more control.

I turn around and gape at the Styrofoam jumble in the back seat. Part of me wants to leave it all in my car, let it melt into one big nasty glob. But then I see Grace peeking out the window at me. I jump out and fling the boxes back into the bags.

A few moments later when I swing open the door, I hear laughter. But it's not Grace; she's in her room. I turn around and see Jane's car parked across the street in the shade. How did I miss that? I guess that's why they call it blind fury.

I walk into the kitchen. "Anyone want dessert?" I flip open one of the box lids; inside it looks like the great chocolate massacre occurred.

Jane wrinkles her nose. "Did someone already, like, eat that?"

"No, I dropped this one." I open the rest of the containers, putting them on the counter. All of them look like I feel: battered, crushed, and, smeared across the takeout box that symbolizes my life. The sweet smells mingle in the kitchen until Grandma and Jane leave their iced tea on the table and accept my offer of plastic forks. We dip into the containers, sampling melting lemon custard ice cream, jumbled strawberry shortcake, chocolate massacre. I'm coming up with various names as I dip into each confection.

Grandma and Jane start laughing, and finally Grace joins us in the kitchen.

I hand her a plastic fork. "These are half yours."

Grace looks wary, but she takes a tentative bite of what can only be termed Fruit Fight Tart.

"Your father went all out, didn't he?" Grandma slurps up a hefty forkful of Mad Mocha Tumble.

Grace looks at me, forked poised halfway to her mouth.

"Naw, Dad skipped out on dessert, so Grace and I went out and robbed a bakery."

No one laughs. Grace looks like she's about to cry. She sets the fork down. "I'm not hungry anymore," she says. "I'm going to go call—" She pauses. "I'm going to my room."

She isn't even going to call Amy?

"Call Amy and invite her to our dessert feast!" I holler after her, but she just shakes her head before disappearing into our bedroom.

"Are you girls fighting again?" Grandma asks.

I shake my head, trying to force a bite of No Longer the Apple of My Eye Pie beyond the lump in my throat. I start coughing and tears blur my eyes.

Jane pats me on the back. "What's going on?"

I shake my head. "I'm choking to death? What does it look like?"

"Honey, this certainly doesn't look like lunch with your tightwad—oops!" Grandma makes a face. "Your fiscally conservative father."

Jane sets her fork into a melting puddle of strawberry ice cream. "Wanna talk about it?"

I shake my head, making a mess of some banana-smelling thing with my fork.

"Of course not." Jane sounds irritated. "This is what I was talking about," she says to Grandma. "She completely shuts me out. How can you have a relationship with someone like that?"

"Hello? I'm standing right here. And *I'm* the one who brought the snacks."

"Quit joking around."

"Sometimes that's all I can do, okay? Do you really want to hear about my crappy lunch with my dad? Do you want to hear how he spent the whole time on the phone? How the only thing he asked me about my summer was the status of my savings account? How he left without finishing his lunch or saying goodbye? He simply sent the waitress over to take our dessert order. Nice, huh?" I pick up a forkful and slop it back down into the I Only Loved You When You Were a Baby Banana Pie Mash. "So we ordered." I toss my hair back from my face.

"Oh my God, Polly." Jane's eyes look moist. "That sounds awful. No wonder Grace is so upset."

Grandma slams a Styrofoam lid shut and pounds it with her fist, sending little flecks of chocolate flying. "That dickwad!"

"Miss Swoon!" Jane says.

"Don't Miss Swoon me. Right now I'm just these girls'

grandma. And one hell of a pissed-off ex-mother-in-law. I'm calling my lawyer. This has gotten ridiculous!"

Jane looks stunned.

I keep trying to tell her that Grandma is Miss Swoon for only 250 words a day. Technically only two days a week. I'm almost frightened for my father's life, not that I'd do anything about that. He deserves whatever he's going to get. I stack the dessert containers on top of each other so I can carry them out to the trash. I'm feeling sick to my stomach. And head. And heart.

A container slips to the floor, slopping melted whipped cream onto the linoleum. "It's not that big a deal."

Grandma smacks her hand on the counter. "The hell it isn't."

I'm not going to mention the cabin. Grandma would probably drive over to Dad's office and do something worthy of imprisonment.

Jane looks at the kitchen clock. "I've gotta get going. Walk me to my car?"

"Sure." I take a deep breath. "So, why didn't you tell me you were coming over?" I ask.

"I needed some advice." Jane rolls her eyes. "In the romance department." Her cheeks blush the color of our neighbor's rosebushes. "Figured Miss Swoon would be the go-to person—and she's so great to talk with!" Jane grins. "I feel so much better now."

I don't even want to approach the Jane and Rowdy romance topic.

"She doesn't exactly follow her own advice, you know. She's got like as many ex-husbands as . . ." I try to think of an apt comparison.

"As you have ex-boyfriends?"

My cheeks heat. "She's just not what she appears to be, okay?"

"Who is?"

"It's just kind of hypocritical. That's all I'm saying. So you might want to, you know, think before taking her advice, or whatever. Her own life is a mess so . . ."

"So? Mrs. Richman sits on her fat butt while she makes us run laps in PE. Doesn't mean that the laps aren't still good for us. Miss Swoon gives great advice."

"I'm just saying."

"God, Polly, it's like you're jealous or something. You can't say anything nice about Rowdy. And now you're, like, upset because I'm talking to your grandma."

"I am not." Grace could come up with a better response than mine.

"Face it. I'm the one with a boyfriend for a change. And we

actually like each other. I'm not just looking for attention like you always do. We have an actual relationship."

That stings! "I've had relationships."

"I don't know—you've always seemed to like the drama more than the guy."

"That's not true."

"Polly, you just raided a dessert menu because your dad—"

"Yeah, well, men suck. All men, Jane. You just haven't figured it out yet."

"Maybe you haven't figured out that all men aren't your dad."

"Twenty minutes talking to my grandma doesn't make you a psychologist. Besides, you're the one having relationship issues, apparently."

"I just wanted advice about taking things to the next level with Rowdy. And you know my mother—sometimes I think her tummy tuck had less to do with swimsuits than masking the fact that I was conceived sexually." She gets into the car with a secret smile flickering across her face. She laughs at my expression. "Don't look so freaked out. I've decided I'm not quite ready."

But it's not that. I hear a skateboard rumbling at the top of the hill. Xander! I run toward the house at top speed.

Jane looks up the hill and hollers out at me, "Who's the hypocrite? Huh, Polly? You're totally into Xander Cooper!"

"I am not!"

I slam the door and lean against it, barricading myself, while my heart beats rapidly, my breath comes in gasps. I peek out the peephole. One of Grace's classmates skates past. All that for nothing!

I've got to get a grip.

Dear Miss Swoon:
I think my friend just comes over to my house to talk to my grandma. That makes me feel extra lame. And my grandma doesn't even know how to take her own advice. And maybe my friend should be listening to me because she's wasting her precious youth dating a dork. How do I tell dear OLD Grandma to butt out and make friends her own OLD age?!?!?
—Can't Compete With A Sex(!)age-
  narian

Dear Can't Compete:
Some of us have it when it comes to

giving advice. Some of us don't. I'd
love to give you some advice about
that. But first, you promised to empty
the dishwasher.

—Miss Swoon

Chapter Twenty-four

$\mathcal{I}$ stand in the middle of Splash Pasture ignoring the screaming kid who fell off one of the rubbery cow statues in a valiant attempt to, you know, violate the no-cracking-your-head-open-and-spilling-your-brains-into-the-pool rule. I look over to the maple tree where Xander usually sits. But he hasn't been here all week. Not since I told him that we had to slow things down, that I wasn't interested, et cetera, et cetera.

I don't really want to think about that conversation again. Not that I've been thinking about it too much—just at one o'clock in the morning, three o'clock in the morning, seven o'clock in the morning (that's skateboard induced), ten o'clock in the morning (when he doesn't show up again), four o'clock in the afternoon (after he still hasn't shown up). Maybe he shouldn't have talked about how I changed in fourth grade after my dad moved out. Why was that desk-licker even paying attention?

"Spending time with Grace keeps reminding me of you in fourth grade," Xander had said.

"We don't look that much alike," I'd joked. "Besides the hair, the sparkling blue eyes . . ."

"No, come on. It's that deep loneliness."

"Lonely? She's practically a Siamese twin! *You've* even met Amy."

"Amy is her distraction. Just like you've got—"

I'd moved in for a kiss to stop him from naming a single ex-boyfriend, but Xander had gently pushed me back. "Come on. Let's talk about this."

"There's nothing to talk about. Except that I think things are probably moving too quickly between us. As you were about to say, I've had way too many relationships this year. And, really, I'm not interested in starting yet another ill-fated attempt at . . . whatever."

So he left sort of angry. I was only trying to be honest. But I didn't mean he couldn't come swimming. Poor Dex and Kyra are probably stuck inside playing video games or something. It's not healthy.

Sonnet's working with—or should I say *on*—Sexy Lifeguard.

She's convinced because of something she read in a magazine horoscope that this is the week she will hook up with him. She even wrote a detailed fantasy date on her blog, as if that wouldn't frighten everyone. Except for the three guys who asked her out in their blog comments, but whatever.

A few boys get too rough on the rope swing, but I don't have the energy to scold them. A kid running from his sister bumps into my legs, making me stumble. I toot my whistle, but he ignores me. I decide to blow the whistle until someone turns around and notices me. I blow it six times before a few moms shout that the pool is contaminated and make their kids get out. I go through a charade of seeing a leaky, not-approved-for-swimming diaper and needing to chlorine boost the water.

"Watch for those diapers, Pollywog," Sawyer says. "Try to catch those problems before they become problematic. Who was it?" He scans the despondent kids standing on the side of the pool.

"I don't see them now." Out of the corner of my eye I *do* see Xander come through the main entrance with Dex and Krya dancing around him. My heart beats fast as Sawyer yells at me again. It's just a coincidence that Xander Cooper decided to come to Wild Waves for the first time in six days at that exact moment.

"You've got to tackle them before they make it to home plate, Pollywog. You can't let them off the hook."

Xander walks through the concessions area shaking his head as Dex and Kyra probably beg for snacks.

"I didn't let him get away. I told him to leave."

"It was a boy?"

"It's always a boy." I pout. Xander hasn't even looked around for me. He's too busy chatting with the O.K. Corral moms. "Except when it's a girl." I think of Jane. "Or girls." Kipper Carlyle and that girl hanging all over Jack.

"You're not even listening to me," Sawyer says.

I glance into his green eyes. "Hmm?"

"Just take a break, okay? You're lacking focus."

I pretend to adjust my swimsuit strap so I can look over my shoulder at Xander again. "No, I'm good." I angle my body so I can see Xander flicking his beach blanket onto the grass.

"I'm standing over here," Sawyer says, touching my shoulder.

"Doing a fine job of it, too." I flash a fake grin. "Now, why don't you run along and save lives over in the Lazy River. Kipper looks like she's focusing on her suntan again." I have no idea what Kipper's doing, but I know that Xander has just finished blowing up Kyra's favorite floaty.

"I'll talk to her," Sawyer says. As he walks off, he mutters something about striking out, but I'm too busy adjusting my swimsuit so I can peek at Xander again. I have such a bad habit of noticing boys. Like Sexy Lifeguard laughing with Sonnet. And Sawyer scolding Kipper. Until she gives him her pouty-wouty, *I'm so saw-ry* face; now he's rubbing her shoulder.

I blow my whistle, signaling that it's safe to return to the pool. I should wait another five minutes, but I can't take any more of this sightseeing. I sneak one more peek at Xander; now he's writing in his notebook while watching a kid climb a tree. I march into the water, trying to convince myself that its tepid temperature causes the goose bumps on my arms.

That cheesy Western music starts up as kids race back to all the waterspouts and start acting extra crazed, as if they've been spending the time on the sides thinking of the worst things they can do. I chastise three kids for going down the slide backwards. I stop another from climbing on the back of a cow statue and jumping off. I'm focused. I'm blowing my whistle. I'm in control. I'm *not* watching Xander take off his shirt. I challenge myself not to look at Xander Cooper for the next sixty minutes.

And I don't. I'm focused. I'm blowing my whistle. I'm in control.

I avoid, through meticulous care and almost mathematical planning, looking toward the O.K. Corral for nearly the rest of my shift.

"Hey, one at a time!" I yell as another group tries to bunch together down the slide.

I hear the little brats complain about my bossiness. Apparently I'm no fun.

"Yeah, well, why don't you go swim in the pools meant for kids your size?" I yell.

"We're allowed to go wherever we want," one particularly mouthy kid says.

"Well, pardner, around here I'm the deputy and I'm kicking you out of this here cow town. Now!" I make my voice sound scary.

I recognize him from Grace's class photo—I will have to warn her against him. He has dimples. Dimples = dangerous.

"Don't have a *cow*." He and his little gang of future ex-ex-ex-boyfriend material leave the pool laughing at his "good one," but I focus on the grateful smiles of the moms walking chubby toddlers through the shallow water.

I am not watching Xander Cooper saunter toward me. Shirtless. Smiling. Now if someone would just send the message to my autonomic nervous system. My heart revs like a three-year-old who has just devoured his weight in cotton candy and missed his afternoon nap. I quickly glance around for Kyra or Dex. But Xander looks straight at me. Maybe. I hate that he's wearing sunglasses.

Trying to act casual, I bend to pick a leaf out of the water. The pool empties of preschoolers as the let's-get-home-before-daddy crowd heads toward the exits.

Xander wades out and stands next to me. "Hey."

"Hey yourself." I keep it light and flirty, *not* serious. "Where've you been, stranger?" It comes out sounding way too sexy by the look of the slow grin spreading on Xander's face.

Xander chuckles. "Are you trying to say you missed me?"

"No. I just happened to notice your absence. The way I noticed when the scabs from my road rash fell off. I mean— Will you take those sunglasses off? They're making me nervous, so I'm talking about scabs and stuff." I splash my foot through the water. We're alone in the pool now. I could be safe in the employee locker room watching Sawyer and Kipper grope. Or better yet, attempting to expire from heat exhaustion in my car. "I didn't miss you, if that's what you think."

I look up. He has pushed his sunglasses on top of his head. "You didn't miss me even just a little bit?"

I shake my head yes, then no. And I'm not even sure which way I'm supposed to be turning my head. I'm all distracted by Xander's eyes, and my face radiates more heat than the sun dipping toward the mountains in the West.

"I didn't, you know, miss you."

Xander leans toward me, his hair brushing my shoulder, lips brushing my ear. "I think you're lying," he whispers. And then he walks away just like that.

I watch him meet up with Dex and Kyra, who wait patiently by the exit, probably bribed with ice cream or something. When he's safely out of sight, I let out a huge scream of frustration.

I'm such an idiot, a babbling idiot. I talked about scabs! I told him his sunglasses made me nervous!

I completely lost focus. No control. Where was someone to blow the whistle at me? Right at that moment, like in a terrible sitcom script, Sawyer walks past. "Why are you still here, Pollywog? You're not going to get any overtime, you know."

"I'm just really committed to my job, Saw-me-in-half, so I'm going to stay until I pluck every used Elmo Band-Aid out of this here pool."

He shakes his head and walks over to meet Kipper, who's somehow now wearing even less fabric than that generously supplied by our Wild Waves uniform. Now there's no way I'm even going near the locker room. Not until I see Sawyer leave.

I stand in the pool watching a few guys from school finish up a miniature golf game nearby. "Hey, Martin!" one of them yells. Another guy makes a remark I can't hear, and all of them start laughing. I fake a big smile and wave and then I run toward the locker room. Sawyer or not. One of the guys whistles at me. Another one says, "Oh yeah!" I'm about 100 percent certain they're not talking about putt-putt golf. Dumb Wild Waves uniform. I should sue the place for sexual harassment or something, making me wear this skimpy outfit, subjecting me to, you know, male eyes.

And I'd better check out Sonnet's latest blog. She told me earlier that she was doing a series called "Undercover Fantasies." I figured that meant her way too detailed ideas for pleasing Sexy Lifeguard. But now I'm wondering if she's just making stuff up—possibly about me. She's obsessed with my nonrelationship with Xander.

I tentatively open the door to the employee locker room. Sure enough, Sawyer's manhandling Kipper's end zone. She looks at me before diving back in. I struggle with my locker combination. Could they stop that for like forty-five seconds?

I need to get my stuff. I'm so over him, but still, I don't need a show-and-tell display about how he's so over me. I hit my locker in frustration, and it bounces open, thank God. I grab my duffel and go, slamming my locker shut. I hear Kipper say, "Buh-bye." Sawyer laughs.

I wipe away a few tears as I walk across the parking lot. I'd love to blame them on sunscreen but it's Sawyer. I was willing to do all that—stuff. I just didn't want to burden him with my problems, talk about my emotions. I mean, who really wants to deal with that? Guys usually *complain* about moody girls, PMS, and that sharing feelings crap.

I reach my car. Hayden's Waxman Way bumper sticker clings like a scab. Omigod, why did I mention my scabs to Xander? And why do I care? I'm trying so hard *not* to like him. I reach down and rip off most of the sticker, leaving sticky white streaks behind. I click to unlock my door, glancing around the parking lot. I'm alone. I'm supposed to like it this way, right? This is what I've been wanting. I pull the door open, and tiny paper cranes spill onto my feet. There must be a thousand of them!

I'm laughing and crying as I pick up the cranes that have fallen all over the pavement. Each one is as carefully folded as the next. Hours and hours of work!

For me.

I carefully move each crane from the driver's seat into the back seat, not wanting to crush any of them. I marvel at the different colors, the various delicate patterns on the thin origami paper.

And I'm sobbing.

I'm crying for the little girl whose mother divorced her father, the girl who wanted to fall in love for the first time but wasn't ready for sex, the girl who dated a boy just because he wasn't the first one, the girl who fell hard for the guy with the easy smile and green eyes, the girl who needed to prove she could hook up on a class trip, the girl who ran for student council just to impress a guy, the girl who lost her best friend, the girl whose father doesn't care anymore, the girl who doesn't have the money for college, the girl who just wants her grandma to fix everything, the girl who can't talk to her mother about anything, the girl who doesn't talk to anyone about anything, the girl who just *can't* fall in love again—even if a sweet guy folds a thousand paper cranes. Just for her.

I barely remember driving home, and I'm relieved I didn't get pulled over. With snot dripping from my nose, tears zigzagging down my cheeks, a rainbow of paper cranes rattling in the breeze coming through my windows still opened a crack, I would have been committed for sure. I pull into the driveway, expecting—

okay, hoping—to see Xander sitting on my front steps. But he isn't there. Not that I'm disappointed. I'm not. Not really.

No one is home. I go back to my car and gather the cranes in a bunch of Hamburger Heaven To Go bags. I take them to my room and spill them across my bed. I pick up a light yellow crane. And that's when I notice writing. I unfold the crane: *wit*. I pick up another one: *kindness*. Another: *great legs*. A blue one: *scared but brave*. A hot pink one: *great kisser*. A green one: *scientific mind*. A maroon one: *scabs*.

I start sobbing all over again. What's wrong with me?

I decide to call Jane.

```
Dear Miss Swoon:
We need to talk. ASAP.
—Torn And Confused
```

```
Dear T & C:
I'm always here to give you some
TLC.
Love, Grandma
```

Not Shakespeare's Sonnet

Okay, so as you know, I've given up on blonds. (See <u>Brain Deadage</u> here.) Oh yeah, and making out in bathrooms. (No linkage: parentals de-manded a delete.) Thanks for your input on Random Picnic Fantasies. Come on Sexy Lifeguard: sunsets and subs. (Read more here, but not you, Dad. Joking!) And sorry, guys, but I'm holding out for quality—no bragging about your six-foot sub sandwiches, okay? (Hi Mom! Hi Dad!)

New feature: Undercover Fantasies!

I'm inspired by my cute, funny, smart, sexy, just-can't-be-a-bad-girl-if-she-tries coworker. P.M., you know you've got some secret lust for a cer-tain tall, dark, wheelie-poppin', guy. GO FOR IT!!! Okay, unrequited lovers. What are your top-secret Undercover Fantasies? Movie passes to the winner!

I remember when my biggest challenge was simply climbing a tree. Branch by branch, sitting triumphantly among shifting green leaves, blue sky above, bird song. Not so simple anymore.
—X.C.

Chapter Twenty-five

So Jane and I have once again achieved best friend status. All it took was approximately three hours of embarrassing soul baring, a bit of sobbing, revealing way too many of my innermost secrets, a three-hour shopping trip for the ultimate bikini, and, um, agreeing to go on a camping trip with members of the yearbook staff—at least there won't be any movie marathons or shopping carts involved.

Jane rips open a package of tortilla chips and hands it to me in the back seat. She's sitting up front with Rowdy, and all I can say is, thank God for seat belts. If she caresses his thigh one more time, leans over to kiss his ear again, or talks about what a blast we're going to have, I'm going to need more than a seat belt to restrain *me*. I'm squished into the back seat of Rowdy's truck, sitting next to a quiet duffel bag and an even quieter sophomore named Emily. Jane allowed me three preconditions. One: no males on the ride up (except for her precious Rowdy). Two: we'd share a tent (not with her precious Rowdy). Three: I'm saving number three for an emergency (but it will probably involve a guy).

The long drive, wide open vistas, and lonely-looking desert landscape precipitate too much thinking. (Ha-ha. It hasn't rained out here in weeks: Get it? Precipitation?) Rowdy speeds along the same route my dad always takes to the cabin, although Jane swears that the campground isn't anywhere near my dad's cabin. Too many memories push into my consciousness as we climb the hills through Pee Pass—where we once made an emergency stop because Grace and I had drunk too much lemonade. A few miles later we pass the spot where we stopped so Grace could take a photo of a black cow munching on sagebrush; she won her school's art contest with it. It hangs framed in our living room. In a few more miles we'll pass through the little town with the candy store where we always "gather provisions." My mouth waters as I think of rocky road fudge.

"Hey," Jane says, almost as if reading my mind. "Isn't that candy store up ahead? We should stop. They have the best chocolate almond fudge ever."

I look out the window, biting my lip hard. "Naw. That's okay." Don't think about it.

"I like fudge." Silent Emily speaks.

"You can bring some back for Grace."

"I don't think so. We've become allergic to it."

Jane gives me a look. "Come on now, Polly. We've talked about this—"

I tilt my head toward Rowdy. "Yes, so we don't need to talk about it now."

Jane goes for the thigh again. "He knows everything. Thanks to Miss Swoon's advice, we don't keep secrets."

Oh, that's just great.

"Then we definitely don't need to talk." I tilt my head toward Emily—unless, of course, Grandma advised Jane to tell nerdy sophomores all my deep dark secrets, too.

For some reason Emily takes this nod as an invitation to speak. "I do like fudge," she says.

Will she please lay off the incessant chatter? My glare frightens her into looking at her shoes.

"Chocolate peanut butter," she mutters.

What a chatterbox!

"Fine, stop. But you can't make me purchase or consume any sort of confections."

Rowdy turns and grins at me, veering toward oncoming traffic, not that there is any traffic out here in the middle of nowhere, but it's the principle of the matter. "Well, with that attitude you sound like you could use some sweets." He leans over and kisses Jane, now steering toward the shoulder of the road. "You're *my* sweetie."

"That's supposed to be funny?" I ask. "Keep your eye on the road there, Rowdy. I plan on surviving this weekend. Somehow."

I'm not sure why. Lacking consciousness would be easier. I close my eyes as if that can prevent the memory of my humiliating phone call to Dad two nights ago. *Please, please take us to the cabin. Just for two little nights? You can do your business meetings by phone.* He said no and hung up to take another call. I phoned several times throughout the day, but he never picked up again. I have a sneaking feeling that he'd break up with me via text message if he could, you know, do it legally with the paternity laws and everything.

I didn't tell Grace. But later that night I overheard Mom comforting her because she'd made her own pathetic Dad call.

Jane came over right after that to bring me a sleeping bag.

"Has it been washed, um, this century?" The plaid fabric smelled musty. "And isn't it kind of big?"

"It's a double bag."

"Are you trying to do some foreshadowing? Maybe change my relationship trajectory?" I joked.

Jane sighed. "Polly you've got to get to know yourself before you venture into a relationship."

"Don't quote my own grandmother back to me," I'd said, searching for a sweatshirt to pack for the trip since I'd given away my blue hoodie. "You realize that she juggles men the way a circus clown juggles balls?"

"Balls, huh?" Jane had laughed. "I know whose balls I'd like to juggle."

I rolled my eyes. "Hanging out with Rowdy has completely ruined your sense of humor."

"You're the one talking about balls." She grinned.

"Next thing I know you're going to start telling Uranus jokes like my mom."

"Oh, she told the funniest one the other night at Hamburger Heaven. Let's see, what does a boy—"

"Jane, don't. I still have a molecule of respect for you. Don't ruin it."

"Oh, you're no fun!"

I wait in the truck while they all go into the candy shop. I only consider hitchhiking home with a dangerous stranger for, oh . . . the entire time they're in the candy store. I feel worse when the stink of fudge fills the car.

We arrive at the campground about two hours and three pounds of fudge later. I haven't ingested a single disgusting, calorie-laden morsel, so Rowdy and Jane blame my reaction to the campsite on low blood sugar.

I drop my duffel on the ground. "Jane! I can see Dad's cabin from here!" The log house looms against the hillside. "You promised."

"Now, don't overact. It's not really that close." She shades her eyes with her hand. "It would take ten minutes to get there—in a boat."

"Maybe even fifteen," Rowdy adds unhelpfully.

"His boat is right there." I point toward the marina. "You totally lied to me, tricked me, fooled me, misled me, bamboozled me—"

"Blood sugar." Rowdy holds out a greasy bag of fudge. "Polly, you've really got to take care of your body."

"Blood sugar is not the issue." I slap the fudge away. "The issue is my father!"

"See?" Jane nods at Rowdy. "That's what I've been saying all along."

"Argh!" I turn away from the lake only to catch Sawyer and Kipper going at it while putting up their tent. "Jane, what the hell is he doing here?"

"Oh, who? Sawyer? He's the new sports editor."

"Do you not realize that he mixes his metaphors—his *sports* metaphors—like, like—" I can't think of a good metaphor of my own. I'm too busy watching Sonnet climb out of Jack's truck. She'd mentioned "wild weekend plans" on her blog—but I never expected that she meant camping. With the yearbook staff! It's like I've entered the portal to the Dimension of Ex-boyfriends.

"Explain," I say to Jane.

Rowdy kisses her cheek and makes a quick exit. "Good luck."

"The yearbook is going to have a blog that Sonnet's in charge of—and Jack is like a whiz at the computer stuff."

"Whatever. I think I need to move my tent to the other side of the lake."

"Come on, Polly."

"What? Since when does playing video games at the mall give you graphic design credentials?"

"He attended that design camp? You watched his dog?"

"Shut up, Jane. Maybe I've blocked out that bad experience because, you know, I'm completely damaged by my lack of fatherly attention."

"God, Polly. Just have some fun for a change." She rolls her eyes.

And then Hayden shows up! "Now I know *he's* not on the yearbook staff," I say. "Did you hire Gareth to be our hiking guide? Maybe get Kurt up here to do some off-road racing for the yearbook crowd? What's with Hayden?"

"Oh, since I invited you, I figured I'd invite another student council member, too. And he's Rowdy's friend."

I squint into the sunshine angling across the campground. "How considerate of you."

"Relax. You're going to have to work with him all year, you know."

"Not if I die trying to swim to my dad's cabin so I don't have to put up this freaking tent. Not to mention the random displays of public affection popping up like mosquitoes." I slap my arm as another bug bites me. I ignore the shadow porn on Sawyer's now zipped tent.

Just to prove my point, Rowdy rushes back over. He sweeps Jane into his arms, rescuing her from my tirade like a gallant knight, and plants a big kiss on her mouth. "Help me gather firewood?"

I kick at our not-yet-assembled mess of a supposed tent. "Just go."

"I'll help you when I get back, unless you find some handsome lad to help you first."

"I don't see any of those around here." Nearby Hayden helps loquacious Emily put up her tent. "Plus, I'm going to be self-sufficient and alone, remember?"

"Yeah, right. That's what you think." Jane gives me a wicked little grin. "Should I tell her?"

Rowdy looks at me seriously, shaking his head. "Not unless she promises to eat some fudge first." He grins. "I'm not even sure that would be enough."

"Just go get your wood or whatever."

Jane giggles like I've said something dirty again. Really! I watch them walk off hand-in-hand, not even searching for firewood. Just a bit of privacy. Good luck! This place is crawling with yearbook staff the way the ground around my tent is crawling with ants.

An hour later the sun dips behind the mountains, casting a shadow across the campground, but I'm still struggling with my tent. I've refused help from several I-didn't-notice-if-they-were-handsome-or-not lads. I'll just roll up in this damn nylon piece of crap and go to sleep.

"Having trouble?" A warm hand clasps my shoulder. I spin around to see Xander standing out here in the middle of nowhere. "I used to be a Boy Scout, so . . ." He tilts his head and smiles kind of shyly. And way too cute.

"Why are you here? You're not—"

"Arts and Entertainment Editor."

I drop the tent pole to the ground. "That figures. I'm killing Jane! This is such a setup."

"Except for the tent."

"Are you trying to make a joke? Because I'm not in the mood."

"Well then, we might be getting somewhere."

"We're not getting anywhere. I already made that clear. You can make a million paper cranes with a million charming little messages, but that—"

"Charming?"

"Yeah, well, I'm not falling for it. So you might as well save your time. I'm going to put this tent up myself." I reach down and pick up a random tent pole; I have no idea where it goes.

"I can't let you struggle. It's against my Boy Scout code of honor."

"Oh! Go find an old lady to help cross the street or something."

I stab the pole into the sandy ground. Xander puts his hand over mine, and my whole body shudders. Does he notice? "Just let me help."

I take a step back, still feeling the warmth of his hand on mine. "Fine, but only because it's getting dark. And Jane has left me all alone. But it doesn't mean anything."

"Of course not."

I do *not* notice the smile flickering across his face. He becomes all business. "Pick up that corner of the tent."

We have the tent up in just a few minutes, and I feel like such an idiot. I barely have a chance to utter "Thank you" before Xander rushes off to help start the campfire.

I decide to walk down to the marina. Not that I completely want to torture myself by looking at Dad's boat, but whatever. I can't stand to be around the uber merriment of roasting hot dogs. And I don't even want to risk hearing Jane make a joke about wieners!

Sonnet has already quoted me a fake Xander love poem: "I put the pole in your tent. A more romantic moment I could not invent."

"I think that might get you disqualified from taking AP English next year," I'd said.

Sonnet giggled. "I love you, Polly. Now that I'm off blonds . . ."

"I'm not interested in humans."

"Kinky!"

"Go jump in a lake."

"Not worthy, Polly. You can do better than that."

"I can do better in a lot of ways."

"Not better than him." Sonnet cut her eyes at Xander standing by the campfire. "He's smoldering hot, like the coals some cute sophomore brought."

"Um, give up the verse," I said. "I'm going to go buy a pack of gum."

"Freshen your breath—"

"Don't even try to rhyme that with death."

"Well, you know what those old-timey poets said about orgasm."

"Go sic yourself on that redheaded sophomore," I'd said.

The little marina store has closed for the day. Briefly I glance at Dad's pontoon boat bobbing at the end of the dock, which makes me feel worse than watching Sawyer with his hands all over Kipper by the fire. I look at the little bulletin board outside the store. Lost dogs. Fishing equipment for sale. Boats for sale. Cabins for sale. I look closer at a newish-looking flyer. Beautiful log home! South side, five bedrooms, fully furnished, great views. A very familiar phone number. Dad is selling the cabin? Now I peer at the boat flyers. He's selling the boat, too!

I run down to the end of the dock. Sure enough there's a For Sale sign stuck to the side. I feel punched in the stomach. How could he just up and sell our childhood memories like this? Does this mean that he never wants to take us here again? It's like he just wants to erase all memory of us from his life. What's he going to do now? Buy a condo in Hawaii where he can create entirely new memories with one of his Barbie clones? Without us?

I stand on the dock staring out at my dad's cabin across from the marina until it gets too dark to see. A breeze blows across the water and I shiver. I left my sweatshirt back with my duffel bag, but I don't want to go back to the campground. I can hear their laughter—and possibly singing, but that might be a pack of coyotes yipping. I'm not in the mood. I stumble up the path in the dark. Clouds drift over the mountains, blurring the moon.

A flashlight bobs toward me, catching me in its glare. I stop walking, hoping for a dangerous ax murder, but not with my luck. It's Xander. Out doing his Boy Scout duty again.

"You okay?" He wraps an arm around me. I let him, but only because I'm cold. He pulls off his sweatshirt and slips it over my head. It's warm with his body heat.

"You don't have to do this," I say.

"I want to."

"I don't want you to want to, and I don't want me to want you to, either."

He takes my hand in his. "Your hand is so cold." He brings my hand to his mouth and blows warm breath on it. "Give me your other hand."

I do. Just because I'm cold.

We walk a bit in silence.

"Do you want to talk about it?" Xander asks like he's coaxing a scared child off the high dive.

I shake my head even though he can't see me in the dark. "I don't ever want to talk about anything. You can ask approximately three quarters of the campground if you need to confirm that."

"I'm just asking you," he says.

"I don't have anything to say."

I watch the flashlight bob along the trail as he nods.

I twist my hand out from his and walk faster, making Xander catch up. I'm so pissed. Why is *he* the one being nice to me? I don't want his sympathy. As soon as we approach the campground, I run toward the fire. A few guys pass around cans of beer. I take one and guzzle it down. And then I make a big show of belching. The guys all laugh. Sonnet actually looks shocked. Polly = bad girl, after all.

"Bet you can't do that," I tease, squeezing between a pair of sophomore boys who are sitting as far away from Xander as I can get.

My performance sets off a huge burping contest. I sit back, feeling a little bit dizzy. I really haven't eaten anything today. Rowdy hands me a hot dog and I take it, wolfing it down, once again impressing the sophomore boys. Hey, they're a whole new dating pool and I'm sure they're more interested in physical than emotional relationships. Maybe I've found my niche!

Not that I'm interested in any relationships. I pretend to swat a mosquito, sneaking a look at Xander. Our eyes meet briefly, but I quickly nudge the sophomore next to me. "Bet you can't burp the alphabet," I say.

The kind of cute—not that it matters—sophomore shakes his head but offers me another beer. I drink it more slowly—no more belching—but I finish it. Jane goes off into the shadows with Rowdy. Sawyer sneaks off with Kipper. Jack leers at me but takes Sonnet's hand (is that other girl watching the bulldog?). Even chocolate-peanut-butter-fudge-obsessed Emily goes off with one of the cute sophomores sitting next to me. Poor Hayden heads to his tent alone.

I stand up, half stumbling. I'm not used to drinking beer.

In the dark I can't tell which tent is mine. Again Xander appears like the total Boy Scout he apparently is. I decide I hate nice guys. And bad boys. Pretty much any and all males. I'm going to turn into one of those rabid feminists who never shaves her legs and writes long essays about how the planet would be a better place without men. They can all go to Uranus! Ha. Ha. Ha. Maybe if I ever get to attend college, I'll even invent a way to reproduce without them. Win the Nobel Peace Prize.

"Take my flashlight."

I reach for it, stumbling. He catches my arm. "I'm not going to let you take advantage of me." I giggle. "Not this time."

The cute sophomore perks up. "I can walk her to her tent."

"I don't think so," Xander says.

On the way to my tent, Xander launches into a drinking-doesn't-solve-anything lecture.

I push his hand off my arm. "Guess we can't all be like you, Mr. Perfect."

He shakes his head. "I'm not perfect."

"Doesn't show. You're always acting so . . . so . . . good. Not like me. I'm so . . . so . . . completely—" I trip over a rock. "Drunk!"

Xander curses.

I laugh. "Ooh! I'm gonna tell the Boy Scouts on yon!"

Xander doesn't help me as I fumble climbing into my tent. *Where's Jane?* I have no idea where Jane is, but I crawl into the tent anyway.

"Just sleep it off, Polly." Xander walks away with the flashlight, which I refuse to keep, leaving me alone in the dark. God, even the tent smells like fudge. I flop down on my air mattress: blown up with Xander's helpful breath. *Don't think about his breath!* I crawl into my sleeping bag: unrolled with Xander's helpful hands. *Don't think about his hands!*

"Ouch!" My cheek hits something sharp. I feel around, finding a small box on my pillow. I don't even need to open it. Rocky Road Fudge. My favorite. I unzip the tent and toss the fudge to the ants.

"How dare you presume to buy me my favorite flavor of fudge!" I yell.

Through the mesh netting above me I watch a bank of clouds cross the sky wiping the stars away like one of the dark gray dishtowels Mom sometimes accidentally brings home from work. I wait for Jane, even though I know I'll pretend to be asleep when she comes back.

I hate him! How dare he sell the cabin and the boat without even telling me? I'm so sick of letting him hurt me, Grace, Mom . . . Tears stream down my cheeks, dampening my pillow.

I spend half the night waiting for Jane, plotting revenge on Dad.

Dear Miss Swoon:
Is there ever a situation in which revenge against an ex is warranted?
—Plenty Of Reasons

Dear Plenty:
You will be much happier if you focus your energy on yourself. Go to my new website and find an affirmation to get you started on the path to Positivity.
—Miss Swoon

My sweatshirt wraps her like a hug, but she refuses the light I offer.
—X.C.

Chapter Twenty-six

I wake up alone. Jane must've stayed with Rowdy. I've got an achy head, but I'm not sure if it's because of the beers, tears, anger, or general suckiness of my life. Above my tent there is a patch of blue sky, but I can see thick gray clouds hovering over the mountains. If I didn't know the difference between cumulus and cumulonimbus clouds, I'd think they were a metaphor for the pain hovering around me. But really it's just going to rain. Literally not literarily.

In spite of the pending rain but because of my sore, puffy eyes, I slip on a pair of sunglasses, along with a Polyamide smile, and exit my tent. A pair of sophomore boys who've failed at the natural selection thing (no hookups) have built a campfire and rigged up a system to set their Pop-Tarts on fire.

"If you're attempting to toast your breakfast pastries, you might want to utilize the indirect heat," I say, peering at the charred remains of several Pop-Tarts. "Any strawberry left?"

They gape at me like I'm speaking a foreign language.

"Do I need to belch that out for you?"

They shake their heads, kind of smiling, and the cuter one hands me the foil package he's holding.

"Watch and learn, boys." I rip open the package and proceed to impress them by toasting my Pop-Tarts to a lovely, even shade of golden brown.

"We have cocoa, too."

"Make mine a double."

They laugh nervously, which confuses me a little until a hand brushes my arm.

"Hey." Xander sounds almost shy.

I turn around, daring to look at him through my sunglasses, which unfortunately doesn't seem to unnerve him at all. "Would you like a delicious, prepackaged but perfectly toasted breakfast pastry? I mean, I don't even know if you like this kind of thing and maybe you already ate something in your tent." My cheeks provide more radiation than the sun now struggling to shine through the clouds. "But you can have one if you want."

Xander takes one of the Pop-Tarts from me, letting his fingers linger too long. "Thanks."

"Okay, well. Where's that cocoa?"

The sophomore goes rushing off. "It's in my tent!" The other guy gets nervous and then runs off to help fetch the cocoa, leaving me alone with Xander.

"You feeling okay?"

I grin, thankful for my sunglasses. "Bright as sunshine."

"The sun isn't shining." He pushes my sunglasses onto the top of my head.

I avert my eyes. "Yeah, well, that's just a technicality."

"Come on Polly. Don't." Xander brushes a finger across the tender part beneath my eye. "What's going on with you?"

I shake my head. Fortunately the sophomores return with the cocoa, allowing me to return to my familiar, comfortable, joking-around mode, and, yeah, I'm reminding myself way too much of my mother.

A little while later, almost everyone decides to hike down near the marina to check out the beach. I decline: I no longer participate in activities in which the word "hike" is involved. It's a matter of principle.

Not that I enjoy being left alone with my thoughts. I try just about everything: affirmations to focus on the positivity, reciting the periodic table of elements in my head, jumping jacks to get my adrenaline flowing, but I just can't shake the painful emotions accumulating faster than the clouds in the sky.

When the hiking group returns, Sonnet complains about the beach conditions. "It's like so gross down there."

"Full of weedy weeds. Rocks. Greasy boat grease," Sawyer adds.

Sonnet sighs. "If only *we* had a boat."

"A boat would totally rock!" Kipper says, intimately leaning into Sawyer. The two of them sounded like rabid raccoons last night.

Everyone else murmurs agreement, makes boat jokes. I look down at the marina, not really able to see Dad's boat, but I'm quite intimate with its cushy seating for fourteen, as well as Dad's hide-a-key location. I glance around, counting. We have seventeen—but I'm sure *some* people wouldn't mind sharing *other* people's laps.

A little bit of my anger releases as I think about how good it would feel to take Dad's precious boat out on the lake without him ever knowing. "Actually . . ." I say.

• • •

After making more than a few wrong turns, we finally enter Horseshoe Canyon, chasing a patch of sunshine breaking through the clouds. I make a joke about the large Swim at Your Own Risk sign at the entrance.

Sonnet grins at me again. "Can I just tell you one more time that your awesomeness is awesome?" I laugh because I know she's making fun of Sawyer.

I smile, actually feeling it. Jane sits on Rowdy's lap while he drives. He practically begged me to let him drive, going on and on about his tremendous boat-driving aptitude. Although I fear his aptitude doesn't extend beyond steering his grandpa's boat during childhood fishing trips, he's doing okay. The lake is huge, plus we only see a few other boats out today. The clouds don't look that ominous! Rowdy overcorrects as the canyon narrows and we slide on the seats. I think about taking over, but he gets back on course, so I settle back against the seat. Heat radiates from the steep canyon walls, and an osprey circles above, searching for fish.

I'm sitting between my sophomore pals, sharing a bag of Doritos and ignoring Xander's way too paternalistic demeanor. He tried to stop me from hijacking—his word, not mine—the boat—oh, I don't know—about six times on the way to the marina. He actually grabbed my arm to prevent me from dropping the For Sale sign into the water. But I've learned a thing or two from those squirmy brats roving the Lazy River, and I managed to twist out of his grip and sink the damn sign.

Rowdy slows the boat, looking at the depth finder. "The water here is nearly two hundred feet deep, and the rocks look great for jumping. What do you say?"

A collective "Yay!" echoes off the canyon walls. I'm the first one in the water, diving off the back of my seat: a trick I've perfected over the last few summers to impress fellow boaters in my acceptable age and attractiveness range.

"Wow," I hear one of the sophomores say.

"Don't get any ideas," says the other one. At least Xander keeps quiet.

It takes me only a few strokes to reach the rocks. I stand on the ledge just below the water and reach up to begin climbing. People on the boat cheer, but it's really nothing. My family used to stop to swim at this spot all the time. I know what I'm doing. I reach a fairly impressive height and without hesitating cannonball into the water.

"Who's next?" I yell.

Sawyer immediately whips off his shirt. Some of the girls squeal as they climb down the ladder into the cold water. Soon almost everyone splashes around in the sparkling sunshine. Only Xander sits on the boat, watching me, when he's not watching the thick gray clouds taunting the sun. I dunk under and swim through deeper, colder water back to the ledge. I'll show him some cliff jumping!

I scramble next to Sawyer, who has reached my previous jumping spot. "Saw-yer Later, alligator," I say, climbing past him. I hear a few oohs and ahs from below, so I keep going until the water looks really far away.

"That's a suicidal height!" I hear Rowdy yell.

Jane shrieks, "Climb back down, Polly."

Sonnet bellows, "Go for it, girl. I've got my camera ready!"

Below me, Sawyer jumps, but no one notices. All eyes fix on me. I decide to put on a bit of a show, since I've already gone way beyond bad girl with, you know, stealing a boat and everything. I'll give Sonnet something to blog about. I sit down on the sun-warmed rocks, stretch out my legs, and prop my head up with one hand like a sexy bikini model. The sun feels good on my face, even though I know I'll pay for it later with freckles and sunburned skin. A few minutes later I stand up and walk to the ledge. Another rock juts out below me, and

I'm not sure I can jump out far enough. The "don't jump" calls now equal the "jump" calls. I'm pretty sure all my ex-boyfriends want to see me jump. Sonnet's camera glints in the sun.

When I bend my knees as a tease, Xander shoots into the water, still wearing his shirt. For a guy who rarely steps foot in the water at Wild Waves, he reaches the cliffs with impressive speed. I'd jump, but the water is too far away, and the ledge does jut out too far. And as pissed as I am, I'm not suicidal. Although part of me thinks Dad deserves it. Mom, too. But even I know that's pretty stupid thinking.

Out of breath, dripping wet, eyes wide, Xander reaches me and yanks my arm—hard—pulling me from the edge. He tries to say something, but he starts crying.

I'm shocked. I've never seen a guy cry before; I'd kind of considered their tear ducts as vestigial organs or something. Silly thoughts float through my head. I try to laugh but it comes out like a choke, and now I'm crying, too. Xander pulls me farther from the edge and closer to him. He's shivering and holding me so tight.

"It's going to be okay, Polly. Everything will work out. Trust me."

I allow myself to sink into him, for a moment. Just to see

what it feels like. He relaxes his body a bit. I feel a shudder ripple through him. Or maybe it's me.

I let myself fall into him.

He holds me tight, not saying anything. But now I *feel* like things will be okay. If I just let them be okay. If I just let myself go. Let myself trust him.

A few minutes later everyone below loses patience. Some yell "jump"; some yell "climb back down."

Xander lets go of me, without letting go of me. Both of his hands hold my elbows. "You ready to climb down?"

I nod.

We carefully climb down the boulders, though groans of disappointment echo with the thunder in the distance; it's much easier going up than down, and I slip more than once. But Xander's right below me guiding me to the next foothold. We stop to breathe when we reach the ledge I first jumped from.

And that's when I grab Xander's hand, pull him to the ledge, and shout, "Ready, one, two, three!" Holding hands, we splash down into the deep cold water. Together. He never lets go and neither do I. We even swim back to the boat holding hands.

And, yeah, it might mean something.

The sun loses its battle with the bank of clouds, so we all climb back into the boat. I find all the beach towels stored under the seats and hand them out to everyone while Jane passes out the snacks she bought at the marina with her mom's credit card. We're starving and devour everything in minutes. Rowdy starts the boat and exits the canyon just as it starts raining. Hayden and Jack struggle with the rain canopy, but it covers only the driver's seat in the back and a few spots on the side bench.

"Which way, Polly?" Rowdy asks.

Low-hanging clouds hide the tops of the high canyon walls, and the rain falls harder now. Everything looks different, plus I'm turned around enough that I'm not sure we've left the horseshoe-shaped canyon the same way we entered. I search for the Swim at Your Own Risk sign, but I can barely see through the sheets of rain now falling. Thunder cracks the sky, and everyone rushes to huddle under the small canopy, tilting the front of the boat out of the water.

Water rushes over the back of the boat, flooding the floor. The engine dips low, moaning in the wind-whipped lake.

"Get to the front of the boat!" I scream, racing toward the front, Xander at my side. Hayden follows. So does Jane. Almost everyone else huddles to keep out of the rain. Our weight is enough to keep the boat relatively steady, though. Rowdy shrugs his shoulders at me. He mouths, "Where?"

I shrug back. I just don't know.

Rowdy pushes the engine into gear and heads toward the left. Xander wraps a towel around my shoulders. He hands me another towel, but I give it to Hayden, who nods grimly. A bolt of lightning strikes the cliff tops ahead of us. I count, waiting for the thunder.

It comes too soon.

I've made a huge mistake. I look at the scared faces huddled together, draped in colorful beach towels like cartoon versions of Arabic sheiks. And maybe it would be funny—if the lightning weren't striking so close, the rain falling so hard, the canyon growing so narrow.

"This isn't it!" I yell.

Rowdy nods, unable to turn the boat around in the narrow space into which we've drifted. He backs up, slowly entering a wider portion of the lake. He speeds up as the canyon widens. Soon we're in the middle of the lake. Huge waves rock the boat, swelling, lifting the hull, dropping us back down. *Clank.* The entire boat shudders. Water sloshes against the canyon walls as if we're in a giant bathtub. The sky darkens. Rain falls harder. Thunder crashes.

"This isn't safe!" I can't tell who's screaming.

A finger of lightning touches the rock wall across the lake from us. The realization hits me: *we're* the highest point on the water. We're like the bull's-eye on a target.

"We have to find shelter!" I scream. "Stay low, everyone."

Rowdy looks scared.

Even though I want to slide to the floor of the boat and huddle against Xander, I take the wheel from Rowdy. Speeding up, I race toward the cliffs and turn the boat into a narrow canyon where the lightning will have plenty of higher objects to hit. I cut the engine to save gas.

With water splashing against the canyon walls we float, rocking with the storm-churned waves. Rain cuts across sideways in the wind, drenching us, even under the canopy. Xander stumbles toward me, kneels next to me, and wraps one towel around us, putting the other soaking-wet towel over our heads. We shiver together. No one talks. No one jokes. A few people pray. The sky turns so dark that I have no idea what time it is.

No one will come looking for us. No one knows that we took the boat. The boat drifts toward the canyon wall, scraping against the side with the wrenching crunch of metal against rock. A few people scream and shift to the other side, tipping the boat.

"Spread out!" I yell. "We've got to keep our weight even."

The boat crashes against the rocks again as we shift positions. I lean into Xander's shoulder, pinching my eyes shut to stop the tears. My thoughtless idea for revenge is going to get us all killed. Oh God. I'm so stupid. Stupid, stupid, stupid. I peek behind me at Jane, looking so afraid she doesn't move a millimeter. She sits with Rowdy, who has tenderly wrapped his arms around her. I've been so blind not to see how much he cares for her, that he really is a decent guy.

There *are* decent guys.

Hayden stumbles toward the front of the boat and sits down. He convinces Sawyer to move to the front to keep the weight better distributed. Sawyer reaches for Kipper's hand, but she shoves it away, wrapping her beach towel around her more tightly.

"Listen," Xander whispers, breath hot on my ear. "The storm is weakening."

Sure enough, the next clap of thunder sounds more distant. The wind eases. The rain falls consistent and hard but not with such force. Still we wait.

I keep expecting the sky to lighten, the sun to peek through the clouds. People start complaining about the cold, being hungry, thirsty, having to pee. Rowdy actually pees over the side of the boat and makes a big joke about it, but no one laughs. Jane gives him a weak smile.

A few stars twinkle through a break in the clouds by the time I restart the boat. Somehow I manage to steer us out of the canyon by following the dark shadows, but there isn't much moonlight. The middle of the lake looks like a black hole, and the engine sounds weak chugging through the water. A huge shiver shakes my body. I'm not sure if I've ever been this wet and cold. Xander pulls me close. I lean my head on his shoulder. "I'm such a fool."

He rests his head on mine. Agreeing, I think.

Something clanks against the hull so I sit up straight, steering through the inky water cautiously, watching for debris. I've been so reckless. I *must* get everyone back safely. What did I think I was going to accomplish with this stunt? Dad's not going to act any differently; if anything, he'll be so angry he won't ever want to see me again. He might not even be able to sell the boat if it's too damaged. *No more risks!* I steer away from a dark mass floating in the water, shuddering again, too exhausted and cold to cry.

Xander brushes my temple with his cool lips. "You're doing great."

I *do* have to learn to take some risks emotionally.

"There!" someone shouts. "I see Rowdy's big old ugly truck!"

I look toward shore. A nearly full moon has broken through the clouds, shining on the campground just above the marina. I push the throttle down and race to the dock.

Later, a huge fire roars in the campground and everyone has changed into dry clothes. Laughter rings in the air as people recount various aspects of our harrowing journey. Beer, food, warmth, and, um, the fact that *they* didn't scratch up *their* dad's boat make everything okay. For them. Sonnet trills with excitement about the blog entry she can't wait to start writing. After eating I return to my tent.

I'm going to have to tell Dad about his boat. I'm going to have to tell Mom what I did, too, before Sonnet blogs about it. Turns out Mom's become a fan after learning about the blog from fellow Hamburger Heaven employees.

A few minutes later I hear footsteps outside my tent. Xander unzips the mesh door, which sounds way too much like his skateboard. He crawls inside, lies down next to me, and we just gaze at each other in the moonlight.

"I think I'm falling for you," I finally whisper. "For real."

"I love you, too."

My smile matches his. Xander pulls me close, and we fall asleep in each other's arms.

Dear Miss Swoon:
How can you tell if you're in love?
—Falling?

Dear Falling:
If you were in love, you wouldn't have to ask.
—Miss Swoon

Chapter Twenty-seven

Even though I can see Grace peeking through the curtains at us, I don't immediately get out of the car. I rode home with Xander after heading down to the dock to inspect the damage to the boat: a deep gash on the right side and some minor paint damage on the left. The guy at the marina thought a couple of thousand bucks could handle it—in other words, about fifteen credit hours of in-state tuition or a summer's worth of Wild Waves savings.

"You sure you don't want me to come with you?" Xander smiles. "Your mom loves me."

"Probably more than she loves me."

"Hey, don't."

"I know." I take a deep breath. "I just think I've got to do this on my own."

He jumps out of the car and runs to open the door for me. I catch Grace grinning at me through the window, and I try to shoot her a dirty look, but I can't help smiling at Xander, acting all proper. He lifts my duffel bag out of the back seat.

"You don't have to walk me to the door or anything now that you've got me, or whatever."

He flashes his eyebrows at me. "Maybe I'm not ready to say goodbye yet."

I feel awkward when we reach the door, since so much has changed between us. We stand there for a few moments shyly smiling at each other. And it feels heart-revving in a nice way. Right as I tiptoe up to kiss him, the door swings open.

"Well, it's about time," Grandma says.

I back up covering my mouth like it's criminal evidence or something.

"They've kissed lots of times before." Grace squeezes next to Grandma. "I've seen them."

"But now Polly doesn't look so frightened, dear. That's what I was talking about."

"Grandma!"

Xander just starts laughing. "You sure tell it like it is, ma'am."

"Don't you dare 'ma'am' me! I've got a date tonight with a man young enough to be your uncle."

"Grandma, please. What happened to Bookstore Guy?"

"Way too much nonfiction, if you know what I mean. Oh, could that man talk about himself!" She says. "I'm headed over to my new health club. Plenty of well-preserved hotties."

"Oh, Grandma, you sound like The Sassy Sage or something."

"Yeah, well, she'd better watch her tight little fanny. I made a breakthrough on my book today—an actual breakthrough with a word count and everything. No more of those ridiculous affirmations. I'm writing a dating guide for the geriatric set."

"Finally something you actually know about."

Grandma fluffs her hair. "You said it! Well, I'm off to do research. I'm sure I'll see you soon, Xander." She turns to me. "You just stay calm, sweetie. He's a keeper."

"I'm not going anywhere." Xander kisses me—in front of Grandma and Grace. And Mom.

"Oh, you're back. How did it go?" Mom raises her eyebrows. "Better than expected, huh?"

"Yes and no." I shrug at Xander. A look of concern crosses Mom's face, and for the first time all summer I realize what a burden she's been shouldering. Making time for Grace, listening to me freak out, reading rumors about me on Sonnet's blog, watching Grandma date up a storm, fighting with Dad, bickering with Grandma, and on top of it all, money problems. "I'll explain everything," I say.

Xander kisses me again. "I'll call you later."

I stir more sugar into my glass, even though I don't like sweetened tea, but then two days ago I didn't like Xander Cooper. Okay, so that's kind of a lie. I didn't like having boyfriends. Well . . . I reach for one of the cookies I've arranged on a serving plate to give our talk a casual, tea party feeling.

Mom sips her tea. "Xander is such a nice boy. A true spirit. Although I have to admit I'm a little surprised. You've been resisting him all summer. Blog love poems aside." Mom laughs.

"Mom. Those aren't real."

"I know, honey. Xander wrote better verse back in the fifth grade. Sonnet, on the other hand, does not live up to her name. Poetry has too many rules to follow." Mom touches my elbow. "What's up?"

"Yeah, well, a lot kind of happened on the camping trip."

Mom's eyes grow wide like she's suddenly realizing that she should've given me another, stronger version of her Big

Talk. One that maybe went beyond her standard keep-your-virginity-until-you're-thirty-five joke.

"Not *that* kind of thing."

"I didn't think so, but you never know, the way you've been chasing boys like a dog chases cars."

"Mom!"

She picks up a cookie but puts it back down. "Sorry, I was thinking of that Kurt kid."

"Yeah, well that ended *because* I wouldn't—" I tilt my head back and forth. "Do that."

"Well, thank the Heavenly Hamburger that you've been listening to *some* of what I've been saying."

"That's not fair." I push away my too-sweet tea. "You're the one who tries not to talk about anything. You're always telling stupid jokes instead. Your heart is broken? At least it's not Uranus."

"All of my jokes are better than that one." Mom smiles. "Although with a little tweaking . . ."

"I'm trying to be serious here. Life is serious. Full of serious problems."

"That's why I need to laugh a little."

"Well, you won't be laughing when I tell you that I hijacked Dad's boat and crashed it into a canyon wall."

Mom's face goes blank. "I thought he sold the boat."

"It *is* for sale! You knew about it and didn't tell me?"

"Wait." She shakes her hand. "You back up and tell me what you did."

She munches down four or five cookies while I explain how Dad canceled our weekend at the cabin, and then I saw it for sale, along with the boat. I tell her some stuff about Sawyer and Kipper and feeling so scared about falling for Xander.

And she just listens. No joking.

"We'll have to pay for the damage to the boat. And soon," she says.

"How can *we* pay? You've got stacks of unpaid bills!"

"Where?" Mom looks around the kitchen.

"I saw them! Stacks of unopened, patented Mom-style unpaid bills."

"Oh, honey. That was back in June. You know how crazy things get at the end of the school year. Yeah, I let things slide for a couple of weeks, but I'm back on track now."

"Then why the Hamburger Heaven job?"

"My undying love of french fries and snarky teenagers."

I shoot her a look.

She unfolds her wadded-up napkin. "Someone around here has to send you to college."

"But that's Dad's job. He's the one with all the cash, even if he won't talk about college."

Mom bites her lip. "No, sorry to tell you, *I'm* the one with the cash."

"I told you not to joke around with me."

"I wish I were joking. Look, your dad's business has been struggling. All along he's been planning to send child support and then pay for your college." Mom looks away. "But he's about to lose his condo. And he just can't."

"Why didn't anyone tell me? I thought he hated me!"

"He's a proud man, honey. And stubborn. Look, we both know I could sit here for hours and recount his various faults, but the bottom line is that he's going through a difficult financial period and I'm left picking up the slack." She frowns. "As usual."

"And Grandma?"

"It's like her condo and Dad's ran off to foreclosure together."

"Absolutely not funny."

"Look, Grandma's trying hard to reinvent herself. I don't know if she will, but it hasn't been too awful having her around, has it?"

"I'm living in a room with six thousand stuffed animals."

"And I'm seriously considering couples therapy—with my mother. But what can I say? She's family."

"Why haven't you told me this stuff before?"

"You've had such a rough year. All those boys." Mom rolls her eyes. "Distancing yourself from Jane. Searching for yourself. I wasn't sure you could handle much more."

"Thanks a lot. I'm not stupid, you know."

Mom sighs really deep. "Look, you have so much admiration for your grandmother. I didn't want to ruin that. And as far as your dad goes, when we divorced, I promised I'd try to keep my feelings about him to myself."

"So instead you let them both lie to me?"

She doesn't say anything but crunches down another cookie.

I consider taking a drink of my tea but set the glass back down. "Mom, I don't like living with so many secrets and pretending everything is okay. I'm not doing it anymore. I want to see the best in people, but I want to be okay with their faults, too. Everyone has them, you know."

"Well, listen to you. The next Miss Swoon." She grins.

I roll my eyes as dramatically as possible. "Yeah, right. Soon I'll have my own TV show and magazine."

Mom laughs. "Sounds like a plan. No more slinging burgers."

"Are you going to keep working there once school starts?"

"One evening a week. And you'll have to do your part—maybe earn a scholarship or ten."

She starts clearing the dishes from the table, signaling that our talk is over. I follow her to the sink with my almost untouched tea.

"Do you think we could maybe make these tea parties a regular thing?" I ask.

"Only if we have special snacks so it won't remind me of a parent-teacher conference."

"Maybe we can do it with Grandma and Grace, too?"

Mom slouches dramatically and rolls her eyes to the ceiling. "I don't know. Like, my mother just doesn't, like, get me at all." After a summer at Hamburger Heaven she does an impressive impersonation of a teenager.

I laugh. "You remind me of someone: Riley McGhee!"

"We've been, like, so burdened with the same, like, shift for like two whole, like, boring weeks."

I glance at the clock. "I'd better call Dad before the guy at the marina does."

Mom turns serious all of a sudden, turning and putting both of her hands on my shoulders. "I'm not sure how he's going to react. But don't take it personally. It's about *him*. Not you. It never was. Do you understand that?"

I nod, shake my head, nod again. My heart pounds in an

entirely unpleasant way. I'm sure there's some kind of medical term for it and some kind of machine at the hospital to fix it. The cookie I ate is suddenly making me nauseous.

Dear Miss Swoon (and Grace):
You're invited to attend bimonthly honest family discussions on the first and third Sundays of each month. 7:30 p.m. Dessert and tea will be provided. No stuffed animals, no af-firmations, and no boys allowed!
—Polygraph

Dear Polly:
Yay! (But not about the stuffed animals—that's not fair.) Will you make something chocolate?
—Graceful
I will be there with bells not beaux.
—Miss Swoon (AKA Grandma)

"Swim at your own risk," the sign read, and we did. Sun, storm, stars, holding each other the whole time.
— X.C.

Chapter Twenty-eight

Jane frowns at her butt in the mirror again. "Maybe I could start a new fashion trend and wear a burqa on the first day of school."

"What about moving up a size?" I grimace, worried I'll offend her. "I mean, maybe that's part of the problem."

"Are you saying I'm fat?"

"I'm only saying that your curvy and totally cute figure might be more size-ten than size-eight. You've gotten like two inches taller this summer."

"I'm never going to stop growing. I'm going to be some freaky giant who can only find love at the circus."

"Rowdy seems to like you plenty."

"What if he's the only one I ever meet who likes tall girls?"

"What if he's the only one you ever need?"

Jane's mouth drops open. "Who are you and what have you done with my neurotic friend Polly?"

I shrug. "Maybe some relationships do end up happily ever after."

"Oh. My. God. You're in love."

I turn around and pretend to look for a sweater I liked, but my smile shines in the three-way mirror.

"Well, I never. Good old Xander Cooper. The guy who in fourth grade—did what?"

"Licked his desk."

"Righto."

"He's metamorphosized since then."

"Glad you finally noticed! So now you're all in love, huh?"

I shrug, not wanting to share everything just yet. "I'm only saying that just because my parents got divorced and my grandma has her lawyer on speed dial doesn't mean that some relationships can't last." I hold a sweater up to my chin. "Wouldn't this color look good for a prom dress?"

"Now, that's optimism! I'm just hoping Rowdy and I can make it through the first yearbook staff meeting."

"You're joking."

Jane slips the larger jeans over her hips. "Oh, they're so comfortable. Promise not to tell anyone my size!"

"I don't know. I've got my new honesty policy and everything." I smile. "Isn't the important thing that you're comfortable and look good?"

"You sound like your grandma's last column."

"I'll take that as a compliment."

"You should!" She glances over her shoulder at her butt again. "So, where did you find this pair? I'm buying all of them."

"You've got your mom's credit card again?"

"I most certainly do."

After paying and gathering all her shopping bags, Jane stops for a frappuccino at the coffee bar outside Macy's. I order a much cheaper iced tea.

"Where should we shop next?" she asks. "I'm thinking I need a miniskirt and some new tights."

I shrug. "We can go wherever you want. Most of my clothing fund is going toward boat paint. I'm thinking I can streak my legs with a mariner blue so they will look almost like designer jeans."

Jane stops walking. "Did your dad freak?"

I take a long sip of iced tea. I consider making another joke. She waits patiently, not even glancing at the nearby window display. I finally whisper, "Oh yeah."

Jane crumples her lips into a sympathetic frown.

"He yelled so loud that several dogs in the neighborhood lost their hearing."

She just widens her eyes.

"He said so much stuff, as if he'd been holding it in for my entire life. It's like I've been disappointing him for *years*. I felt like I'd gone through his office shredder when he was done."

A tear drips down my cheek, and Jane hands me the napkin wrapped around her frappucino. I dab my eyes. "It hurts so much. And I'm not even sure how to talk about it. I'm not very good at this feelings stuff."

"Who is?"

"I don't know. Sometimes it just seems so much easier to pretend that things are okay."

"But that leaves you carrying your burdens alone."

"It's not like they're as heavy as your shopping bags." I smirk at her.

"Yeah, well, these come with their own set of expectations—like perfect grades and majoring in prelaw at Stanford. You think I'm going to be allowed to take one single photography elective?" Jane looks down at her shopping bags, and I can tell she feels a little guilty. "We all have our crap to deal with—"

"Some of us are just better dressed for it."

Jane laughs so loud a couple of extremely well-groomed old ladies stare at us. "Yeah, and some of us have petite little figures that make all the boys swoon."

"Well, I'm not going to swoon back. Not anymore." I sip my iced tea.

"Now that you have your tall, mysterious, poetic Xander Cooper."

"X marks the spot." I grin around my straw.

Dear Miss Swoon:
Is it true that clothes make the man? My girlfriend is always nagging me to dress up when we go out with her friends. I say, shouldn't they like me for who I am?
—What's One Little Hole

Dear What's:
You seem to have a hole in your head when it comes to acceptable manners. Just because it's your favorite T-shirt doesn't mean it belongs in her favorite

restaurant. Make her day and let her take you shopping!

—Miss Swoon

Not Shakespeare's Sonnet

HOOK-UPdates:

Polly Martin and Xander Cooper: Finally, guys!

Emily Wright and Luther Smith: Cutest s'more-making sophomores ever!

Me: Nothing. But I'm okay with that. (See, Mom? Dad? No need to phone a therapist.)

New Contest: Prom Partner Predictions!!!

Let's start the school year by pairing the new seniors into Prom Partners. You predict the breakups, makeups, make-outs, and wanna-be-left-outs. There will be prizes for most accurate, most creative, and most delusional!!!!!

Chapter Twenty-nine

I watch the breeze ruffle through the leaves above me as I lie with my head in Xander's lap. Such a simple thing, a tree. Yet, it takes this complicated process of roots and photosynthesis to make it grow. And I've realized that everything is that way: complex. We've walked down to a small park in our neighborhood. Not too far away Dex and Kyra play on the playground equipment. Xander twists one of my curls around his finger.

"You sure I can't talk you into joining the academic team? We could use a science geek like you."

"I'm not a geek."

"Just thirty seconds ago you were explaining xylem and phlegm to me."

"Phloem. Just remember the phloem helps the nutrients *flow* throughout the tree."

Xander smiles. "Like I said, we could use a geek like you." He tickles my neck with his fingers. A leaf falls, brushing his hair, falling into mine. "The tree says yes."

"It's just that I don't want to join another club for a boy. You realize that if I do in fact score a college interview, when they ask me about my interests, I'll have to say, 'Oh yes. I joined the Nature Club because, you see, there was this guy.' I don't even need a diary. I've got an academic transcript that details my broken hearts."

He tilts my chin so that I'm looking at him. "I'm not going to break your heart."

I smile, even as fear prickles through me. He keeps saying things to reassure me, but I've started to focus on *actions*, not words. More than one drunk guy at a party has proclaimed undying love for me—if only I'd join him upstairs in an empty room. I've given up affirmations, snappy advice columns, blog gossip—I've got to find something that fits my scientific mind. Actions = empirical evidence.

"You keep saying that, but isn't it just words?"

Xander puts his finger over his mouth, asking me to hush, and closes his eyes.

"Okay, what little moment are you capturing now?" I've made a game of guessing notebook-worthy moments. "Is it Dex's laughter?"

Xander shakes his head.

"Rustling leaves?" No. "The weight of my enormous head in your lap?" A smile. "My hair wrapped around your finger." Slight head tilt. "My sky blue eyes staring up at the sky—ugh. I sound like Sawyer."

Xander laughs. "It's the way the skin on your forehead crinkles just a little bit when you're thinking of something that scares you."

"Well, that's just great." I push myself up so that I'm sitting at an angle to Xander. "I'm going to need Botox injections by the time I'm nineteen. I've got as many worries as the periodic table has elements."

"Let me be your oxygen." He bumps against me.

"That's the problem with being poetic all the time," I say. "Sometimes you just don't make sense. See, you need more than just oxygen, which happens to be highly combustible—"

He stops me with a kiss. "There. A little carbon monoxide or is it dioxide?" He squiggles a finger across my knee. "My bio notes aren't so great."

I take his hand off my knee. "We're so different. How is this going to work? Shouldn't we have more in common? I bet you're not even signed up for a science class are you?"

Xander shakes his head, but he's still smiling.

"And, yeah, I'm in AP English because I'm in AP everything, but I don't like it. I'm just good at knowing what the teachers want to hear, and I know how to use proper grammar."

"And don't forget all your big vocabulary words."

"You're teasing me."

He flashes his eyebrows.

"I'm serious! What if you decide, you know, after dating me for a few more weeks that we don't have enough in common?"

"We have enough in common."

"Like what?"

"I like you. You like me. Isn't that enough?"

"But it's not based on anything. It's just all that mushy feelings stuff. What if we hate each other's music? What if we never read the same books? What if—" A butterfly lands a few feet away, resting on a dandelion. "Take that butterfly. I see it as an amazing insect that's transformed from an egg to a caterpillar to a chrysalis and finally a colorful butterfly."

"I see a metaphor."

I roll my eyes.

"I'm going to ignore that," he says.

"See? It *is* a problem!"

He shakes his head. "Let's say we wanted to catch that butterfly. So we get up and run around this field, falling, tripping, never quite reaching the butterfly, the way some people go chasing after love. I won't mention any names."

I whack his arm. "Hey!"

He puts his arm around me to protect himself. He says. I lean my head on his shoulder, and we watch the butterfly flit from flower to flower, landing just briefly.

"Or we can wait, quietly, thinking our own thoughts, being our own selves." The butterfly floats in the air right before us, yellow wings almost transparent.

I sit completely still, watching the butterfly floating. And then it lands. On my shoulder! Out of the corner of my eye I watch the insect resting on my sleeve.

Xander whispers, "And the butterfly will land on your shoulder."

"How did you know?" I whisper back.

"We don't know. We just have to wait and see what happens. We can't capture it, control it. We can only enjoy it."

The butterfly opens and closes its wings, exposing an intricate, almost magical pattern of gray and yellow. A few moments later it flies away from me, but the feeling stays.

I will just wait and see what happens. A butterfly did just land on my shoulder.

Dear Polly:

Help! I think this might be the real thing! I've never felt like this before. Not with four husbands and who knows how many dishwasher repairmen. Why didn't you tell me?

—Miss Swooning

Dear Grandma:

He's a dog. He's a cute dog, but he's a dog. However, I will love him even more if he eats a few more of Grace's stuffed animals. Glad you've found true companionship at last. Now go write your book and let me work on my scholarship applications in peace!

—Polly

Acknowledgments

Dear Miss Swoon:

I just wrote a book and want to thank all the people who helped me along the way. My clever and insightful editor, Julie Tibbott, my ever-supportive agent, Ted Malawer, my mom, Rondi, and daughter Emma, who read early drafts, my daughter Sophie, who gave me "no talking" coupons, and my wonderful husband, Mike, who cleans the kitchen better than I do. Oh, and so many other friends and family members who simply listened, offered advice, and cheered me on. How do I say a big huge thank you?

—Grateful Author

Dear Grateful Author:

I think you just did.

Sydney Salter has never had an ex-boyfriend or worked in a water park, but she did once babysit a bulldog. Sydney now lives in Utah with her first and only boyfriend (now her husband), two daughters, two cats, two dogs, and a pair of tortoises. She loves reading, writing, traveling, and really tall, really twisty water slides. She is also the author of *My Big Nose and Other Natural Disasters* and *Jungle Crossing*.

www.sydneysalter.com